Sergeant Tom & The Battle Of Crete

Joseph Taylor

Contents

Prologue

Chapter 1

Chapter 2

Chapter 3

Chapter 4

Chapter 5

Chapter 6

Chapter 7

Chapter 8

Chapter 9

Chapter 10

Chapter 11

Chapter 12

Chapter 13

Chapter 14

Chapter 15

Chapter 16

Chapter 17

Chapter 18

Chapter 19

Chapter 20

Chapter 21

Chapter 22

Chapter 23

Chapter 24

Chapter 25

End-piece

Prologue

Sergeant Tom Lane of the Welch Regiment, British Army, lay in the lee of a large boulder, one among many scattered around the arid, northern slope of an outlier of the White Mountains. The Cretan sun, as on any other day in late May 1941, had heated up the air and even the rocks on the ground, and sweat was beginning to soak his body. Despite the deepening darkness, flying insects, attracted by the salty moisture, were beginning to land on his arms, his legs, neck and back but he paid them no concern. All his attention was focussed on the small, rather dilapidated group of houses at the bottom of the slope, and what was happening there.

Next to Tom lay Yannis, a young Cretan man of twenty or so. Like Tom, he watched the developing events below, with scarcely a blink. Both men, one dressed in worn and dusty working-men's clothing, the other in British Army battledress, lay with loaded rifles, ready to shoot when and if it became necessary. Neither wanted to set off a gun battle but if it had to be, neither man would hesitate.

In the tiny hamlet about one hundred yards below, illuminated by the lights of a grey kubelwagen and an oil lamp, eleven people were lined up facing a wall, hands against the old stone, as they were roughly searched by two grey-clad German infantrymen, while another stood back, sub-machine gun in hand, watching for any sudden movements. An officer observed events from underneath the branches of an olive tree, giving what sounded like orders in a harsh and hectoring tone. Other soldiers could be heard inside the three houses, presumably searching, as broken furniture, cooking pots and ancient clothing came hurtling out of the doors, to lie in the dust. Having seemingly found nothing of interest or value, these three soldiers joined their comrades outside to watch the interrogation. Full of arrogance in their own superiority to these helpless peasants, neither the officer nor the NCO had set a sentry or had troubled to examine where any opposition might lie.

The inhabitants, comprising a boy and a girl of around ten years, two women in their late twenties who could have been their mothers, four elderly women dressed in the traditional Cretan black, and three old men, cringed as the officer moved and stood behind them, lashing what looked like a riding crop across their backs, and shouting questions at them in poor, broken Greek. All screaming in pain and fear and not apparently giving the officer the answers he desired, he quickly grabbed the young boy around the neck, dragging him towards the tree. The prisoners, now desperate and hysterical with terror, fell to their knees, imploring the officer not to hurt the boy. One of the younger women, perhaps mother to the boy, tried to crawl towards her son but was immediately kicked to the ground by one of the soldiers and was held there, his military boot squarely in her back. A rope was thrown over one of the branches of the sturdy olive, one of the soldiers quickly fashioning what looked like a noose at one end. As the remaining prisoners wailed in realisation of what was about to happen, Tom and Yannis made their move.

With no more communication than the slightest nod to his companion, Yannis took the first pressure on the trigger of his rifle, checked his target then squeezed harder, enough to send the first shot crashing down into the group. The heavy bullet took the officer, a Leutnant, in the left side of his back, exiting at sternum level and missing the young boy held under one arm. He collapsed instantly, a mist of blood hanging in the air for a second or so.

Within that same second, Tom's first shot entered the belly of the Feldwebel holding the machine gun, blowing out a portion of his spine. He lived, but it would not be for long. He fell to the ground, over his gun, a lake of blood beginning to pool around him.

Years of experience now paid off as Tom, having quickly recycled the bolt of his rifle, ejecting the spent round and pushing a live round into the breech, fired a head shot into one of the soldiers who was beginning to lift his rifle. He dropped instantly, reminding Tom of rabbits he had shot as a boy in England.

The surviving four soldiers, desperately beginning to look for cover and to find the source of the firing, quickly became three as Yannis' second shot bowled the nearest soldier off his feet, to lie still and dead beneath the tree.

One of the three, thinking quickly, turned to capture the boy, now lying on the ground in a pool of the officer's blood. As he did so, one of the older women, pulling a long, rusty knife from a niche in the wall, plunged it into his neck, his severed carotid artery spraying bright red blood over her and the boy. As he fell, dying, he snapped off a short burst from his carbine, shattering her upper chest and shoulder and throwing her to the ground.

The two remaining soldiers, lucky to have avoided death so far, lifted their semi-automatic carbines and loosed off several shots in the direction of where they guessed their assailants were concealed. Yannis and Tom ducked as rounds ricocheted close to their heads but before they could rise again to continue firing and finish off the German survivors, two single shots crashed out from below, echoing around the stony surroundings of the valley. There was a silence, broken only by the moans of the surviving villagers. Tom lifted his head, to see the final two troopers lying sprawled out, both with bloody chest wounds, neither was moving, their weapons dropped by their sides.

Tom and Yannis rose from the rocks and cautiously made their way down to the houses, checking the German casualties for any sign of life, with rifles ready to shoot again if any further soldiers unexpectedly appeared. The older villagers were huddled around the wounded woman, while the younger women clutched the terrified children.

One of the older men, moustached, burly, dressed in worn, dusty clothing, caught sight of the two armed men as they made their way towards them, appearing out of the surrounding darkness. 'Ha, Yannis, son', he said. 'You took your time. They were looking for you but we told them nothing. Another minute with the boy, and we would have told them everything. Where is Giorgos? And who is this with you? Is this a British soldier?'

Before Yannis could reply, cries of despair and grief rose from the people grouped around the shot woman. She was still and pale, blood spread around her head and shoulders. 'Ya-ya!' shrieked the boy, hugging her body in his shock and disbelief. One of the other old men, her husband, held her hand, tears dropping fast onto the ground where she lay.

'Later. You cannot stay here', said Yannis, his eyes fixed upon the dead woman and her grieving husband and grandchild. 'The patrol will be missed, and the Oberst will send out another, with dogs, to find you. Anyone left in the village will be tortured and killed, whoever they might be. You must leave with us, now!' The old man nodded, hugging his grandson and whispering to him, 'Philip, Ya-ya saved us for another day. We will honour her memory and her love for us by living for as long as we can'.

Tom turned towards the houses. 'George, Davey', he shouted, 'All clear, come on in and bring Giorgos with you. And good shooting'. Heads turned as the two men moved cautiously into the light, George holding his rifle under his right arm, with his left hand resting on the shoulder of the boy walking next to him. At the sight of the dead woman on the ground, the lad threw off the protecting arm and ran to the group around her. He flung himself into the arms of the old man, alongside the other boy, who hugged him tightly to his chest. The boys seemed to Tom to be of a similar age, maybe brothers, he thought to himself.

George looked across at Tom. 'Found the bodies, two locals, an old couple, shot. Both squaddies too, beaten, tortured I reckon, then throats cut'. He was shaking in his fury. 'What could they tell them? They had nothing to tell them! If you hadn't shot the rest of these fuckers then I would have!' Tom had never seen George as angry, and it was as well for the perpetrators that they were already dead.

With help from the three soldiers, the dead couple along with the woman just killed were buried in a shallow trench, with small and then larger stones over them to deter foxes and any other scavengers, and a small amount of clothes, food and water was divided among the adults. The two dead soldiers, New Zealanders, were buried together, their would-be rescuers saluting them over their makeshift grave. The German soldiers were left where they fell.

The small group of survivors with their rescuers, trudged slowly across a boulder field, disappearing into the folds of the mountain, and were soon lost in the quiet darkness of a Cretan summer's night. Above the now deserted houses, vultures would circle at first light, in anticipation of their next meal.

Chapter 1

Tom Lane, sergeant in the Welch Regiment, 1st Battalion, Company B, was a regular soldier with ten years' service, originally enlisted in the Royal Welch Fusiliers, then posted to its sister regiment two months after Dunkirk. He had served in the Western Desert campaign during the winter of 1940 but in February 1941, with Tom newly promoted to Sergeant, the 1st Battalion had transferred to Crete, to initially deter but perhaps to deal with any future invasion. Crete was seen as strategically important in the eastern Mediterranean, with a few useful if small harbours and decent airfields that should be denied to the Axis powers.

At that time, Tom fitted the standard image of what one might expect a British Army sergeant to be. Blessed with a loud voice and a strong physique, together with a love of regiment and its traditions, he was already seen as efficient and reliable by his officers. Some of these officers thought him a little unimaginative, mistakenly. His view of discipline in his men was robust, and woe betide any man who either shirked his share of the work to be done or let down his mates or the regiment. His was the rank that made sure that the officers' orders were translated into viable action, the backbone of the army. His men viewed him as hard, even ruthless when he had to be, but knew that he would never ask them to do anything that he would not or could not do himself.

He was a couple of inches under six feet tall, with broad shoulders and narrow waist. He had boxed at light-middleweight for the Fusiliers before the war but although out of training, he retained a great strength and stamina, able to march and fight as long and as hard as the best of the men under him.

Short dark brown hair, and a previously broken nose in a kindly but determined face completed the picture. The impression was of a man who knew his job and meant business, with the more sensitive observer detecting a degree of wisdom and experience that others might miss. He loved his work, and demanded that those responsible to him at least tried to follow his example. His only regret was that he was still a single man, having had little opportunity to meet a woman who would marry him, or more importantly, that he would choose to marry. At just twenty eight years of age, he remained at his physical peak, backed up with a gradually increasing maturity.

The late winter and spring of 1941 passed for Company B in a mix of preparation of defensive positions and physical, weapons and other training. Tom and his immediate superior officer, Lieutenant Chalmers, were both determined that their platoon would be the best organised and fittest group of men in the company.

The battalion was initially placed at the village of Galatas, then after handing over the position to Australian troops, moved to about half a mile to the south of Chania, a picturesque and historic town, with a busy harbour. Their role was to act as reserve for the defending troops, mostly New Zealanders and Australians, and to guard and defend Force Headquarters on Akrotiri, the rocky peninsula that overlooked Souda Bay.

Behind the battalion's position, there was a narrow, coastal plain that merged into foothills mostly covered in thousands of olive trees and behind them, the hills steepened, becoming more bare and rocky, eventually forming the imposing and grand White Mountains. The battalion was spread over an east-west line of about two miles, with the eastern flank sitting above Souda Bay, a well-sheltered natural harbour thought to be an obvious potential landing place for an invasion. A series of slit trenches were dug around Force Headquarters, with anti-aircraft positions, mortar pits and machine-gun nests all looking down onto the bay. To begin with, a stand-to at dawn and dusk was seen as adequate security, with all but the necessary sentries using the hours in between in following whatever training Tom and the lieutenant could come up with, on top of their normal duties.

Range practice would be followed by weapons maintenance, keeping everyone's eye in and the weapons in battle-ready condition. Then they decided that standard PT, physical jerks in lines of sweating men, was too limited. Why not break down a three-inch mortar, all one hundred and fifteen pounds of it, into its constituent parts of baseplate, barrel, bipod and mortar shell (unfused), then get each section to run up the six hundred foot hill a mile behind the camp, reassemble the mortar, break it down again and race back to the base, with an extra beer for the quickest section? The extra beer never replaced the sweat lost but the thought of it helped keep everyone going! They even tried the old standard of dropping off sections in unknown areas of the locality, at night, with instructions to find their way back to camp as quickly as they could, under their own steam. This was less than successful, with more than one section begging lifts on donkey carts or taking long, liquid breaks in the first kafeneion they came across.

Everyone had the chance of a few hours twice every month in Chania. A beautiful old city with mazy little streets and a bar seemingly at every corner, the men spent what little money they had on beer, the local, potent raki, egg and chips and whatever female company was available. British and Commonwealth troops were there to defend the island and were made welcome by the local people, as the 5th Infantry Division of the Greek Army, raised in Crete, had transferred to mainland Greece to fight the Italians in Albania.

Crete in early spring was a beautiful place. The countryside was green after the winter rains, with countless wild flowers beginning to burst through the soil. Nights remained cool but the days could be either blazing hot or less warm but with showers of rain. After almost a year in Egypt and Libya, Tom and the Division were well acclimatised, tanned and fit.

By late April, Tom began to feel that the platoon, and Company B as a whole, was beginning to lose its edge, despite all the work and exercise. Meeting Lieutenant Chalmers one morning after stand-to, he decided to tackle his officer about it. 'Sir, this endless training and waiting around is buggering up the men. They are bored, finding trouble for themselves just to pass the time. Jones B had a black eye this morning, wouldn't tell me how he'd got it. I didn't push it any further, he would never live it down if he dropped one of his mates in the shit. And there's trouble brewing with the New Zealanders on our left. Too many fit, fighting men with no one to fight, that's the problem, sir'.

'Tom, I know. I've had more lads up for defaulters in the last week than in the last three months'. He paused, appeared to come to a decision and spoke again. 'Tom, this is for your ears only, I trust you to keep it to yourself'. 'Of course I fucking will' thought Tom to himself but permitted himself only to say 'Sir'. 'Sorry, Sergeant, I'm exceeding my authority in telling you this but you need to know, it'll be out soon anyway'. Taking a breath, he continued. 'The decision to evacuate Greece was made two days ago. The Germans are pushing our forces, and the Greeks, south as fast as you like and they'll evacuate here to Crete. There's nowhere closer. You can bet your last penny that the Germans won't be far behind, so I think we'll soon have more than a little fighting to do. The CO thinks that way, so they tell me'.

Tom was surprised that things were moving so fast. Like everyone, he had heard that the Nazis had invaded Greece, replacing the ineffectual and badly-led Italian army. The buzz was that it would be like the 1940 blitzkrieg all over again but Tom had been sure that the British Army, unimpeded this time by demoralised French allies, would put up a good show and, if not stop the Germans in their tracks, they would make them pay dearly for every mile.

'Sir, the boys are ready, more than ready. We're well dug in, well supplied, we can drop a bomb on a ha'penny!' Chalmers smiled at his enthusiasm as he continued, 'Sir, permission to step up training further? The boys will take it when they know they'll be doing the business soon enough'.

'Wait until the news breaks officially, Sergeant. I would only give it a couple of days at most before it is common knowledge. That'll give us a breather to plan how best to use the time we have before they come. I don't think it would do any harm though if you checked out the mortar pits again. They're good for size, is there more we can do to protect the men and the bombs though? You can bet your life that once we're spotted from the air, we'll be a target'.

'Sir, I'm sure the roof we put up on both pit shelters will take another layer of sandbags. We used bigger supports than we really needed to, seasoned timber on a firm base so it should be fine. I'll get onto it straightaway'. Saluting Chalmers, he strode off, shouting for his corporal to begin to organise the work. He was sure though that the boys would guess that something was up.

Sure enough, the news was out by breakfast the next day, and the atmosphere within the whole company perceptibly changed as the days passed. Officers and men appeared more purposeful, defaulters lists shrank to a minimum and weapons maintenance took place almost of its own accord. Tom was happy with the platoon again now, even his 'hard bargains' were beginning to pull their weight, perhaps understanding at last that they were part of a team, part of the machine, and they had to do their bit or the team would go down, taking them with it.

Evidence of the retreat from Greece was not long in arriving. Tom, inspecting the eastern of the three inch mortars, watched as HMS Glengyle, a troopship, along with two cruisers, crept into Souda Bay, to land four battalions of the 2nd New Zealand Division. He was shocked to see how beaten and dishevelled many of them looked, some lacking rifles, others without their helmets and other kit. The Welch, as other regiments, were quick to offer tea and sustenance to the soldiers as they straggled past them, and Tom was able to ask a few questions of a tough-looking platoon sergeant before he moved on. 'Mate', said the sergeant,' they are quick bastards, and no mistake. You get no time to get organised, they keep coming and coming. You push 'em back in one place and they put the pressure on somewhere else. Only way to beat 'em, I reckon, is to shoot first and keep up the scare. Turn the tables on 'em. We tried but without the reserves, we couldn't keep it going. If you ask me, your Churchill didn't give us enough men to do the job. And there ain't many of you either'.

Thousands more soldiers arrived as the days passed, sent up to camp beyond the coast road, Souda Bay becoming more and more an attractive target for the Luftwaffe, as it filled with so many ships discharging these troops. Tom and his men had their first view of the Junkers 87, the Stuka, as they toppled down from the sky, sirens wailing. Ships in the bay could not manoeuvre in that congested space and it seemed to Tom that the dive-bombers had more or less a free hand. Carcases of bombed ships began to dominate the waters of Souda, despite the brave efforts of the very few Hurricane fighters remaining on the island, and the hopeful shooting of the scarce anti-aircraft batteries. It didn't take a genius to work out who was going to be next on the receiving end and slit trenches were deepened and overhead protection was thickened even further, for the trials to come.

Chapter 2

Yannis felt guilty, but there was nothing he could practically do to change how he felt.

Like many young Cretan men, he had volunteered to help defend Greece when news of the Italian attack in Albania came through, joining the Cretan Division. He had arrived on the battlefield in mid-November 1940, in the north-west of the mainland, in time to help throw the Italians back over their starting line, and with enormous casualties. Winter had come in fierce and early, killing Greek and Italian alike and disrupting supplies for both armies, but it seemed that the Greeks, defending their homeland, could endure and suffer yet still fight, while the Italians were encouraged only to retreat. Yannis had agonised in the cold, along with his comrades, short of food and without winter clothing, but it was an Italian bomb that had brought his service to an end.

The morning sun had peaked through the nearby mountain pass, bathing Yannis in an illusory, golden heat. It was illusory because at five thousand feet in the Pindus Mountains in late December, real warmth was just a memory. He and Petros, his oldest friend from the village of Panadiki, eventually brother in law and now his comrade in the Royal Hellenic Army, sat huddled together for warmth as they tried to eat their breakfast, a hunk of frozen bread. It was all they had, after no rations the previous day, so they persevered for there would be no more. They had worn all of their clothes, in an effort to keep at least some of the cold at bay, supplemented with a greatcoat each, inherited from dead comrades. They had just pulled back two hundred yards from the present frontline after a literally freezing night on guard duty, hoping that a little food might warm them enough to allow to sleep for a little while in their shelter between three boulders that peeked above the snow. A couple of cypress branches had sufficed as a roof for their temporary home, and both of them felt that sleep, however brief and uncomfortable, was calling them. Yannis could remember that Petros had cocked his head, saying 'Planes, must be Spics, none of ours left'. Yannis recalled hearing the increasing roar of aero engines himself, and glimpsing the silvered shapes of tri-motors in the clear sky but that was where his memory stopped.

He had awoken slowly and painfully, aware of warmth and bright light and the murmur of quiet voices around him. Warmth! Where had that come from? Where was he? What had happened? He had struggled to rise on his elbows but had felt gentle hands pushing him back and a calm, female voice asking him to lie still, telling him that he was safe in hospital. He learned that he had been blown up by an Italian bomb, that he was the only survivor of his section and he had been lucky because the only supply truck for miles had arrived by chance, soon after the bombing, and had agreed to shift him down to the valley, to where there might be some medical care. He had asked about Petros but they could only repeat that he was the sole survivor from his section. His injuries were serious enough; a left arm that ended below the elbow, a broken leg that should mend, concussion and a partially collapsed lung caused by the blast of the bomb. His war seemed to be over.

His good luck had continued, being transferred first to Athens, to a military hospital for more treatment, then near the end of April 1941, to the port of Kalamata in the far South, ordered to find his own way back to Crete. Doctors had told him that, obviously, he would never again be fit enough to fight. His broken leg had mended, albeit leaving him with a slight limp, and the crashing headaches and dizziness caused by the concussion were also in the past. They had told him that his lung would never fully inflate again, the damage had been too great, but the clincher, the decisive injury, was the loss of his forearm. How could he load and fire a rifle with one hand? His war really was finished.

Yannis had not seen any good fortune in his situation, and had used every argument he could think of to persuade the doctors to pass him as fit for service. He was deeply patriotic and wanted to defend his country, just like everyone else. He had lost his closest friend, his second sister's husband, presumably blown to shreds by the Italian bomb, and he wanted some payback for what the invaders had done and the only way to achieve that was by fighting them as hard as he could. He had left unsaid his fear of returning home and having to tell Cristina of the death of her husband and the father of their two sons. Begging the medics to change their opinion had achieved nothing, he had been told that he should be grateful for what they had done for him, and that better men than he had been left to die in the mountains. 'Go to Kalamata' they said, 'find a boat going to your island and go home. Be grateful you are alive'.

So he had gone to Kalamata, hitching lifts all the way because he had no money. He slept in the open when he arrived there, begged food, drank water from a public well and tried to find a passage home to Crete. There were plenty of boats in the harbour but a journey down to Crete would cost many drachmas and Yannis had none.

His problem was eventually solved by developments in the war on the border. While still in hospital in Athens, Yannis had heard that Germany had joined in with the despised Italians and had invaded Yugoslavia and Greece. Within ten days, the first troops of the retreating armies, British, New Zealanders and Australians, were trickling into the capital as Germany smashed through their defences in the North. Within ten more days, that trickle had become a flood and the Allied plan was to evacuate as many fighting men as possible to Crete, the nearest friendly territory.

Every ship in Kalamata harbour was hired or commandeered for the evacuation, and suddenly, crewmen to work the boats were at a premium. Yannis was no seaman, no fisherman, he was the son of a shepherd, but he could cook and surely the soldiers and crew would need feeding? It had not taken him long to find a captain of one of the larger fishing boats, the 'Pelican', who needed hands of all descriptions, and who was about to take as many soldiers as he could squeeze into his hold and on his decks all the way to Crete. Yes, he needed a cook and Yannis could work for his passage, no wages. In reality, Yannis had little choice. He could sail or starve.

Captain Pappadakis had reckoned on a passage of thirty hours maximum to Chania, God willing, and thus Yannis had started his journey home. They had cast off from their moorings at ten in the morning, the boat buzzing with conversation and laughter. Intending to pass the Tenaro lighthouse at Faros just as night fell, Pappadakis reckoned that they should make as far as the island of Antikythera by middle morning the next day, and Chania perhaps four hours after that.

The first day and night went smoothly, with no sightings of enemy ships or aircraft, and the boat making solid if steady progress through the calm water. Yannis had been kept busy, cooking fish and making bread for the crew, helping the troops to heat their rations and cleaning up after them. He had worked all the afternoon and most of the night, helped in turn by a few soldiers sympathetic to his efforts. 'Here, young un', one of them had said, 'you needs some help, give us them brushes, me and the boys will help you out a bit, take our minds off this fuckin' sea too!' Yannis had some English, having worked before the war with an archaeologist from Cambridge, John Pendlebury, excavating Minoan ruins in Crete. Their kindly intention was clear enough and to be honest, his injured arm was so painful after many hours work that he was grateful for the help. Together, they made short work of the galley and by four in the morning, Yannis was able to lie down on the galley floor, and lulled by the gentle rocking of the boat and by the rhythmic thud of the old engine, he dropped off to sleep.

Daylight was breaking as Yannis gradually surfaced from his exhausted sleep on the galley floor. As every morning, his first feeling was of an overwhelming guilt, for he had lived when Petros had not, he had had his wounds tended to and would have a life and now, he was safely on his way home. How had he lived, when Petros and Andonios and Nikolas and the others had all died? How would he explain that to their parents when he met them? They would hate him, surely? Yes, of course he was glad that he was not dead but couldn't they be alive too? It was all too much to bear!

'Up, boy! Earn your wages!' It was Spiros, Papadakis' oldest and most senior seaman. 'Captain's breakfast first, then mine and the crew'. He added kindly, 'That means you too, boy, you're crew same as us. After that, get these English moving, fed and out of my way, they're making 'The Pelican' look untidy!' Yannis had told him about his recent past and Spiros, wise old hand that he was, reckoned that keeping busy would help keep his mind of it and besides, there was so much to do.

'How long to Antikythera, Spiros?' asked Yannis. 'About three hours Captain says, then four to Chania, if the Saints deliver us. He's worried the Germans will try to catch us, they know Crete is where the Allies will have to go. They've only got to send a few of their fighter planes, whatever they're called, and we're fucked. Look around us' he said, pointing through the galley scuttle. Yannis obediently put his head through the porthole and whistled in surprise and understanding. Within a mile of the 'Pelican', he could see three other boats, all with khaki-clad men on their decks, all heading in the same direction as they were. 'Two more on the port side, lad, now isn't that a target for them planes, if they sees us?' Yannis could only nod in agreement. 'So do your job, lad, and we'll have you home by tonight and these English too, they'll be drinking your wine and chasing your virgins! You do have virgins in Crete, do you?' he guffawed, and turning, left Yannis to his work.

The next three hours passed in something of a blur for Yannis, immersed in all his chores. A couple of the Australians, Bert and Al, had helped him out again and in between jobs, had tried to teach him a few more English words.

To begin with, he didn't let on to them that he knew some English but as he collapsed in laughter when they told him that he should greet the Captain with 'Fuck off mate', every morning, the penny eventually dropped. 'You cheeky bastard, you knew what we was saying all the time, didn't yer? Now, how about you givin' us some Greek lessons, how do I say to a girl, do you believe in love at first sight, or should I walk by again? I'll be needing all my best lines when we land on yer island!'

Before Yannis could even begin to answer, his thoughts were scattered as the booming thunder of aero engines and the rapid percussion of gunfire overwhelmed his senses. He dropped to the deck, echoing his two companions, and crawled to the door in the bulkhead, leading out onto the main deck.

Chapter 3

Men were pouring up on deck, not wanting to be trapped below if the worst happened. The Pelican had not yet been attacked but to starboard, he could see a single fighter plane, a Messerschmitt, painted in grey camouflage with a yellow nose, black cross on the fuselage, hurtling down from the sky towards one of the other boats, its canon and machine guns tearing into the vessel. The boat was a cloud of smoke and flame and flying debris, and already it was down by the stern. Yannis shuddered at the thought of the hell that the men, crowded on to the boat, must be going through.

The Messerschmitt pilot wasn't having it all his own way though. Bert pointed at the tracer converging on the plane from the other two boats to port, shouting 'Hit the fucker, hit him!' at the top of his voice. There was a cheer as smoke began to leak and then pour from the fighter's engine. Within a few seconds, the pilot had broken off his attack, turning north and, keeping low to avoid more hits from the defenders, heading back towards the mainland and eventually, out of sight.

The two surviving boats to port headed for their sinking comrade but Pappadakis made no attempt to join them, remaining on a direct heading for Antikythera, which did not go well with the Australians on board. 'You dago bastard, turn this tub around and help our guys' and 'Leave 'em to drown would you, you Greek fuck' were two of the comments thrown at him, and for a few moments, it seemed as if they were going to storm the wheelhouse and force a change of direction. Pappadakis appealed to Lieutenant Perkins, the only army officer on board, who stood between him and the angry soldiers. 'Sir, space on other boats, little space here. More planes come, will sink us also, must get to island quick. Stay until dark then go Chania'.

Yannis lifted his arm, pointing out at the rescuing boats, which seemed to have done all that they could and were moving away from the wreck, which was awash and about to go under. Everyone could see that no one was left in the water, other than bodies, and the complaints died away. No one protested as Pappadakis wrung a little more speed from the old engine, heading for the rocky island of Antikythera, now lying about a mile ahead and to port.

Yannis knew the island from when the Cretan Division had embarked for the mainland nearly six months previously. He described in his best English what he could recall for Al and Bert. 'Small island, only ten kilometres long. Few peoples, more sheeps! One harbour, Potamos, Pappadakis takes us there, I think'. Sure enough, the captain steered the Pelican to the east of the island, which seemed to the watching Aussies to consist of rocky cliff and hillside, and not much more. There was no easy landfall in case of an aerial attack, and many nervous eyes scoured the sky.

Within half an hour, the coast curved around to starboard, opening up in to a small bay, with the harbour and village of Potamos visible at its head. The remaining four boats, all ahead of Pelican, altered course for its shelter but again, Pappadakis surprised them all by carrying on southwards, continuing to follow the coast. On this occasion, the Captain did not wait to be questioned by the troops.

'My friends', he boomed, so that all could hear, 'We not go Potamos. Is trap, shallow water, small space for five boat. I know better place, two kilometre only. We stay there, safe, then Chania tonight'. 'I hope he's fucking right, my young fellah', murmured Al, 'I don't want to meet no Jerry planes out there, and only a rifle to shoot back with'. 'You'd miss the bastard anyway, mate', laughed Bert, earning himself an elbow in the ribs.

Ten, tense minutes later, Pappadakis throttled back and swung the wheel, steering apparently head-on for the cliffs that marked the shore. There were some curious looks aimed at the Captain, was he going to run them ashore? Spiros pointed forward, 'Look'. As they neared the sheer cliff, a narrow entrance about twice the width of the boat became clear, and with great care, Pappadakis manoeuvred the boat, stern first, into the cleft. Three members of the crew, with boathooks, fended the vessel away from the walls of the fissure, while Spiros and another threaded ropes through mooring rings already fixed into the rock. Moored fore and aft, the Pelican was invisible from seaward, and could only be seen from directly above. 'Great move, mate', laughed Al. 'We'd be bloody unlucky if the Jerries found us here. How do you think he knew where to hide out?' he asked Yannis, who in turn asked Spiros. 'Ah', he laughed, 'Pappadakis is not only a fisherman, he sells cigarettes from Turkey, very cheap! He knows all the small places to disappear into'. 'Smuggler', Yannis reported, to nods of approval.

The troops were told by Pappadakis, through Lieutenant Perkins, that no one would be allowed on shore during the day, it was too dangerous with the Luftwaffe likely to be returning to look for the boats, so they should take the chance to rest. A guard would be set for the day though, to warn of any approaching danger.

Bert drew the first duty, and scrambled his way, armed with rifle and binoculars, up to the grass that pushed through the thin soil at the top of the cliff. He took a look to the north and quickly called down to the officer, 'I can see that Potamos place, sir, about a mile away. Looks like half a dozen boats in the harbour, all quiet. Plenty of guys on the beach, stretching their legs, lucky bastards!' 'Just keep looking, Private, any changes let me know immediately' answered Perkins, 'You'll be relieved in an hour'.

Yannis went back to his duties in the galley. More Aussies came through to brew their tea and Yannis, with some olive oil, onions and the last of the potatoes, helped them to try to turn their bully beef into something more appetising. They managed to fill two huge stock pots with their version of beef stew, which smelled surprisingly good, and had placed them on the top of the cooker to warm through, when they heard Bert shout down from his perch.

'Planes coming from the north, beyond the island, looks like a dozen or so. Can't see what they are, hang on, they're circling around, they're goin' to come over the top of us'. As he stopped shouting, the men on board could hear the roar of aircraft engines growing louder and louder, then begin to fade. Bert shouted again, 'They're turning back towards the port, they must've seen the boats, they're diving, looks like they're attacking'. The Lieutenant shouted back up to Bert, 'What are they, fighters, bombers?' 'Stukas, sir', was the reply. There was a thoughtful, momentary silence. All of the soldiers had recent experience of what Stukas could do, and many had lost mates by their actions.

The silence was broken by the wail of sirens and the crash of exploding bombs as the planes pushed home their attack. Bert continued to report, 'Sir, I can't see much in the harbour now, it's all smoke and flames down there. I saw one boat go up then everything's hidden in the smoke. There's bodies on the quay, on the beach. Oh, the bastards, they're machine-gunning the village!'

The sounds of destruction and devastation could be heard for a further ten minutes, then all was quiet. Engine noise was fading. 'All heading back north again, sir. Nothing left to bomb, I reckon. Harbour's still in the smoke, can't see much'. 'OK, come down, Private'. Another sentry took Bert's place, and a debate began, between Perkins and the Captain about what to do next.

Pappadakis refused to sail back up the coast to Potamos to look for survivors. 'More planes come, more bomb. We sink too, and dead!' 'But there will be casualties, Captain, perhaps some troops who can still fight. My duty is to save anyone who can be saved, we don't abandon our comrades!' Perkins' voice was raised, and Yannis could see that the Aussie soldiers listening in would not willingly leave their mates without at least trying to help them. Pappadakis could find himself with a mutiny if they could not agree a plan.

Yannis spoke in Greek to the Captain. 'Sir, would there be time to sail back to Potamos in the darkness tonight, pick up any survivors then reach Chania before morning?' 'Yes, that would be possible, young man, but not if we have to wait around in Potamos while they decide who to take and who to leave. We could stop there for thirty minutes only, any longer and we would be an easy and lonely target for any passing German before we made Chania. Tell him that!' Perkins was looking irritated at being left out of the conversation but brightened when Yannis quickly translated the Captain's remarks. 'Captain Pappadakis, I am happy with that, and thank you for your consideration. I will send a small patrol with a medic to the village, in fact I'll lead it myself, we'll see who can be moved and we will be ready at whatever time you tell us'. Pappadakis had lost the gist of the Lieutenant's remarks and looked to Yannis for clarification. Yannis' grasp of English was being stretched further than it ever had been but he managed to get Perkins' meaning across. 'I will moor at the quay in Potamos at 2200 tonight', said the captain, 'and at 2230 we must leave. No later, do you understand, no later'. 'We will be ready', replied Perkins firmly, and left the wheelhouse to set up the patrol. He stopped in the doorway. Turning back, he asked, 'Yannis, will you come and translate for us? There will be villagers to talk to, I'm sure, and perhaps they will need some help'. Yannis looked across at the Captain, who nodded back at him. 'Go if you wish, young man. They will need you but you must make sure that they are ready to load at 2200 and you must be ready also. I will not wait'. He looked back at Perkins, 'Yes, I will come'.

Thirty minutes later, the patrol was ready to leave. Each man had had a belly-full of stew to sustain him through the remainder of the day, and after a swift weapons check, they made the short climb to the top of the cleft. There were plenty of hand and footholds in the rough and shattered rock, and Yannis found that he could use the stump of his arm for balance, while hauling himself up with the other, and relying upon the strength of his legs. He hadn't been given a rifle to carry but he did have a knapsack filled with wound dressings and someone had slung him a steel helmet, just in case they ran into trouble.

From the cliff-top, the ground, covered in short grass and small bushes, sloped gently down towards the village. There was no real cover, in case of surprise attack, but all seemed quiet now and Perkins led them steadily down towards the harbour below. To Yannis, in the brilliant sunshine, it seemed like a typical and beautiful Aegean spring day, the heat tempered with a gentle breeze off the sea. The illusion lasted only until he looked more closely at Potamos, at the bottom of the hill.

Some of the smoke had cleared, and he could see the smashed and burned remnants of three boats in the water. Where was the other? The quay itself, an old stone and concrete construction, had taken damage too but Yannis was most shocked to see the remains of the tiny village. Every house was damaged, some were completely destroyed, and some were still burning. Bombs had cratered the street that led down between the houses to the water and even the olive grove behind the houses had been blasted, leaving swathes of trees splintered on the ground.

It only took minutes to walk to the village, and the scale of the human destruction became plain. Casualties were lying in rows at the edge of the beach, and two men, medics at a guess, were working from one end to the other, bandaging and offering comfort. Other men in uniform could be seen giving water to those that wanted it.

Not all of the casualties were military, Yannis could see that some of the wounded were in civilian clothing, men and women, and perhaps children too, judging by the size of some of the bodies. As the patrol moved closer, the crying and wailing of the wounded reached them. It was the saddest, most disturbing sound that they had ever heard, and would hope never to hear again.

Yannis watched as Perkins approached the two likely medics. They spoke for a few moments then the Lieutenant made his way back to the men of the patrol and snapped out orders, 'There are no surviving officers from the other boats so the job falls to me. Privates Wilson and Roberts, take the dressings down to the medics and do what you can to help. Yannis, stick with me while we find out the damage and get a better idea of numbers. I'll need you to speak to the villagers, see what they need'. Then, looking at the four remaining soldiers, 'I want two of you on that headland, to the north, you and you', pointing at the two closest to him, ' fire a warning shot if you see anything coming then get back down here damned quick, it wouldn't surprise me if the Boche made a return visit'. Then, to the final pair, 'You two, I want an inventory of what weapons are here, and ammunition. Take a look in the wrecks if you can, there might some stuff there that we could still use. Leave people their personal weaponry if they're fit to fight but otherwise, collect it up and tell me exactly what we have, it'll not be much. Report back to me in an hour. Questions? No, off you go. Yannis, with me'.

Perkins and Yannis walked down to the line of casualties. According to the two young soldiers trying to perform medical duties, there were thirty five wounded, twelve of whom were inhabitants of Antikythera, but they reckoned that only twenty seven were fit to travel anywhere. The other eight, all soldiers, were severely hurt, requiring sophisticated care and treatment and would be unlikely to survive any sea journey. Perkins made his first decision. 'If they are going to die anyway, they can die in the company of their mates, not left on some bloody island. They are coming with us. They don't need to be at the quay yet but be ready to move them when I give the order. How many blokes managed to avoid getting blown up?' He was stunned at the reply. 'Just twelve, including us two, sir. We've got thirty eight dead over there', pointing to a line of bodies that neither Perkins nor Yannis had noticed until then. He added, with a catch in his voice and horror visible in his eyes, 'Sir, there's bodies still in the boats, sir. Can't say how many, some of them are in a terrible state, sir, blown to rags they are. We couldn't move them, sir'.

Lieutenant Perkins stiffened, but quickly responded. 'Corporal, there they must stay. We must look after the living now. Carry on doing what you can and I promise you, we'll get all the help we need when we get to Crete in the morning. Now, release a couple of men if you can spare them and we'll get some of the dead identified and covered up for now. Maybe Jerry will give them a proper burial but we can't. Yannis, get back to the boat and tell Pappadakis he needs to make room for another forty seven passengers, eight of whom are critically wounded. He won't like it but we're not leaving them. Make sure you tell him that a dozen of them are Greeks, wounded civilians from the island. He won't want to leave them for the Jerries. Don't argue with him, just get back here as quick as you can. We have work to do'. Yannis saluted from habit and as he ran back up the hill, he saw the Lieutenant pick up a spade and make his way over to the line of corpses.

Pappadakis had made no comment, just nodded, and Yannis was back in the village well within the hour. Perkins was still wielding his spade, having excavated the shallowest of graves with the help of two troopers sent by the corporal, and they were now spreading what soil they could over the old tarpaulin that covered the dead. Noticing the approach of the young Greek, he spoke to the two men working with him, carefully propped his spade against the wall and walked over to where Yannis had stopped. 'That was quick, young man', he remarked. 'I am twenty, sir', answered Yannis, 'my arm may be gone and I have a damned limp but I can still run better than most. I was raised in the mountains, sir, and spent my childhood chasing our sheep and goats'. The Lieutenant gave a wry grin, 'Twenty, eh? Well, as it happens, I am nineteen, so you are my senior!' They both smiled, and made their way towards the village, or what was left of it.

As they turned into the main street, they were stopped by an older man, dressed in a plain black cassock and hat, clearly the village priest. He looked pale and shocked, his clothing covered in dust from the bombing, and with what looked and smelled like blood. Eyes bulging, he roared in fast Cretan dialect, 'You soldiers, you have brought death to our island! My flock was forty souls only, now only twelve! Twelve! You will take the twelve hurt with you, but sixteen will never leave, they are all dead!' As the words continued to spill from him, tears pouring unregarded down his thin face, Yannis translated for the Lieutenant. 'I will stay, twelve and me, all that are left. May God forgive you for bringing so much death here'. 'Now hold on, Padre', interrupted Perkins, 'We are helping you to defend your country. This is not our doing', he remonstrated, gesturing at all the destruction, the collapsed houses and the reek of death, all around them. 'We have dead also, dying for your country'. But the priest was not to be mollified. 'Why did you not sail past and leave us in peace!'

Yannis plucked at the Lieutenant's sleeve. 'Sir, we waste time. He is beyond reason, he has seen too much. I will ask him if any more people are trapped and tell him we will help. Then we must get the wounded ready to move'. Perkins was still irritated at the priest but quickly realised that Yannis was right, and nodded. To Yannis' question, the priest replied, 'None, all dead', and turned abruptly away.

Before Yannis and the Lieutenant could retrace their steps back to the harbour, a sharp crack, crack, crack of rifle shots echoed across the bay. On the headland to the north, the two sentries posted by Perkins were waving their arms urgently, the enemy was returning. Perkins burst into action.

Chapter 4

'Take cover!' he bellowed. 'Everyone out of sight, leave the wounded where they are, no firing unless I order, move!' 'Sir', protested one of the troopers tending the wounded, 'We can't leave them, what if the Boche see them, they'll massacre them!' Perkins knew that any delay could mean even more casualties, that if an enemy pilot spotted Commonwealth soldiers, then they would be bound to attack. 'Private!' he roared, 'Get out of sight, now! Don't fucking argue. Move!'

Within a minute, the soldiers were out of sight, hidden among the ruins of the village and behind the rubble of the quay. There was a short silence, broken only by the moans of some of the wounded, then abruptly, all could hear the slowly increasing buzz of a single engine, getting louder and louder. Risking a glance above the rubble sheltering him from sight, Yannis looked in the direction of the sound, down the bay towards the open sea.

Flying low and slowly above the water, only perhaps two hundred feet above it, was a monoplane, painted in brown camouflage, and with a tall, fixed undercarriage hanging below. He became aware that the Lieutenant was next to him, at his shoulder, eyes fixed on the plane.

'Storch, Nazi reconnaissance plane, checking us out', murmured Perkins. Raising his voice, he shouted again. 'Nobody move. No one looks up, stay still until I order you to move!' He sank down into the shade behind the rubble, pulling Yannis with him. As they crouched there, the noise of the little plane increased as it reached the top of the bay and the harbour, then seemed to amplify then reduce as it slowly circled the village. This carried on for a few minutes then steadily, the clatter of the little engine began to fade away to the north.

Perkins shouted again. 'Stay under cover, they could be back yet'. No one moved for a further ten minutes, then he relented. 'OK, lads, well done.

Let's get the wounded as near to the jetty as we can, feed and water them if you can, then yourselves. I want all weapons and ammunition together for distribution. We've got just over two hours before the boat comes and we can evacuate'. To Yannis he added quietly, 'Let's just hope that Jerry didn't spot anything to make them hurry, and by the time they do get here, we'll be long gone'.

The next two hours, as the light faded, were frantic, as the wounded were gently moved near to where Pappadakis could moor. Everyone managed a snap to eat and a drink, even if it was only well-water. Perkins sat Yannis at the seaward end of the ruined quay with a torch, to signal the Pelican in, as soon as he heard her engine. Sure enough, as close to 2200 as he could judge, Yannis picked up the subdued thud of the old boat's single cylinder engine, as she unhurriedly made her way up the bay. Someone, Spiros perhaps, signalled back to Yannis with a shaded light and within a few moments, Pappadakis brought her snug against the end of the quay.

Perkins and Yannis leapt down onto the deck and were quickly in conversation with Pappadakis. There was a problem, the captain told them, with so many wounded taking up space, there would not be room for everyone else, not on one boat. Could they find another?

Perkins was in despair. The boats that had taken refuge at Potamos were utterly destroyed, there was no other boat! But everyone must leave tonight!

A tired voice contributed, from the quayside. It was the village priest. 'There is a boat further up the beach, out of the water for painting. Take that, you must save my people'. Spiros and Yannis took a look, it was about six metres long, no engine, no deck but sound enough. They reported back to the captain and Perkins that it should take a dozen men at least, and could be towed. The priest was thanked, and the loading began.

It was after 2230 by the time Pelican puttered back out to sea. Fourteen protesting soldiers were jammed into the towed vessel, christened the Jolly Roger, for the slow journey to Chania. Pappadakis explained that he would have to reduce his speed by a couple of knots because of the tow but they would still make Chania before morning. The atmosphere among the soldiers was still tense but tempered with some relief that the journey's end was in view.

Remarkably, the night was uneventful and by 0400, the island of Crete loomed in the warm darkness in front of them. Yannis was glad to see home again but could not help thinking about Petros and how he would explain his death when he returned home to the village. What would people think of him?

As the old, stone breakwater of Chania drew closer, and Pappadakis prepared to tie up and land all his passengers, Lieutenant Perkins made his way across the crowded deck to Yannis, stepping carefully over the recumbent bodies of the wounded and dying, as they lay waiting to be moved. He smiled, and offered his hand to the young Cretan. 'Yannis, thank you for all that you did to aid us, I could not have sorted things out with the captain without your help. We'll get these people some medical care, then find our regiments, if we can. What about you, what will you do?

Yannis shrugged. 'I don't know. My division no longer survives, it is smashed by the Germans. They will come here so I will find another unit, or perhaps become andarte'. As Perkins looked puzzled, he continued. 'Andartes is what you would call guerrillas. Fight and hide, disappear, fight again. Cretans fight good in the mountains, so instead of fighting each other, we will kill Germans. Even with one hand, I will kill'. His eyes glittered, taking on a hard glare at the thought of battles to come. Perkins was impressed, 'Well you frighten me, old chum, and I'm on your side!'

'Sir', added Yannis, formally, 'I have question, if you can help me'. 'Go on', said Perkins, intrigued, 'ask away'. 'Sir, if I am to shoot Germans, I need rifle. My rifle is in Pindos Mountains. You collect many rifles in Potamos, please to give one to me, so I may fight?'

Perkins first, instinctive thought was to refuse outright, he couldn't give the King's property away, it wasn't his to give. This first thought, though, was quickly followed by another. Yannis was a soldier, he wanted to defend his island, his home, his people. How would he, Perkins, feel if the Jerries were coming ashore in Auckland, his home town? He would want to fight them, wouldn't he? He made up his mind, and to hell with the rules!

'Yannis', he asked, 'Do you have dog-tags, or your identity papers as a soldier?' Yannis smiled, guessing where this was going. 'No papers on me, sir', he answered, 'but yes, in village. I have', he said, struggling for the correct words in English, 'I have my metal round, disc, with my army number. That shows I am soldier, Cretan Division'. He put his hand down the front of his shirt, pulling out a two tarnished metal discs on a chain, marked with numbers and Greek characters. 'Number is me, letters is Fifth Brigade, which is Cretan Division', he explained.

'In that case', grinned Perkins, picking up a Lee-Enfield from the small pile on the deck, 'The British Army, through this Kiwi, is happy to help its Greek allies. Make sure it's a good 'un and take a couple of hundred rounds too and some spare magazines. I know you won't waste them!' Yannis was about to express his thanks when another voice butted in.

'You goin' huntin' mate? Be a bit slow with one hand but that won't stop you, will it mate? Good luck to you! Give us yer hand, and give 'em hell' It was Bert, who had helped him in the galley. They seemed like old friends after the past couple of days, although both understood the nature of war, how you entered the lives of people around you for minutes or hours or days then moved on to the next fight and the next group of strangers. Friendships were short but nonetheless, real.

Pelican tied up, and as helpers jumped onto the boat to help disembark the wounded, Yannis clambered up the short ladder to the quay. He had thanked Pappadakis and Spiros for their kindness in taking him on, and with a final wave to Lieutenant Perkins, walked into Chania.

Chapter 5

On the morning of the 14th May, a beautiful, sunny spring day with perfect visibility, it began. Tom was watching Corporal Ralph Jones, together with Williams J, Lance Corporal, finishing a kit inspection. Heads lifted as the men began to hear a subdued roar, slowly increasing in volume as it came closer. 'Air raid, to your positions, wait for my instructions!' roared Tom. Already he could distinguish the unsynchronised stutter of the German bombers' engines, for that is what they were. Lieutenant Chalmers joined him,' Sergeant, mortar teams under cover, nothing they can do for now.' The men got the message and dispersed to their positions.

Nodding in reply, Tom jumped down into Pit A. All their equipment was squared away under cover, as were the mortar team. 'All OK, Ralph?' he asked the corporal. 'Yes, Tom. Just as long as we don't get a direct hit!'. 'Let's hope not, eh'. Ducking into the men's shelter, Tom had a quick word with them all, and made sure he spoke to Williams D, Davey. Davey was 18, a big, strong-looking lad, fresh from his basic training and the least experienced of his men. 'Davey lad, just remember your job, do what Ralph tells you and you'll do well.' Davey looked pale and worried but nodded at Tom and tried to smile. 'He'll do alright' thought Tom.

Now outside the shelter, Tom could see that the bombers, it looked like about 30 of them, had lined up to bomb positions to their west. They were in range of anti-aircraft artillery placed around the town and already, black clouds of smoke and the crack and blast of shells indicated that the defence had started.

One Dornier bomber had smoke and flames bursting from one engine but kept its place in the line of planes, already dropping their destruction over the hill-side village of Galatas, down to the hospital on the coast. Tom could see and hear a ragged series of explosions and shuddered at the effect that high explosives, shrapnel and incendiaries would have in the narrow streets of the village. Clouds of black smoke and thick dust began to rise, mercifully hiding the destruction from Tom's view, but the pounding continued. To their east, more planes were attacking the remaining shipping in Souda Bay, adding to the smoke and noise. One German plane, obviously hit, tipped onto one wing and crashed into the water, exploding with a roar and surge of spray and debris, almost lost in the cacophony around them.

Then, all was quiet. Men started to come out from under cover, but were ordered to stay where they were by Tom, and by other sergeants along the line. They guessed that this was the beginning and certainly not the end. Sure enough, within a few moments, more planes were heard and the few anti-aircraft guns began to fire again. This raid ignored the bay and Tom realised that the Division was its target. 'Mortar teams stay under cover', he roared and ran a few yards along the slit trench to where the Bren team were set up to fire. 'Now then, George, you know the score,' he murmured, 'only fire if they're in range. You'll not bring one down but you might put them off their stroke!' 'Don't you worry about me, Tom Lane,' replied the gunner, an older lance-jack with thin, greying hair, 'I was aiming a gun when you was still on your mother's tit!' Only George Parry, with more than twenty years' service, would ever speak to Tom in such a manner, and Tom smiled despite the imminent danger. George had taken him under his wing more than ten years previously when he had signed up with the Fusiliers, looked after him and taught him to be a soldier, more or less, and had been posted to this regiment with him, and others, after Dunkirk. Tom knew, as did everyone else in the Division, that George had forgotten more about soldiering than most of them would ever learn, and would always do his job, whatever the pressure. Sergeant's rank would have been his if he had wanted it but George had always refused, he was happy where he was.

The noise overhead grew louder and Tom looked up. 'Time to earn your money, George', he said, raising his voice to be heard above the increasing racket of aero engines, and moved out of the way to the back of the pit. He watched George pull back the cocking lever of the Bren and it was ready to fire. A tracer, after every fifth round, would help him track his shooting, or so it was hoped but with an effective range of 600 yards, it would only be of use if the enemy employed dive bombers or strafed from low level. Both were likely.

The Germans must have registered the anti-aircraft gun emplacements to the west of the Division because they were obviously the first targets. Dive bombers, all Stukas, peeled off from the group and with great discipline, dived vertically towards their targets, engines howling and sirens screaming. Tom could see this being repeated all along the valley out towards the Maleme road, huge crumps as their bombs exploded and clouds of black smoke rising into the clear sky. They were not getting it all their own way though, shells were bursting around the planes as they dived and Tom could hear the crackle of small arms fire, aimed at the Stukas as they bottomed out before climbing again. George had held his fire, the range being too great as yet.

After about a quarter of an hour of this relentless assault, Tom began to notice that the defensive anti-aircraft fire was lessening. He guessed that guns and their crews were being destroyed and that the line of attack would now gradually move east, and would include the Welch boys in their targeting. Planes were seen to be heading north, back to the mainland where they came from but fresh planes were taking their place. This must be their first big effort at reducing the defences before an invasion, he thought. 'George,' he cried, 'give 'em some stick, George!' George looked across, winked, and settled back behind his sights, his loader behind and to his side, fresh magazine ready in hand.

A huge, penetrating engine roar, accompanied by the ear-piercing shriek of the sirens seemed to burst into Tom's head as the first plane dived over them. Louder and louder and louder as the Stuka reached the bottom of its dive, then changing in tone if not volume, as it began to slowly accelerate away. At the same time, Tom heard the chug chug chug of the Bren as George began to fire. He dragged his eyes away from the retreating plane to see George swinging the automatic rifle on the tripod, tracking the Stuka at its most vulnerable point in the manoeuvre. 'Must have hit the bastard' exulted Tom!

Another split second passed, then Tom felt himself hurled to the ground, all the breath pushed from his body, his ears and head in agony from the huge explosion of the 500kg bomb dropped by the plane. George and his second were also thrown down violently and for a moment, Tom feared that everything was over, that all their training had been for nothing and they had failed in their first action. He struggled to move, he couldn't seem to shift but then felt a strong hand pulling him upright, then onto his feet. 'Now then, Tom', shouted George, for it was him. 'No lying down on the job. They missed us, we needs to be shooting back, come on!' George's loader was still lying on the ground, arms splayed out. Tom couldn't see a wound, maybe he had been knocked unconscious. There was no time to check, because the next plane was well into its dive and would be releasing its bomb soon enough.

Tom took his place as George's loader but before they could shoot, the diving Stuka suddenly vanished in a huge blast, and the two of them dived into a niche built into the sandbagged wall of the trench, dragging the unconscious loader by his webbing, as pieces of wreckage, large and small, fell to the ground, some falling with great velocity and landing with a massive thump, others spiralling down slowly, like burning paper from a fire. 'Good shot, somebody' grinned George, pulling Tom back out to man their gun, which by good luck, had not been hit by any debris.

They seemed to be completely surrounded by guns firing. Artillery, light weapons, some Stuka pilots were strafing as they dived. It was utterly deafening and confusing but George already had the Bren to his shoulder. Tom was able to do all the duties in the platoon, and knew the routine for Bren loader. George began to shoot in short, controlled bursts as the next plane, seemingly attacking an artillery placement about 150 yards away, neared the bottom of its dive. As it began to flatten out before climbing away, George shouted 'Mag!' This was the signal for Tom to quickly remove the empty magazine and replace it with a full one. Tom had practiced this routine many times in the last few months and the new magazine was in without delay. George fired again, scoring hits around the engine, then the canopy. Others were firing at the same target and at the exact moment that the artillery emplacement was obliterated by the bomb delivered by the Stuka, the plane seemed to stutter, twist in the air as if unbalanced then dive headlong into the ground in front of the trenches, a huge pall of flame and smoke marking its position. There was no time though to celebrate, as more flights of enemy planes were seen to join the battle.

'Take cover!' bellowed Tom, diving again for the shelter of the trench wall, for he had spotted more planes, this time manoeuvring to fly parallel with the line of the trench, to strafe and annihilate the defenders of this frail line. He was astonished to see George calmly sighting his gun, waiting for the first Messerschmitt 109 to come within range as it began to traverse the length of the trench line, firing its 20mm cannon and machine guns at men and guns alike. Without conscious thought, Tom found himself back out in the trench with George, who grinned and nodded towards the small heap of filled magazines. Looking west, they could see black smoke beginning to fill the valley and hear the burst of cannon shells, above the deafening roar of aero engines. In a few seconds only, the first fighter was on them, shells landing in front and behind them, somehow missing the two soldiers but finding the shelter in Mortar pit A. George got off a few bursts at the 109 but it was so low and so fast that it was in and out of range in a matter of a few seconds. There was no time to check for casualties in the shelter before the next plane erupted along the line of the trench.

This time, George gave a good lead to his bursts, the German plane flying into and through his cone of fire. They could see a plume of white smoke venting from the engine but again, the plane was gone before they could take another shot at it.

The raid continued for the next four hours, with sometimes a few minutes to bring up more ammunition, take a much needed drink of lukewarm water and take casualties to safety. The four man mortar team in Pit A, their shelter hit by cannon shells, no longer existed. Ralph Jones, the corporal in charge, was killed instantly. Of the two privates whose job was to keep the mortar supplied with bombs, one was silently clutching a chest wound, with blood frothing between the fingers of his covering hands, the other lay, disembowelled and dead, beside him. Young Davey Williams, whom Tom had taken time to encourage, was untouched, lying as if frozen among the bodies of his pals. George helped Tom pull him out of the remains of the shelter, sending him up for a rest at the medical tent, with his wounded mate carried on a stretcher alongside him. 'Have a brew and a fag, Davey, then come back, we need you'.

By the time Davey returned, the raid was over. Both George and Tom had been cut by flying stones, but not seriously, and they could still fight. The Pit B mortar team was still intact, ready to fight another day. Of the three other Bren teams, one man had been killed, blown to pieces by a direct hit. Three others were injured but only one seriously, the other two had returned as soon as their wounds were dressed.

Tom sat for a few moments on the fire-step with George and Davey. 'And how is Evans', asked George, referring to the private with the chest wound. 'He died', whispered Davey. 'He was dead before we got him to the MO'. George placed a consoling arm around his shoulders, while Tom sighed, stood up slowly and moved off, to find Lieutenant Chalmers and then to reorganise the remains of the platoon.

The next five days brought more of the same, more bombing and strafing by the Luftwaffe which steadily reduced the defenders, and their ability to defend. Anti-aircraft artillery, never generous in number, was almost wiped out. Even more dead ships lay in Souda Bay, and supplies of food and ammunition were hard to come by. Men grew weary and hungry, there were signs that morale was beginning to fray and Tom had a feeling that a full attack was bound to come soon. He and the Lieutenant did all they could to prepare their men for each new day, knowing that tomorrow might be the day that decided all their futures.

Chapter 6

May 20th began as any other day, with stand-to at dawn and a hurried breakfast of bully beef and tea, taken in position. If the previous few days were anything to go by, there would be an early morning bombing to endure, with precious little anti-aircraft defence still operational. Tom was feeling the strain of six days under aerial assault, and knew that his men were suffering too. If they were not being bombed, they would be soon, they realised, and that kind of pressure gets to a man, thought Tom. Increasing casualties had made it increasingly difficult to give people time out of the trench, as the mortar and Bren teams had to be able to work at a moment's notice. Lieutenant Chalmers stepped up to Tom. 'Sergeant, I have a feeling we won't have to wait for much longer before the Jerries make their big push for the island'. 'I think you are right, sir. Not much point in pounding us like this for much longer, they'll want to get on with job. I would, if I was in their shoes'. 'What about the men, Sergeant? They look tired to me'. 'They are tired, sir, we all are' replied Tom, 'including me, but they'll do fine when it starts. They haven't been able do much as yet, trying to bring planes down with small arms is never going to win it for us but when they have some proper targets, you'll see their mettle, sir'. 'I'm sure you are right, Tom. I don't doubt them, good men'. Both men paused and looked up as they heard the familiar drone of aero engines. 'To your post, Tom, and good luck!'

The attack started with a short but heavy bombing run from an altitude beyond the range of any small arms. Bombs thundered down either side of the trench line but there were no further casualties, the trenches now being deep enough to protect the men from anything except a direct hit.

Ending the short pause after the final explosions, the swelling thunder of multiple aero engines again caused Tom to lift his eyes to the sky. Looking north, he was astonished to see a swarm of grey planes coming in from above and behind Chania, having just dropped their tow lines from the tug planes that had dragged them across the Mediterranean from mainland Greece. Momentarily stunned at the sight, he noticed the huge wingspan of the planes, out of proportion to the size of the fuselage, and then the absence of engines. No engines!

'Stand to, stand to!' he bellowed. 'Gliders to the north, fire when ordered!' Tom watched as the twelve or so gliders, still out of range, separated into two groups, six carrying on towards the Akrotiri peninsula while the remaining six continued to bank until they were flying directly east, swooping down and down, aiming to land astride the road that lay between the Division and the outskirts of the town.

Stacked between about two hundred to eight hundred feet, and spread over half a mile of sky, the gliders moved into range, and Rangers to the right of Tom's division beginning to engage with small arms and a surviving Bofors gun. They took some hits but losing altitude as quickly as they were, they dipped one by one behind a low hill, to the frustration of the Rangers' gunners.

As they dropped the last few feet, and moving out of the shadow of the hill, the six gliders landed safely on either side of the road, slowing down quickly on the stony ground. Before they had the chance to fully stop and begin to deplane their troops, Lieutenant Chalmers was heard to roar in a huge voice that carried the length of the trench, 'Range four hundred, give 'em everything! Sergeant, get your mortars onto them!' Unfortunately for the troops inside the gliders, they had landed directly to the front of Company B.

It was as if all the frustrations of the last few days were poured into the unlucky German troops as Bren gun and rifle fire smashed into the gliders, passing through the canvas walls as if they were paper. An explosion inside one of the gliders, probably as a result of a grenade or an explosive detonating from small arms fire, blew it in half and as two survivors staggered out of the wreckage which was beginning to burn fiercely, they were cut down before they had taken more than a couple of steps.

George Parry now showed his skill. With the Bren on the bipod, balanced on the lip of the trench, George swept fire backwards and forwards along the length of the right hand glider, firing three, thirty-round magazines before he was satisfied that no one would emerge from the wreckage. As Tom watched, George calmly switched his aim to the next glider in the line. He shot three troopers as they attempted to dash away into cover, then moved his aim back to the glider, pouring burst after burst through the pilot's position and down through the length of the plane. At four hundred yards, it was slaughter.

The mortar teams in pits A and B were not going to be left out of the battle. Four hundred yards was almost point blank range and both mortars were on target within two shots. 'Fire for effect' yelled Tom, acting as spotter for Pit A, and bombs started to hail down upon the gliders, with near misses driving shrapnel through and through their thin walls. A few German troopers, realising that immediate deplaning was their only chance of survival, were able to find low cover in a shallow ditch along the road but were quickly exposed by mortar fire, which wiped them out to a man.

Tom could see that, further down the valley to the west, to their left, more gliders had landed or were coming in. They seemed to be taking huge punishment and he knew that if this was how the Nazis hoped to take Crete, then they would fail. Trained, entrenched defenders would always win out.

Minutes passed, then the throb of multi-engined planes was heard again, to the north-west. In a line from the coastal hospital, south to beyond Galatas, Junkers 52 transport planes were disgorging countless black figures who quickly sprouted white canopies and drifted slowly towards the ground. Parachute troops! As they descended, Tom could hear the rattle of fire and explosions as the defenders found their range. Unknown to the German command, Prison Valley and Galatas village were heavily defended by the New Zealand Division's 10th Brigade and the 6th and 8th Greek regiments, who poured fire into the paratroopers as they neared the ground. Tom could see troopers slumped in their parachute harnesses, dead before they reached the ground. Others hurtled into the hard, rocky ground as their chutes burned above them. It was carnage, and Tom thought fleetingly of these young men descending to their deaths, unable to save themselves. 'Is this what we've come to', he thought.

It remained a passing thought, quickly forgotten, because at that moment Lieutenant Chalmers roared, in a bellow heard the length of the trench.

'They're here!' Tom looked up, amazed to see a line of parachutes, maybe sixty or more, drifting directly down around them, on both sides of the slit trench. 'Wait till they're in range,' he screamed, 'don't waste a shot!' They hardly needed telling, as the paratroopers were met with a huge volume of fire. Some landed within ten yards of the trench, either already dead or immediately blown off their feet by close range fire.

'Aim at their feet!' shouted Tom, thinking that would compensate for the drop of the descending soldiers. He emptied a ten-shot magazine into the men, hearing screams and cries as they floated down to their destruction. Canopies and bodies, and parts of bodies, littered the ground around the trench, as the platoon continued to engulf the invaders with their firepower.

But not all the paratroopers landed so close to the line. To Tom and his section's astonishment, as a batch of them alighted in and around an olive grove between their line and the city, they were immediately attacked, ferociously, by a baying throng of Cretan locals, all armed with whatever weapons they could find, and led by what looked like the local priest. The Germans managed to bring down a few of the attackers before they closed with them, but they were rapidly overwhelmed and massacred. Hunting rifles, augmented with axes, knives and clubs, and wielded by old men and women, were enough to rout the invaders in short order. Some troopers, having landed in the branches of olive trees and struggling to release themselves from their parachute harnesses, were despatched as they hung, suspended above the ground. Others were simply smashed off their feet, then bludgeoned and battered where they lay. None were spared.

A group of about twenty landed around an old monastery, about six hundred yards away from Tom's section, in the valley. They were engaged with Bren gun fire but nearly all of them gained temporary shelter in the building, from where they began to return fire. A further, larger group of troopers, having landed behind the house in a fold in the ground and thus having avoided massacre in the air, were seen to join them. The monastery, an old and substantial building, looked strong enough to defy any amount of small arms fire, enabling the new inhabitants to return fire at the Division. 'We must break this up', thought Tom, ducking as fire from the monastery cracked over his head.

Lieutenant Chalmers clearly had the same idea. 'Sergeant, we have to winkle them out of there before they do some serious harm. This is what we'll do. We'll take half of the platoon each, except for the mortar teams. On my word, both mortars will drop smoke in front of the monastery. You move right, and get around the back. I'll attack from the front with grenades and we'll soon shift 'em. Any that try to move through the back, you take care of 'em. Collect your men, we move in five minutes, understand?' Tom could only say 'Sir!' in acknowledgement, and rushed away to assemble his men.

With all gathered, the lieutenant gave the signal for smoke and Tom immediately heard the thud of the mortars firing. Grey, impenetrable smoke billowed up in front of the monastery and Chalmers and Tom led their sections out at a crouch.

The passage to the monastery took longer than Tom had anticipated, as the Germans in the monastery, guessing that an attack was in hand, began to fire at random through the smoke. A man behind Tom collapsed as a stray shot took him but Tom allowed no one to stop, they had to reach the monastery. More smoke bombs added to the fog, someone was using their initiative, thought Tom, enabling the group to locate the side wall of the building and follow it around to the rear.

At the back of the building, a courtyard was entered through a gateway large enough for a wagon. He considered placing his men outside the courtyard to pick up stragglers but it seemed to him that it would allow anyone escaping from the back of the building to take cover behind the courtyard wall and cause more trouble. So, leaving three men outside the courtyard in case anyone got through, he and the remaining ten men, including George Parry, moved towards the gateway. Gesturing to George, they both rolled smoke grenades into the courtyard. The ten men moved through the gateway, dividing into two groups of five and moving as quietly as they could up both sides of the courtyard. 'George', whispered Tom to Parry, standing next to him. 'Sight your Bren on that door', pointing at an old wooden double-door which stood at the top of some stone steps. 'If they come this way, that's where it'll be'. Parry nodded, unfolding the bipod under the rifle.

They didn't have long to wait. Tom recognised the boom of a grenade, quickly followed by another and by automatic gunfire from the front of the building. Shouting and screaming came from inside and outside the monastery, the usual hubbub of battle as Lieutenant Chalmers started his attack. Almost immediately, the door in front of Tom's men opened and a group of German parachutists, perhaps a rear-guard taking their chance to escape, all armed, burst out of the building and onto the top of the stone steps. They paused, noticing the remains of the smoke but took no further steps as, before they could move, George's Bren burst into life. At such a short range, they were killed where they stood, bullets crashing through bodies and into the ones behind. One magazine was enough to turn half a dozen armed and fit young men into so much torn and abused flesh, in a spreading pool of their own blood. There was a very brief, stunned silence as the thud of the Bren gun died away, then Tom led the way into the monastery.

It seemed dark inside, compared to the brightness of the day outside but some light was coming from in front, from under a door, and from behind where they had entered, so there was enough to get by. Ahead they could hear more firing, more voices as the battle continued at the front of the building. Tom was well aware how easy and stupid it would be to lead his men into the line of fire from their comrades and indeed, he could hear rounds thudding into the thick walls that seemed to separate him and his men from the defending German troops. As his eyes gradually adjusted in the gloom, he could see a heavy door to his right, from behind which he could not only hear the sounds of battle but also of German voices, raised in rage and fear, as their owners fought for their lives.

Gesturing to two privates, armed with rifles and bayonets, to move alongside him, he was surprised when George Parry quickly elbowed one of them out of his way and took his place, next to Tom. He grinned at Tom, 'Well, what's keeping you?'

Tom, resigned, nodded. The door had been left unlocked and the three of them burst through into the room behind, the others close behind.

They were lucky. The door opened into one side of the room, not the back, and the defending parachutists were lined up across the room in front of them, facing left, in the direction of the Lieutenant's attack. Without knowing the layout of the room or of the monastery, Tom and his men had flanked the defenders, giving themselves a great advantage.

Tom lunged at the nearest soldier, a tall blond private holding a machine pistol which was beginning to swing his way. His bayonet took the man above the sternum, Tom howling in his fighting rage as he twisted the blade between his ribs. As he withdrew it from the soldier's body, it jammed in the bone and he couldn't shift it! Beside him, he was aware of George firing from the hip, his whole body swinging as he hosed a full magazine around the room, dropping trooper after trooper. As George quickly paused to change to a full magazine, a paratrooper who had been out of his line of fire raised his carbine to shoot him. Without a thought, Tom let go of his rifle and flung himself across the room, cannoning into the midriff of the trooper who brought the butt of his weapon down onto Tom's head as he fell. The last Tom knew, as consciousness left him, was of bullets crashing all around his body, then all was quiet.

Chapter 7

Tom slowly, gradually, became aware of a crashing pain in the left side of his head. Eyes still closed, his left hand automatically moved up to where the pain was, coming across a bandage wrapped around his head, with a thick dressing underneath. Even a gentle touch gave him an excruciating, sharp pain, and he must have groaned. 'Ah, you're coming to, and about time, Sergeant' said a friendly voice. 'What happened', croaked Tom, opening his eyes, 'and where am I?' 'You're in the sick bay, it's a bunker now, not a tent, it was too dangerous. You know me, Parsons, sick bay orderly. The hospital is where you should be but there are too many Jerries around it to get you there. You took a hell of a crack to the head but as far as the M.O. can tell, there's no fracture. You'll have a headache for a while yet but unless he's missed something, you should be fit to return to duties in a couple of days. Now, I'll get you a drink and something to eat if you think you can manage it'.

'Hang on, Parsons', said Tom, 'how long have I been out of it?' 'You were brought here at about eleven yesterday morning, and you've been unconscious for about thirty hours'. Tom was astonished. 'And what's happened to the platoon, and the lieutenant? Are we still fighting?' 'Tell you what, Sergeant', answered Parsons. 'Your lance-jack, Parry is it? He's been by a couple of times to see if you were woken up yet, it's quiet again outside, I'll see if he can give you a catch-up for a few minutes, I can see you won't rest until you know. And I'll fetch you a brew, alright?' 'Until I know what?' said Tom but Parsons was gone. Tom closed his eyes and sleep claimed him once again.

He awoke to a hand gently shaking him by the shoulder. 'Tom, wake up, I only got a minute'. Tom recognised George's voice, and was glad to hear it. 'George, what happened? Where's Chalmers? What about the boys?' There was a pause before George replied. 'Well', he said, 'we took the monastery all right, killed and wounded two dozen or more of 'em, took twenty five prisoners. We'd six casualties, miracle there wasn't more. Two dead, four wounded including you, two serious'. 'What about the lieutenant?' asked Tom, getting a feeling that George was holding something back. 'He copped it, mate. Shot him as he lobbed in the first grenade. Reckon they'd still be in there if we hadn't surprised 'em from the side, and after we shot the one that clobbered you, they started to give up, surrender. Lads is sorry 'bout Chalmers, he were a good 'un for an officer'. 'Yes, he was' answered Tom, knowing that there would be plenty more deaths to come.

'Take your rest, Tom, the boys will be glad to know you're still in the land of the living. We needs you, mind. No more drops here but plenty towards Maleme, we hears. And still some of them parachuters bothering us, sniping and all. Plenty more fighting to do yet'. Tom nodded. 'George, I'll be back in the morning, tell the lads. I'm sorry about Chalmers too'.

George went back to the line, leaving Tom with his thoughts. He managed to drink a brew from Parsons but passed on the bully beef sandwich. 'A few hours' kip', he thought, 'then back to it'.

Tom still felt groggy the following morning but knew he had to get back to the platoon. He gingerly made his way back down the hill to the trench, returning before stand-to. There were a few smiles and nods from the men, pleased he was back with them in the line. Men always fought better with leadership, and they knew that Tom would provide it.

George approached him. 'It's a good morning to you, Sergeant Lane', he said with his usual smile, but looking pale and tired under his tan. 'Welcome back. While I remember, we had a visit from Captain Thomas last night, when I got back from seeing you. There's no lieutenant to sit in for Mr Chalmers, he said, we'll have to make do, he said'. 'Yes, George, I thought that might happen, too many casualties. You're my corporal now, with Ralph gone, I'll sort it out with the captain. Look after stand-to for me, I want a weapons inspection, you take the Bren teams, and Richard Smith'll look after the mortars. Get me an ammunition count too, Richard'll do the same, we'll have gone through plenty. We might have to scrounge from the Rangers, if they can spare any. I'll find Captain Thomas and see what his orders are, meet you and Richard in thirty minutes. Right, Corporal?' 'Sergeant'. George nodded and carried on.

Captain Thomas was receiving orders himself, in the command bunker, further down the trench and Tom had to wait until he came out. 'Ah, Sergeant Lane, I was just coming to find you, there's a job for your platoon. We've knocked off most of those paratroopers and glider bods but there's still some out there with a heavy machine-gun, we reckon a mile or so out and the CO wants them taken care of before they build up into something substantial. I want five in a patrol, corporal in charge'. 'Sir' interrupted Tom. 'No, Sergeant, I know just what you are going to say. You don't have a lieutenant, your platoon cannot lose you as well, not now. The Division is short of NCOs and there's more trouble coming, Maleme airfield is lost we're hearing, so the Jerries will be bringing in reinforcements as fast as they can. We need to reduce them at this end, do you see, and we need you in one piece, at least for now'. 'Yes sir', said Tom, reluctantly. 'Parry will be your new corporal, I imagine? Tom nodded. 'A good man, knows his work, tell him he's promoted. Choose another four to go with him'. He handed a map to Tom. 'I want the patrol out here, to the north-east, no further than a mile and a half. Tell them to take a Bren and rifles, there's a Thompson spare too. Everyone carries grenades. Get them out by 0700, they should take that gully behind you for the first four hundred yards or so, then they'll have to find whatever cover they can. Tell Parry to take his time, do a reccie first if he can. There's a machine gun up there somewhere, bear that in mind, the way the ground lies he might be able to flank it from the right and get above them. Parry might want to call in a mortar if he finds a fixed position though. He can send a runner back with the map reference and your boys can have a crack. Sentries along the line will be warned your men are up there, they may not come back down the same way. Anything else for now, Sergeant?' 'No sir, we'll get cracking, they'll be ready for 0700'. 'Thank you Sergeant, report back later, and good luck'.

Tom knew that Captain Thomas was right but it grieved and angered him that he was sending men off to do a dangerous job without himself in the lead, he was used to being the man at the front, leading by example. He wasn't worried about George Parry's leadership, he would be able to pull it off if anyone could. You couldn't call it a properly thought-out plan either but these were not normal times, he conceded. George would have to improvise, make it up as he went along but that was war, and it would probably suit George anyway.

Tom made his way back down the trench line, calling for George to join him. Running through the Captain's orders quickly, he told George that his promotion was approved and then they deliberated who should be in the patrol. As George was in charge of the patrol for this action, Tom allowed him to make his choices, knowing that if he was confident enough to choose them, then their chances of success were improved. He interrupted though when George said he wanted Davey Williams. 'Are you sure, George? He looked really rattled when Ralph Jones and Evans bought it. Shouldn't you leave him behind with the mortars? That's what he's trained for, after all'. 'No, Tom', answered George, firmly. 'He was rattled but wouldn't you be, covered in blood and guts from your best pal? Him and Evans joined up together, both of them from Swansea. Didn't know each other before but you know how it is, they chummed up, helped each other out, got pissed together. He wants the chance to get his own back a bit, for Evans and for himself'. Tom was about to interrupt but George got in first. 'And he's a bloody good soldier, first-class shot, can lob a grenade further than anyone. Shouldn't be in the mortars, really. Wasted, he is'. Tom knew when he was beaten and when all came to all, he knew that George's judgement was reliable, and that he wouldn't take a passenger on such a tough job.

Together, they rounded up their 'Chosen Few' and briefed them to their task. Davey Williams was offered the Tommy-gun but said he would rather just use his SMLE, his Lee-Enfield. He knew it better and it was well sighted-in for him.

Everyone had a bite and a drink, and was loaded up with a generous amount of ammunition, two Mills bombs each and a canteen of water, for the day was already hot. Five minutes before the starting time, the patrol was ready, Tom with them as they waited for the last few minutes to pass.

To his surprise, Captain Thomas appeared at his elbow. 'All set, Sergeant?' he queried. 'Yes, sir', he replied, 'ready as they'll ever be'. 'Parry, good luck. Give 'em hell and we'll see you in a few hours' said the Captain to George, as he steadied himself to scramble over the edge of the trench. 'Thank you, sir', answered Parry, grinning. 'Hell it is'. He motioned to the patrol to follow to him and one by one, they disappeared over the lip of the trench, crouching low as they moved into the gully.

'Sergeant' said Thomas. 'Keep some men standing-to, in case they need covering fire on their return'. Tom's face must have betrayed his feelings because the captain quickly continued, looking tense and worried, 'Sorry, Sergeant, you know your job, of course, but if you don't mind, I shall stay with you until they get back. My orders, my responsibility'. Tom had always thought Captain Thomas to be something of a cold fish but he had clearly misjudged the man. He was strong enough to give difficult orders but also human enough to understand the possible cost. Together, they waited.

The following hours felt like the most endless of Tom's army service, and he would have given anything to be up there with George and his men, where he thought that he could do some good. He felt useless, just waiting. Fortunately, the Luftwaffe seemed to be either having a rest or attacking another part of the island-wide defence, because they were not troubled by further bombing or strafing that morning.

All was quiet for the first hour and a half, then both Tom and the captain jumped up as they heard the rapid firing of a machine gun, the repeat so fast that it was almost impossible to pick out separate rounds. 'MG 42, know it anywhere', said Thomas, 'heard enough of them in the desert. They've been seen!' Before Tom could answer, he began to hear the more deliberate thud thud thud of a Bren gun, and the whiplash crack of more than one SMLE. The exchange of fire continued at more or less the same rate for the next few minutes, with brief intervals as people reloaded, then restarted firing. Gradually though, the volume of fire started to reduce. The buzz of the MG 42 continued unchanged for a few more minutes, interrupted by the occasional snap of a British .303. Then, it seemed to Tom and the captain, the machine gun was firing on its own.

The officer and NCO exchanged glances, both downcast, both thinking that the patrol had failed, had been wiped out. But before either could speak, their heads jerked up at hearing a muffled boom from up the hill, perhaps half a dozen rifle shots then silence. 'Sir', pleaded Tom, 'Let me take a couple of men up to the top of the gully, see what's happening, they might need some help'. Captain Thomas looked at him, hesitated, then nodded. Quickly, Tom pulled two men from the B Mortar team, telling them to bring their rifles. He stuffed a pack full of field dressings and collected as many syrettes of morphine as he could from the remaining men in the platoon. He joined the two at the trench wall and they quickly scrambled over the sandbags, through the same gap in the barbed wire that George's patrol had used, then down into the gully.

The gully was long and very dry, seeming to catch and magnify the heat of the sun as it climbed higher into the sky. With Tom leading, the three of them scrambled carefully upwards, each one taking a turn to watch for the enemy as the other two climbed. It was almost an hour later that they reached the top, and as Tom went to step out onto the hillside, he froze as a shower of pebbles ran down the slope alongside him. Signalling to the other two to stop, he took his rifle from his shoulder, pushing the safety catch forward, ready to fire. Slowly, he lifted his head to see over the lip of the gully, rifle ready to catch whoever might be coming down the hill.

Twenty yards further up the stony slope, carrying a man on his back, staggering as he carefully negotiated the uneven rocks and sharp edges of an indistinct path, one hand clapped over a bloody dressing on his side, came George Parry. He looked all in, his tunic soaked in blood, and Tom quickly moved out of the gully, followed by the two mortar boys, and up the hill to help him. George smiled in relief as Tom approached, gently laying the man he carried onto ground beside him.

'No questions, Tom, not yet, no time!' he murmured in a dry, cracked voice, hardly recognisable as his own. 'First thing, you two get Jones down to the MO, quick. He copped a round in the knee, a lot of bleeding, put a new dressing on it if you've got one, no morphine, I've given him a shot already. Tell the captain we need a party up here to help us bring down the other three. Sergeant, I need you to help me bring young Davey down first, he's just up the hill but the other two, well….they're dead'. Seeing Tom's shocked face, he added, 'Davey's wounded, Tom, Jerry bullet clipped the side of his head, tumbled him over, banged his head on a rock, knocked him out. He's woke up now but he don't know where he is. He's too big for me, the great lump, but the two of us should manage him'.

He paused for breath and Tom quickly asked him, 'What about you, George, are you hurt bad and the Jerries, what about the Jerries? Do we need another go at them?' 'Ah, bayonet slid along my ribs, just a slash. As for the Jerries, no, no need for another go. Me and Davey fucked over the lot of them, but they killed two of my boys first'. A few, slow tears slid down his face, cutting through the muck and the dirt of the battle he had fought, and won.

Chapter 8

Later, when the two casualties were safely in the care of the MO, and the two dead had been brought down to await burial, George met with Tom and Captain Thomas to give his report. He was handed a mug of gunfire, tea laced with rum, as he sat down, and sipping at it, began to talk.

He addressed himself to the officer, but looked across to Tom often, sharing with him the closest personal knowledge of all the men in the patrol. 'Sir, everything was smooth and easy to start. We was up that gully in an hour, going dead slow, nice and quiet. I split us up into two groups, like we planned, about thirty yards between them, after we left the gully. No trouble then either, we snuck up that first slope and as far as I can tell you, no one picked up we was there. We took off round to the right, like you said, Captain, carried on up for ten minutes or so then I reckoned we should move back left, we was running out of hill you see. Damn me, there they was, about fifty yards below us. I could see half a dozen or more of them, they'd built a good sangar, plenty of loose rock all over the place, a frontal assault would have been murder! They was talking, hadn't heard us by then. Davey and me moved off down and further right, real quiet. On my signal the other four would pour it into them and while they was engaged, me and Davey would rush them, finish them off'.

George paused, his eyes seeming to go out of focus as he put himself back on the side of that parched hill. He continued, 'I gave them the signal and it worked real well to start with. Them Jerries dived into cover and Jones and the other two was really giving it to them, kept up a good rate of fire. But they was quick to recover, they wasn't hit serious, see! They fired up a couple of rifle grenades, they done for Evans and Dobson, then Jones got his shot in his leg. But them boys did their duty, sir, because by then, me and Davey was nearly right on top of the sangar. Davey shot the gunner, I got his loader, rolled a grenade down and then we was in amongst them, bayonets and butts after that. They couldn't move to aim see, they got a couple of shots off and when Davey went down, I got the last two'.

He paused again, then continued. 'Then I went round the boys, saw who'd copped it, started bringing Jones down first because he'd lost a lot of blood, and there was Sergeant Lane, sir, thank you for sending him up. You know the rest, sir'.

There was a brief silence. 'Corporal Parry', said Captain Thomas earnestly, 'you all did your duty and more. That was as remarkable a piece of soldiering as I have come across. All five of you either wounded or dead but the job was done, and you will have saved many lives. I will get my report in and my guess is that Lieutenant Colonel Fraser will want what you did to be recognised with an award'. As George looked up, with the beginnings of an angry and scornful look upon his face, the captain hastily continued, 'I know, I know, Corporal. You don't want personal recognition or a gong, and no award will bring back Evans and Dobson, or fix Jones' leg, I understand that as well as you do. But if it happens, and I think it will, look on it as something for your section, for your platoon and for the whole division. What you and your lads did today was to the credit of the regiment, and will not be forgotten'. With a final nod to Tom, Captain Thomas stood up and walked off down the trench-line.

'How is Davey, George', asked Tom. 'He'll be alright', replied George. 'Sore head, bit of concussion, right as rain in a day or two' 'And you?' pressed Tom. 'Me? Good as new. MO put a few stitches over my ribs, still a bit sore. Better than those poor sods we killed up the hill, most of the blood on my kit was theirs. I know Thomas is doing his job and means well but I don't see no glory in shooting up German boys. It needs to be done, yes, because otherwise they would slaughter us, and I would do the same again and will do, won't hesitate, but don't ask me to be proud of it, no'.

'George, have a rest for a couple of hours. I don't want to see you until stand-to, I'll get someone to bring you some grub. I shall go and see Davey, then get the sections sorted out. There'll be more fighting to do yet'.

Chapter 9

The next days brought more disasters to the force defending Crete. Despite inflicting huge casualties upon the paratroops and glider-borne soldiers, the New Zealand 5th Brigade were withdrawn further and further east, towards Chania. The German army was able to then reinforce by air through Maleme and gradually began to gain superiority in manpower and equipment. The battle to defend Crete was beginning to be lost.

It was two days after the patrol's ambush of the machine gun team upon the hill. Strafing and bombing of the Company's position was still happening with regularity, and although the number of casualties was not catastrophic yet, they could not be replaced. Tom and George worked hard to maintain organisation and discipline but inevitably, the platoon was becoming makeshift. Only one mortar could be fully manned and both of the Bren teams were looking thin. Tom reported the state of the platoon to Captain Thomas, knowing full well that neither he nor any other officer could put things right. 'Sergeant' said the captain in response, 'if you need to move to one Bren and one mortar team, so be it. I would rather you had two functioning teams than one and two halves'. 'Then I'll get on with it, sir', replied Tom, and with his corporals' help, he used the rest of the morning to move the right men into the right teams, so that both were as strong as they could be.

Tom looked up as heard the gathering thunder of approaching aero engines. From the west, he could see ranks of enemy planes heading in their direction. There seemed to be no accompanying fighters though, and over the next few hours, he came to understand why.

Ignoring the dug-in troops this time, and contemptuous of the pitiful anti-aircraft fire coming up at them, the fleet of bombers started to drop their explosives, ton after ton, onto the city of Chania. Within a few minutes, it was lost in increasing clouds of smoke and dust, punctuated by the concussion of detonating bombs and the crash of collapsing masonry. There was no way of defending the city, no friendly fighter aircraft remaining on the island, so the bombers were free to do as they wished.

Tom cursed and swore as he watched the picturesque little city being systematically destroyed. 'Those fuckers, all those good people they're killing and for what? Fuck all! There's no military in Chania, it's not defendable, everyone knows that. The bastards, and we've got nothing left to throw at them!' Around him, the remainder of the platoon watched in disgust and increasing anger. In the few months they had been on the island, they had all spent time and money in Chania. They had been made welcome, in the hospitable Greek fashion, as if they were family friends, come to help out. Some of the lads had met girls in the town, sometimes in a bar but often as a result of a friendly family invitation. They liked the people, they liked the city, and they felt some responsibility both for the place and for the people who lived there.

While the bombing continued, no one could venture out onto the city streets. After three hours, there were no more planes, no more bombs and Tom began to field requests from the men for permission to help in rescuing survivors. He sought out the captain, to ask for authority to send out volunteers but received the immediate response that he expected. 'No, Sergeant, they bloody well can't. If we were up to strength, it might have been possible but we are not. We are down below half, as is the rest of the Battalion, and they know that. We need every man here, the skirmishing is nearly over, and the Jerries are going to come head on at us soon, they have to. I am sorry about the city but we can't help this time. Tell the lads, the best way to help their friends in the city is to do their job and shoot as many of the enemy that they can, when they get the chance. And they will have the chance very soon'. 'They understand that sir', answered Tom, 'but they feel bad about their friends with no help, mostly women and children, old people. They're fucking angry, sir'. Thomas sighed, still for a moment then looked at Tom directly in the eye. 'I am sorry, Sergeant, but my order must stand. Tell your lads I know how they feel but there will be no rescue attempts. We're expecting a full attack by tomorrow at the latest and the Battalion needs every man to hand. Company B, including this platoon, will do its job'. 'Yes, sir', answered Tom, knowing that Captain Thomas had his own orders. He would pass the news back to the lads and get their minds back onto the task in hand. If Captain Thomas was correct, then they would be busy soon enough.

It was the middle of the evening, as Tom walked around the remnants of the platoon, checking that everyone had been fed and having a quiet word with whoever he thought needed it, that he noticed the captain climbing down into the trench. Thomas beckoned him over, Tom noticing that he looked grim in his expression. 'Sergeant, I want you to ready your platoon. Arms and as much ammunition as they can carry. Also any extra rations they can manage, water too'. His voice was quiet but strong and steady. 'The Regiment is ordered to march on Galatas and form a defensive line. There will be some help from the New Zealanders and the Aussies, our job will be to hold off the Jerries while the rest of Creforce begin a withdrawal to the south coast for evacuation'. Tom was astounded.

'Retreat, sir? We've held them for a week, with a bit of reinforcement we could hold them for longer! We're down on men and supplies but....' Thomas interrupted, 'It's orders, Sergeant, from General Freyberg to Lieutenant Colonel Fraser. There will be no reinforcements coming. The decision has been made to evacuate Creforce, as far as is possible, and the job we have been given is to cover their withdrawal for a minimum of twenty four hours, longer if possible, then get out ourselves'. Tom laughed, but with no smile. 'Lucky if we manage that, sir, being tail-end Charlies'. Before Captain Thomas could reply, Tom's professionalism and pride in his profession, honed over the previous ten years, overruled his immediate anxiety. 'We'll do a job, sir, give the Jerries a proper fight. Holding for twenty four hours shouldn't be beyond us, ammo might be short after that. What about casualties, sir, any transport available for their evacuation?' 'Yes, Sergeant. Company B has two trucks allocated, they'll be bringing up extra ammunition behind us to start, then they'll be used for casvac only. The MO will be one mile behind where we think our front line will be, make sure your lads know that. We're to head direct for Galatas, New Zealanders below on our right, then Australians down to the coast. There's no heavy weapons, I'm afraid, the infantry tanks were lost so if the Jerries bring up armour, we're in trouble'. Tom interrupted, 'We have the Boys rifle, sir. We've not had the chance to fire him yet, not in action'. 'Well, this might be your opportunity', answered Thomas, drily. He left Tom to organise the platoon, telling him to be ready to move at 0200 hours.

Tom got hold of Richard Smith and George Parry, his two corporals, and told them the situation. Both looked shocked and Smith started to complain, 'Cover their withdrawal? We're fucked then. There'll be no transport left for us, will there? No one to cover our withdrawal!' Before Tom could respond, George interrupted his fellow corporal. 'Now then, Richard, think on. Somebody has to cover the retreat, and it's us, it's just how it's dropped. We was in reserve, after all, and we'll do a job for them. We don't have to like it. I tell you, I would rather be first out but not this time. We'll get the lads lined up, Tom will tell them the job, then you and me will do our job. The best chance for all of us to get out of this is to fight harder and better than the Jerries. You with me, Richard?' Smith had the grace to look a little shamefaced at his first reaction, answering 'Course I am, George, course I am. Sorry, Sergeant, bit of a shock, that's all. I shall do my job, never fear, and my lads will do theirs'. Tom nodded. 'Speak to your lads, both of you. It's not easy on them, I grant you, but it's our job now and by God, we'll do it right. I shall keep close, it's only half a platoon now, and we'll carry them through between us. Anyone you're worried about, let me know, and I'll see what I can do to help. Off you go'.

As Smith walked around the corner in the trench line, George murmured quietly 'I'll keep an eye on him, Tom. He's a young feller, needs a steady hand, that's all'. 'Thanks, George, do that'.

It seemed to Tom that the next few hours flew by. He and the two corporals were busy checking weapons and ammunition, making sure that everyone had a full water bottle and a little food and answering any questions that the troopers needed answering. The lads did not look happy, but there was an air of professional competence and preparation. He looked for Davey Williams, thinking that he might need something of a buck-up, and found him helping one of his mates to stow a little more ammunition in his pouches. Williams had made a quick recovery from the effects of his concussion following his fall in the attack on the German sangar, and Tom wondered if his confidence and spirit were still intact after that violent attack.

'Alright, Davey? Ready for the off?' asked Tom. Davey looked up, with a grin. 'I'd rather be somewhere else, Sergeant', he replied with a grin, 'but yeah, ready to go, time we got stuck into them again'. 'That's the way, boy, just remember your training and you won't go far wrong. Stick close to Corporal Parry, he'll help you if you need it'. Tom moved along the trench, pondering how Davey seemed to have grown up a year's worth in just over a week, stronger in his confidence and in his belief that he was up to the job. Combat and brutality had that effect on some men, Tom reflected, while others went into their shells, a little or a lot. Davey was beginning to show that he could be a very useful soldier, and Tom hoped that he would get the chance, and the time, to show it.

Just before they were due to leave the safety of the trenches, Captain Thomas returned. 'All ready, Sergeant?' he queried. Tom nodded. 'Sir'. 'Right-o then, Sergeant. We are routed along the southern edge of Chania, coast road for a mile, then up past Panadiki towards Galatas. You know the route well enough, don't you? That was your first stop here, Galatas, wasn't it? Your platoon should end up just below the village, as long as Jerry hasn't advanced further since this morning. There won't be time to dig-in but there's plenty of stone about, build a couple of sangars maybe? This platoon has the furthest to go, so you're out first. Any questions, Sergeant?' 'No sir', Tom replied, then asked, 'Will we see you later, sir?' The Captain smiled. 'I shall be moving between your platoon and three others, Sergeant. Send a runner if you need a word, I won't be far away. Good luck to you, Sergeant Lane, carry on'. He saluted, then stuck out his hand. Tom shook it briefly, not used to such informality from his officers.

Tom turned to the platoon, or what was left of it after the losses they had suffered. Nodding to the corporals to bring the men along behind him, he climbed out of the trench and headed for the city. It was full dark but he was able to avoid the bomb craters and rubble that littered the rough ground. He stopped and turned, behind him the fourteen surviving lads of the platoon followed him in loose order, rifles carried across their bodies, ready to hand if needed. There was no talking, as instructed, just the occasional clink of equipment and crunch of boots against stone. Tom carried on and within a few minutes, was jumping down onto the road that ran along the southern edge of the city and waiting as they formed up behind him.

To their right, even in the darkness, they could see the enormous devastation caused by the German bombing. There were old stone houses, either flattened into heaps or gutted so that, even if still standing, their pathetic contents were revealed to the world. Roads into the city were blocked with debris, Tom could see a flattened car poking out from under a heap of masonry. The stench of burning filled his nostrils, even though the fires were long burned out.

What unnerved them most was the silence. This had been a lively, typically Greek, town, full of chatter and argument and song, full of movement and chaos, at least to a British eye. It had been full of life but now it was dead. No sound, no people, not even a dog or a cat, prowling the streets. The silence of the soldiers, tramping quietly through the desolation and the wreckage, became even more profound.

Tom breathed a sigh of relief when, after a further half an hour's steady march, the platoon began to leave the city behind them. The houses began to thin out, spaced apart with small olive groves. There was less bomb damage out here, less to aim at, Tom supposed. It was even possible to imagine what life here might have been like before the coming of war, but these comfortable thoughts were driven out of Tom's mind, as a voice called from out of the darkness behind him. 'Sergeant, sergeant, you there?' It was a runner from Captain Thomas. 'Sergeant, Captain's orders. Ten minute break for your platoon, and there's six platoons from the 2nd New Zealanders, let them pass through your line then continue your march. Captain says turn up towards Galatas, then wait for further orders'. 'Understood', replied Tom. 'Tell the captain, no contact as yet, all quiet'. The runner nodded, and at a gesture from Tom, jogged back into the darkness.

Tom turned to Corporal Parry, who had moved up behind him. 'George, you heard that. You and Richard, stand the men down but I want sentries fore and aft, and above and below. Tell the lads, no chat, no smoking either, could be Jerries close to us now. Tell 'em to go easy on the water, don't know where the next lots coming from and they're going to need it in the morning'. George nodded, and carried on.

The ten minute stop turned into nearly an hour and a half. The New Zealanders came through in dribs and drabs, cursing and complaining. 'It's a bugger's muddle, mate', one of them answered, when questioned quickly by Tom. 'Some bastard took a wrong turning and we'd gone two miles or more before the penny dropped. But you know what they say, shouldn't have joined if you couldn't take a joke!' A hundred men had had to retrace their steps in the blackness of the night, but there didn't seem to be much wrong with their spirit and they were ready to fight.

Tom felt himself becoming more and more restless, he knew that the enemy wouldn't all be curled up asleep somewhere, they would have patrols out, looking for the British front-line, if you could say that there still was such a thing. Furthermore, although full dawn was almost ninety minutes away, they would barely have time to get past Panadiki before it became properly light, and certainly they'd be building sangars in daylight, maybe even under fire.

Eventually the last New Zealander had moved through and Tom was able to pull in the sentries and restart the move towards the valley. The night was still again and all Tom could hear was the quiet movement of the men behind him. Two men were sent forward on point, and for three quarters of an hour they made careful progress, Tom reckoning by then that the junction that would take them up towards Panadiki and Galatas was only a few minutes ahead. Then, without any warning, everything changed.

Chapter 10

From down the road they had just walked up, back towards Chania, the tranquillity of the swiftly passing night was shattered by the rapid percussion of machine guns and the din of exploding grenades. Flares exploded in the distant night sky, flooding the hillsides with a blinding white light which slowly faded, to be replenished as more flares were fired.

'Everyone off the road!' shouted Tom. Men ran for the shelter of a low stone wall which bordered one side of the road, while others dived in among the sparse bushes which separated an olive grove from the track on the other side. George appeared at Tom's side, 'That's Spandau fire, Tom, not one of ours. The Jerries have got behind us'. Tom nodded. 'For all I know, we're surrounded, George. They're in front of us, we know that, now there's some in the rear. Maybe it's just a patrol, if it is, it shouldn't take long to sort 'em out'. Tom thought quickly, as Richard, the other corporal arrived, looking shaken.

'Richard, send a runner back to Captain Thomas. Tell the Captain we're going to carry on to the junction, see if we can make a strongpoint there, and we'll wait for his instructions. Now!' Richard scurried off. Turning to George, he carried on. 'Form 'em up, George, we're going to double to the junction, you know where it is. I want the Bren and the mortar set up as soon as we're there, and a sentry on each of the three roads, fifty yards out. The rest will pile up as much stone as they can find, make a start on that sangar. Best we can do until Thomas brings the rest up. Go to it!' As George turned away, calling the men back onto the road, Tom headed on towards the junction, hoping to himself that he was right about its location, and that they had beaten the Germans to it.

He was right, and there were no enemy there, so he rapidly looked around the immediate area for a potential site for their strongpoint. To the right of the road as it turned up into the valley, in the rapidly improving light, Tom could see a flat, rocky area, roughly circular and perhaps forty feet across. The hillside dropped away from it for about three quarters of its circumference, with the final quarter bounded by the hillside behind it. It wasn't a perfect spot to defend, far from it, but it would have to do. At least it dominated the road from Chania and the road that carried on to Maleme. If they were outflanked from the direction of Galatas, further up the hill, then they were finished anyway but this was the best they could do for now. Perhaps they could find somewhere better, later. Davey was close behind him, and Tom sent him up the track in the direction of Galatas to provide some early warning.

The racket of gunfire seemed louder and closer to Tom, as the platoon dashed around the final corner in the road below him. George had passed on his orders, because without any delay, the mortar and Bren teams carried on up to where Tom stood and began to deploy their weaponry. Tom and George, with the help of the final four troopers, began to haul in the loose rock that surrounded their tiny plateau and pile it up into a rough wall. By now, stray bullets were cracking over their heads as they worked and as Tom took a glance down the hill towards Chania, he could just see clouds of black smoke rising, perhaps a mile away, no further. He could hear nothing heavier than machine guns and the crump of what must be mortar shells, so that was something to be grateful for, at least there was no armour or artillery.

As Tom peered at the action below, Richard staggered around the final corner in the road, almost carrying another soldier. There was a trail of blood left in the road behind them, and Tom ran down to help them up into the shelter of the strongpoint, laying the wounded man down in the lea of the wall. Richard gasped, 'He's a runner from the Captain, Sergeant. I sent Davis back with your message but now he's sent Pearson, this lad, back. Looks like he took a packet'.

Blood was continuing to pool around Pearson, and they quickly located the wound. He had been shot in the thigh, and as George worked to tie a tourniquet above the gaping hole in the muscle, hands slipping in the blood and pulverised meat of the wound, Tom leaned over to Pearson, hoping that he could pass on whatever message he had before losing consciousness.

Pearson was fading as his blood continued to flood around him, but he roused himself enough to speak for a few seconds. 'Captain under fire, can't move forward. Hold your position'. He had more to say but, as he opened his mouth to speak further, his eyes rolled upwards and he was gone. Everyone seemed to freeze for a moment, then George leaned over Pearson to check for a pulse. After a few seconds, he shook his head.

Tom shook himself into action. 'Richard, get back down the hill, I want the earliest warning if the Jerries get through the Captain's position. Slow 'em down if you can, then get back. We'll make 'em attack us here. George, you do the same on the Maleme road. I'll keep an eye up the hill, understood?' They nodded, Richard asking as he turned away, 'What if they come from all directions, Sergeant?' 'Then we're fucked, Corporal!' he replied, 'but we'll do our job anyway. Move!'

The three of them, Tom, George and Richard, ran off to their posts, Tom jogging up the rough lane that led eventually up to Galatas. As he rounded a corner in the lane, a stern voice called out from among the scrubby trees that bordered it. 'Halt, who goes there?' 'It's Sergeant Lane, Davey, come to join you', answered Tom, glad that Davey had followed procedure and hadn't shot first. 'Advance and be recognised' came the reply, and as Tom continued around the corner, Davey stepped out into the road, rifle at the hip and aimed directly at him. 'Sorry 'bout that, Sergeant, but you might have been a Hun' he grinned.

'Never apologise for doing your job right, Davey. Now, is all quiet up here?' he asked. 'Seems to be, Sergeant. All the action seems to be down below, back the way we came. I can't hear anything above us, heard some vehicle noise to the west, faint like, about half an hour ago but nothing since'. 'That's how we like it, Davey', Tom replied. 'I shall watch up here with you for now, but we'll have to move back down if anything starts below us. Not enough of us to cover everywhere'. Davey dipped his head in understanding.

Looking down in the direction of Chania, they could still see smoke spreading out across the valley and hear the rattle and crash of rifle and machine gun fire. Gradually though, over fifteen minutes or so, the firing seemed to die down, almost to nothing. Maybe we've knocked 'em out, Tom allowed himself to hope, but before he could put that thought into words, he turned, startled, as the rippling crash of rifle fire broke out below them, further down the hill, below the strongpoint. 'Come on boy!'

he roared, 'They've got trouble!' They both clattered down the lane, just about holding their balance on the rough surface of the road and within half a minute, were leaping over the low defences of the sangar. Below the strongpoint, Tom could see Richard and two other men running around the corner at the bottom of the slope, no longer firing but racing up the short hill towards them. Below them, and to the left, George and his sentry must have been able to still see the attacking force, because they were shooting rapidly as they edged their way closer to the track that would bring them closer to their comrades in the strongpoint. Tom cursed, he could offer them no covering fire because their attackers were still out of sight beyond the corner and a mortar bomb could also knock out George and his mate, but he had not reckoned on George's well-learned skills. As he watched, George and his comrade hurled a grenade each in the direction of their tormentors and at the exact second that the thump of the explosions reached the strongpoint, both men sprinted for the track, heads down but still clutching their rifles.

As Richard and his two companions reached the little fortification, George and his companion were still fifty yards or so behind them, starting to flag as the angle of the hill began to slow them down. As their friends cheered them on, drowning out the cries of pain from where the grenades had landed, Tom was horrified to see a small group of grey-clad figures emerge from around the corner in the road, firing from the hip as they spotted the two runners in front of them. Without the need of an order, fire crashed out from the sangar, six rifles, leaving three German infantry still on the ground, the remaining three diving back around the corner into cover.

The cheering died away in the sudden silence as George's comrade seemed to trip up and fall flat on his face, unmoving. 'Covering fire!' shouted Tom, and dashed down out of the shelter, as George stopped to see what had happened to his mate. Bullets snapped around them as, grabbing a shoulder of the man's battledress each, Corporal and Sergeant hauled him rapidly into the shelter of the sangar. Helpful hands took him from them as they dived headlong through the narrow entrance and lay panting on the rock-strewn ground. Tom could hear the rasp of George's strained breathing, but before he could move or look around him, a grave, deep voice spoke to both of them.

'I am afraid, gentlemen, that your efforts will go unrewarded. Your comrade was killed instantly, I fear'. George did not recognise the voice and puzzled for a second before turning his attention to more urgent matters. As he started to get up from the ground, he bellowed, 'Get that mortar firing, there's Jerries behind that bank, range two fifty', pointing at the corner at the bottom of the hill that Richard and his two pals had appeared from behind. They wouldn't be able to see the fall of the rounds but there was a good chance that their attackers would be forming up there, prior to making their attack on the strongpoint.

The first mortar shell climbed into the brightening sky, just clearing the bank in its descent, and its crashing explosion, closely followed by a cloud of black smoke and clatter of shrapnel and debris caught everyone's attention. 'Fire for effect, three rounds, then the Bren must take them if they get onto the hill, rifleman you too, they'll overwhelm us if we let 'em get too close', he ordered then turned his attention to his corporals. 'George, Richard, what are we up against, what about a counter attack?' Before either could reply, the unrecognised voice from a minute before again broke into Tom's thoughts, from behind him. 'Sergeant, you can have my sitrep'.

Tom turned sharply, wondering who the hell was interrupting him, then gaped in surprise. Veteran that he was, his turn transformed itself almost instantaneously, as his heels crashed together and his right arm shot up in salute. 'Sir, Lieutenant Colonel', he began but couldn't get any more words out, he was so surprised. What was the CO doing here, things must be bad! At his side, he could hear George suppressing a snigger and even Lieutenant Colonel Fraser cracked a smile at Tom's discomfiture.

'Good morning, Sergeant. What's your name, man?' the CO asked. Tom told him, and Fraser continued. 'Here's my sitrep, Sergeant Lane'. In the background, Tom felt and heard the last mortar bomb leaving the tube, and the steady crack crack crack of the Bren gun, as the number one gunner acquired a target. 'Somehow the Hun has got behind us, must have traversed the north side of Chania, by the harbour, as we took the south. So, we have the German army in front of us and behind us, west and east. We haven't seen the Jerries in the West this morning but they'll be supplied direct from the airfield at Maleme, so we must assume that they will be fully equipped, and plenty of them. The force in the East, well, as you know, I got here just before they did so I had a good look at what's chasing us. They've rolled up the platoons behind you, I was taking a report from Captain Thomas, when they attacked from behind and below us. Mortars, machine guns of course, plenty of infantry, no tanks that I could see or hear, thank God, but I did spot a couple of armoured cars back along the road. No doubt they'll be calling in ground attack soon, Stukas I imagine'.

As the Lieutenant Colonel paused for breath, Tom tentatively interrupted, 'Sir, how did you manage to avoid capture, I mean...?' He broke off in embarrassment, not wishing to appear to be questioning the CO's conduct. Fraser looked blank for a second then seemed to understand Tom's query. 'I was at the head of the platoon with Thomas when the attack started. He dashed back to organise his defence and while my radioman was trying to reach the rear-guard, Jerries cut the road between us and the platoon. Couldn't get to them. My adjutant knew one more platoon was ahead of us, suggested we try to reach you. Radio chap got shot on the way, I'm afraid, then the Adj and I ran into your corporal'. A wave of pain seemed to cross the CO's features, and then was gone.

Before Tom could speak, to apologise for his curiosity, the officer began to speak again. 'Sergeant, these are my orders. We can only hold this point against those odds for minutes, once they range in a mortar or strafe us, we're done. There's no force to rescue us, everyone else is either halfway to Sphakia for evacuation or in the bag, and I'm not going to lose any more of my boys for nothing. The Adjutant and I will hold them off for as long as we can, while you and your platoon, what there is of it, heads up the hill towards Galatas, then south into the mountains, see if you can get to Sphakia in time for a boat'. As Tom began to protest, the CO cut him off abruptly. 'Sergeant, these are my orders. Obey them!' then, more kindly, 'your duty is to preserve your platoon for another day, mine is to give you the opportunity'. Tom felt stunned at what he was being ordered to do but discipline was all. He would do as ordered.

The Bren behind them rattled out a longer burst of firing, augmented by rapid fire from the half a dozen rifles in the sangar. As Tom looked downhill, he could see the front half of an armoured vehicle as it moved around the corner, out of the shelter of the hillside. In brown camouflage, it was no bigger than a small truck but was crowned with a turret. Tom knew that these vehicles, thinly armoured, eight wheels, with no tracks, were vulnerable to even light artillery but he might as well have wished for the moon, and as the vehicle emerged, the gunner started to fire. Tom knew that they carried twenty millimetre automatic cannons, which at this range would make short work of their defences. He didn't have time to shout 'Down!' before shells were crashing into their stone ramparts, sending shrapnel and pulverised rock in a deadly tempest onto and around the defenders. The noise was utterly deafening and all Tom and the men with him could do was to press their bodies into the rocky ground below them and hope.

From the corner of his vision, distorted by the shock waves of the explosions and the clouds of dust and smoke, Tom saw a pair of feet, the end of a body as it shimmied out of the narrow entrance of the sangar. 'At least someone's getting out', he thought. Through the barrage of noise and flying fragments, he crawled to the gap and looked out.

To his amazement he could see Richard, his younger corporal, together with one of the troopers, it was Davey, on the other side of the track, out of sight of the armoured car and moving slowly down the hill towards it. Richard was carrying a heavy-looking, very long-barrelled rifle, while Richard carried an ammunition box. It was their Boys rifle, the only weapon they had that could penetrate armour, with its .55 rounds. Richard and Davey had a chance of knocking the bugger out but they needed help.

There was a brief lull in firing as the crew of the German vehicle paused to reload. Tom screamed 'Bren gun, lay down some fire on that bastard, mortars at two hundred yards, shoot!' They wouldn't disable the vehicle but they might distract the crew, until Richard and Davey got close enough to fire the Boys. This had to work, or they were finished.

The hail of .303 bullets against the armour and the thunder of mortar shells exploding next to the vehicle seemed to divert the crew inside it and it was almost a full minute before they were ready to fire again. Tom could see that Richard and Davey had used the time to get within about sixty yards of the car, out of the enemy's view, behind a group of stunted trees. Between them, they had loaded the rifle, and were ready to fire. Because of the powerful recoil, it had to be fired from a prone position and as Richard rolled out directly in line with the enemy and prepared to fire, the crew of the armoured car opened up again at Tom and his comrades.

As they ducked down behind the fragile protection of their disintegrating ramparts, they heard a series of loud reports, followed by another, larger explosion and the sound of heavy material thumping into the ground around them. The shell fire had abruptly stopped, and the defenders, to a man, lifted their heads above the level of their little defences and looked down the hill to the junction. They were stunned by the sight in front of them.

Richard's aim had been true. The half-inch rounds had been enough to penetrate the armoured car, especially at that short range, and must have ignited cannon shells ready to fire. The resulting enormous explosion had shattered it, sending the turret into the air and spreading bits of engine, fragments of armour and body parts for hundreds of yards around it.

Richard was lying still, next to the Boys, and as Tom watched, holding his breath in his anxiety, he saw Davey leave the cover of the trees and bend over Richard for a moment. He seemed to touch his corporal's face quickly, then pick up the rifle and ammunition box and dodge back into the cover at the side of the road, beginning to stumble back up the hill towards them.

In the temporary, relative stillness, with the sound of the armoured car burning below them, with rounds still cooking off inside its carcass, Tom quickly ordered, 'Mortars, three more rounds at two fifty, keep the buggers at a distance, and get that Bren ready to pile it on if they send in infantry'. The mortar team began to move but there was no acknowledgement from the machine gun crew. Tom turned to berate them but quickly bit off his words as he saw that Lieutenant Colonel Fraser and his adjutant had gestured the Number One gunner and his loader to move away from the weapon, and were in the process of taking their places.

'Carry on, Sergeant, your order stands. Leave now, before the Hun reorganise. Take your weapons and as much ammunition as you can, and good luck. Here, have my binoculars too, I won't need them. We'll hold the buggers off for as long as we can, give you a start'. Sensing Tom's hesitation, and over the sound of the mortars, he added, abruptly, 'Go. Now!'

Tom's innate discipline took over and, after saluting the CO and his adjutant, turned to his men. Before he could give his first order, he noticed Davey, as he stumbled back into the sangar. 'Corporal's dead, Sergeant', Davey murmured. 'Piece of armour right through him, nearly cut him in half'. His voice began to break as he continued, 'I shut his eyes, couldn't do no more for him'. Before he could continue, Tom interrupted, they had to move now! He would speak to Davey about his and Richard's brave action later. 'Private Williams, we're withdrawing immediately, orders of the CO. Drop the Boys, it's too heavy to carry far, find your rifle and as many rounds as you can carry. No questions! Same for the rest of you, leave the mortar, we go in two!'

Tom snatched a rifle up from the ground for his own use, ramming some of the .303 ammunition scattered on the stony ground into his pouches. The Adjutant was busy loading rounds into magazines for the Bren gun, while the CO, having made himself Number One, was sighting the rifle down the slope of the road, waiting for any attackers to show themselves. Tom was about to request permission to proceed, but thought better of it, he had his orders already and time was short.

He turned to the remnants of his platoon. There were just seven men remaining, and himself. 'Davey, you alright? I want you on point, no more than a hundred yards ahead though, I'll be first man behind you. We're following the road up to Panadiki, stop when you can see the first house. Wait for us there. George, you're tail-end Charlie. The rest of you, single file, alternate sides of the road, no more than twenty yards between you and the next man. Be ready to support if firing starts. Keep quiet as you can, no smoking. Got it? Go!' Davey nodded and jogged steadily up the rough lane that led eventually to Galatas. One by one, the small group of survivors followed him out of the sangar, leaving their commanding officer to delay any pursuit.

Chapter 11

All was quiet in the first few minutes of their stealthy departure, lit by the rising sun as it rose above the mountains further to the east. The little road was deserted, and Tom could see Davey moving cautiously ahead, staying to the side of the track so that concealment was never far away. Looking back, Tom could see the remainder of his party, with George Parry just coming into view around a bend in the road. As he stood there, he saw George quickly stop and unbutton, about to empty his bladder against an old olive tree, when from the direction of the strongpoint, machine guns were heard, crashing and stuttering into action.

Tom picked out the unmistakable sound of the Bren, and was that a Jerry MG34, yes! More than one! Rifle fire too, then the thud and concussion of high explosive, mortars? His instinct was to return to his CO, to support his officer, but he knew that he could not. He had his orders. He gestured to the man ahead to continue, to increase the pace, and spotted George moving up the slope again behind them. He knew his duty, the CO's sacrifice was to enable as many of his boys to survive as possible, and he would do his best to make it happen. The exchange of fire could be heard below them for another five minutes or more, then suddenly stopped.

The small band double-timed for a further half an hour, before Tom signalled a stop for a water break. The men were sweating hard in the bright morning sunshine, already hot at the end of May, and with a long day ahead of them, Tom couldn't risk any heat exhaustion. Davey and George didn't join them, they had their drink but kept up their watch, above and below the central group.

Davey had not signalled, so the village could not yet be in sight. Perhaps, Tom thought, they could refill their canteens there, maybe buy a little food, for they had no rations with them. It was possible though that German troops had already taken Galatas, he knew that they were in the vicinity. Would they be able to defend themselves, eight men? Was he leading them to their deaths? He sighed, and cursed himself. Of course there were questions he couldn't answer, there always were. All he could do was be guided by what he did know, and do his best for his men. It might be enough.

The road, now little more than a track, dipped between two high banks, rather like a railway cutting. It looked about two hundred yards long, Tom guessed, with no natural cover and with the only easy entry and exit at either end. The banks on either side rose to between twenty and thirty feet, mostly composed of bare rock, interspersed with small patches of grass and mountain herbs. At this time of year, the plants had not yet become parched by the fierce sunshine and still retained some green. The bank to the east provided a little, temporary shade and as the men entered the defile, one by one, they savoured the short respite. Tom directed two men up to near the top of the bank, one on either side of the track, to give the earliest warning if the enemy was attempting an ambush or a surprise attack. Both gestured to Tom that there was no one in sight.

As Tom reached the halfway point, Davey, up ahead, had left the little ravine at the far end and had disappeared from view, tracking carefully around the next turn in the road. Looking behind him, he saw that George had cut the distance separating them and was trotting to catch him up.

'Tom, I can hear an engine, maybe a mile or more back, one of them armoured cars again, I reckon. We needs to get well off the road, there'll be plenty infantry with 'im, too many for us!' 'Thank you, George', Tom replied, calmly. 'Rest of you men, at the double', and at that, the remaining six men of the platoon jogged quickly behind him to the end of the cutting and around the corner, Tom intending them to join up with Davey quickly then find a route to take them away from the road and hopefully, out of sight of their pursuers.

Davey was about a hundred yards further on, in the shade of an old olive tree, and he stepped out into the road as he saw his mates hurrying towards him, a small boy of about ten years or so standing shyly with him. The lad was thin, scrawny even, and barefoot, dressed in an old vest and dirty shorts.

Tom quickly told Davey of their close pursuit. 'Panadiki village is about a mile further on, Sergeant', Davey answered. 'Perhaps the villagers would help us out'. 'No time, Private. Never get there in time, we need to get off this track now. Besides, we can't take the battle to the village, wouldn't help us or them'. Just then, the sound of the engine echoed up the hill, their chasers were getting closer, he needed to make a decision but where to go? He felt a sharp tug on his sleeve.

Looking down, he saw that the boy, now that he had Tom's attention, was pointing urgently towards the olive grove that bordered the road to their left. He took a few steps towards the trees, gesturing that Tom and his men should follow him. Tom shared a look of uncertainty with George, it didn't seem right that their next move was to be determined by an unknown boy! George didn't speak, just nodded in the direction of the youngster. What else could they do?

'Right, lads. Follow the kid, quiet as you can', he ordered and motioned to George to be the last man again. Within twenty seconds, the eight men, led by the ragged little boy, had disappeared into the deep shade of the olive plantation.

The boy set a fast pace, hurrying them along between the rows of trees. Although they were on the side of a steep hill, the ground had been terraced to provide for easier cultivation, so they were moving on flat ground. Rocks poked through the soil in places but most had been used to build the retaining walls between the terraces, so the going was easy.

The roar of a loud engine and shouting voices behind it, as their pursuers reached the point in the road where they had branched off, served to speed them on, and Tom was relieved when the noise of their hunters seemed to fade as, seemingly, they carried on past where the platoon had diverted.

They hurried on, every few minutes climbing over one of the rough retaining walls and moving up to the next, higher terrace. Tom felt increasingly uncomfortable, having no idea where they were being led, but also knowing that he had no choice in the matter. As for the little boy, he seemed tireless and if he felt that Tom and the men were beginning to flag, he would gesture them on with more urgency, speaking words that they could not understand but managing to convey that they needed to keep up a good speed. Tom grinned as he overheard one of his lads mumbling, 'Little sod, he's not carrying what I'm carrying!'

Then, without warning, the boy held up his hand, wanting everyone to stop, they had reached the limit of the trees. Putting a finger to his lips, he gestured to Tom to follow him and together, they crept through the undergrowth for a good fifty yards, mostly tall grass and thistles that grew behind the last of the trees. Tom and the boy carefully parted the long stalks and looked through.

To his surprise, Tom could see the tiny hamlet of Panadiki, a hundred feet or so below him. It was so familiar, it had been close to the Regiment's first base on the island and he knew it and its people well, having spent a month camped out at Galatas, further up the hill. He had spent a few happy evenings in in the village, drinking their thick, sweet coffee alongside the potent raki made by the inhabitants. It had been a wonderful introduction to the culture of the island and he had loved the place and the people, but he had never expected to return under these circumstances.

The olive trees that had hidden the platoon so far had been planted up to the edge of a shallow cliff which led down to a thin stream running in a rocky bed. The ground rose a few feet from the far bank, up to the first of the three old stone houses that comprised the whole village. To the right of the houses, Tom could see the final stretch of the road that they had followed, as it reached its destination.

Within the village he could see field-grey uniforms as they moved among the houses. The soldiers had arrived. There was no engine noise, instead he could hear shouting and screaming and crying, echoing around the rocky surroundings. Then a rifle shot, then another. More screaming followed, chilling him inside, and next to him, he felt the boy stiffen and begin to quietly sob. He placed a hand on the lad's shoulders, but the sobbing continued.

Moving the boy and himself back into thicker cover, Tom started to think furiously. His orders from the Lieutenant Colonel were to try to get his men to Sphakia for evacuation. That was never going to be easy, they were a day behind most of the force trying to escape and the island seemed to be overrun with German parachutists and infantry but he had his orders and it was his duty to follow them.

The other side of the argument was that they were here to defend the people of the island and it didn't feel right to him to leave the people in the village to resist the Germans alone. But could he order his men to delay their own escape, to rescue non-combatants? He knew the answer to that question, he could not. Army discipline would prevail. Their escape attempt would continue, and they would have to leave the villagers to the mercy of the invading Germans.

Tom heard another burst of firing from the direction of the houses, and decided to take a further look before returning to brief the platoon and carry on towards Sphakia and hopefully, freedom. Leaving the boy, he crept forward once again, this time pulling from his pack the binoculars given to him by the Lieutenant Colonel. There seemed to be some movement along the road as it neared the village and Tom put the glasses to his eyes for a closer look. What he saw, brought close by the power of the lenses, suddenly made his imminent decision even more difficult.

Two soldiers, in British uniform, were being marched at bayonet point towards Panadiki, one holding up the other as they both limped painfully onwards, four German infantrymen chivvying them along. For a moment, Tom thought that Lieutenant Colonel Fraser and his Adjutant had escaped but he realised that neither man was in officer's uniform, they were squaddies. They were too far away for him to tell which mob they belonged to but that did not matter, they were comrades! They stumbled onwards, eventually moving out of sight behind the first house. Where the enemy would take them, thought Tom, and what they would do with them, he had no idea but he would find out.

Tom carefully backed out of the undergrowth, taking the boy, who seemed to have dried his tears, back with him. George and the lads were waiting for him and listened intently as he described what he had seen, and what he wanted to do. 'If there's a reasonable chance, I want to get those two boys out. We have our orders to get to the coast but I reckon that we can do both, it doesn't sit right with me to save ourselves and leave them with the Jerries, without at least trying to take them with us'. He could see that not everyone was convinced, as a few of the men shuffled their feet and looked everywhere but directly at him.

He continued, 'I won't order any of you to come with me, it'll be volunteers only and there will be no comeback on you if you decide you want to carry on straightaway'. Heads looked up at this, and Tom noticed some of the men exchanging glances. 'You would be obeying the CO's orders, so no problem there. Think about it, five minutes, then come back to me'. Tom turned on his heel, with the boy still in attendance, intending to walk deeper into the olive grove, to be out of earshot of the men. Before he took more than a few steps, a voice called out to him.

'I'm with you, Tom'. It was George Parry. 'Don't sit right with neither, leaving them fellas to it'. As he stood to follow Tom, another voice was heard. 'You two will never manage on your own, count me in'. It was Davey, grinning as he moved next to George and looked back at the five remaining troopers. There was a still silence for a moment, then the two volunteers turned to follow Tom and the boy, leaving the rest to decide what they were going to do.

Twenty yards into the trees, Tom stopped, sat and leaned back against a tree, gesturing to the others to join him. As he passed the canteen around, welcome in the building heat of the day, George looked hard at Tom, 'You know, it'll be a bloody miracle if we manages to rescue them lads. Even if them five decides to volunteer, we shall still only be eight up against God knows how many. If it turns into a battle, we're fucked'. 'I know', replied Tom. 'It'll have to be a quiet job, in and out before they know what's happening. Don't know what state them two boys are in either, we need more info. Pity this lad can't speak English'. He looked around for the boy. 'Hey, where is he?' The boy had disappeared, and although they searched immediately around where they had been sitting for a few minutes, there was no sign of him.

'We'll never find him', concluded Tom. 'This is his home ground. I can't think he'll go rushing off to the Jerries though, he was crying fit to burst when he saw what they were up to in the village, poor little bugger. Lucky we know the place, that'll help us when we go looking for them'. They began to discuss how they would quarter the village when the time came to search for the two unknown men but were interrupted when one of the other men joined them, looking a little shamefaced and hesitant. It was Davis R, one of the mortar crew.

'Now then, Rodri', said Tom. 'Spit it out, what have you lads decided?' Davis gulped, looking at the three men in turn then started to speak, hesitantly at first then more confidently as he realised that he wasn't going to be shouted down. 'Well, Sar'nt', he said, 'The boys said for me to speak for 'em. Sar'nt, we feels that we've done our share and we should get off the island, like the CO said. We reckons that if we leave now, we might get to the coast in time. We knows them two boys needs rescuing but there aint enough of us to do it, is there? We're not deserters though, so we'll only go with your permission'.

'And you have it, Rodri', interjected Tom, 'you have it. I would rather you stayed, and the other boys, but I understand why you think you can't. Like I said, there'll be no comeback on you, you're sticking to the CO's final order. If you are quite sure of your minds', and Rodri nodded, 'take your arms with you, half of the ammunition, water if you can find it, and head south. The port is called Sphakia, can't tell you any more than that. The Navy is evacuating from there but I don't know for how long, so you'll need to hurry, it's about forty miles but hard going, all mountains. You never know, we might catch you up! Off you go'.

Rodri look confused but then realising that he had completed his task and had been dismissed, he nodded again, tracking back through the trees to where the other four were waiting. Within a few minutes they were gone, following the olive terrace away from the direction of the village, towards the high mountains and the south.

Tom and his two companions watched in silence. With a sigh, Tom turned to them. 'OK, we're on our own. I want a watch kept on the village, see what's going on. Two hours on, while the other two sleep, I'll take the first duty, then you, Davey. Get your heads down somewhere out of sight, don't know about you but I'm knackered'. They all were, having marched through the night, fought a small battle then bolted up the hill. 'What rations have we got?' They emptied their packs, finding that Davey had managed to squirrel away a couple of tins of bully beef, while George had some hard bread and some chocolate. Tom had nothing.

'Let's eat something now', said Tom, 'we need it, might find more in Panadiki. I shall take a bite with me, back to where I was watching the

village with that lad. Relieve me in two hours, Davey'. With that, he was
gone.

Chapter 12

Tom crept quietly back to his viewpoint, confident that he wouldn't be seen from the village, as long as he laid still. He knew that movement could give him away, but it would take very bad luck for someone to identify a human face in among the tall grass. Settling back, sandwich in one hand and binoculars in the other, Tom started his watch.

There was no more gunfire, no more screaming, and Panadiki seemed deathly quiet. Tom began to feel drowsy, a combination of extreme fatigue and long-delayed food but sat up, startled, when the sound of a big engine starting up in the village echoed across the valley. Clouds of black exhaust billowed up behind the houses as the vehicle manoeuvred in the narrow street then slowly emerged into Tom's view. Remembering the binoculars hanging around his neck, he lifted them to his eyes and took a closer look.

It was an armoured car, he presumed it was the one that had pursued them up the hill. Quite a beast, an eight-wheeler, the same as the one that Richard had destroyed, it mounted an automatic cannon in a small turret, with a machine gun visible through an open flap below. They had no weapon between them that would touch it now, having left the Boys behind but to Tom's relief, the machine carried on down the hill, preceded by a screen of a dozen infantry. Perhaps their luck was in, perhaps the Germans had searched the village and found nothing?

Turning back to the village, Tom quietly cursed. He could see soldiers in German uniform as they moved between the houses in the main street, they had left a small garrison. At least the armour had gone, he thought, along with twelve or so troops. They were still in with a chance.

The remainder of Tom's watch was quiet, occasionally noticing a field grey uniform in the village but there was no more firing. Hearing a rustling behind him, he turned as Davey's face emerged from among the undergrowth. 'Time to relieve you, Sarge', he murmured, 'get your head down'. Tom passed on everything he had observed, instructing Davey to wake him if there were any changes. He needed to think hard about how to attempt the rescue of the two prisoners but he was so tired after the hours of combat and flight, he couldn't think straight, sleep had to come first.

George was not where Tom expected to find him, asleep under a tree. Perhaps he's hidden deeper among the trees, Tom thought, but before he could decide what to do next, George appeared, moving quietly from the direction of their path in and explained himself. 'Didn't fancy sleeping with no guard, Tom, not with them Jerries around, so I took a bit of sentry duty'. Before Tom could respond and tell him to rest himself, he continued, 'You need the kip more than me, I shall keep a quiet lookout for a bit longer and call you in a couple of hours. Then I shall have a snooze and Davey can take over'. Tom considered objecting but realised, before he even said a word, that George was right. He just nodded, lay down with his head resting on his haversack and was asleep in seconds.

Tom gradually surfaced from the depths of his exhaustion, as a hand gently shook him by the shoulder. He faintly heard a voice calling him, seemingly from a distance to begin with, then louder as consciousness fully returned. 'Tom, Sergeant, we got visitors, wake yourself up'. It was George's voice, what did he want? 'Wake up, Sergeant, it's not polite to keep your visitors waiting, come on, wake up', the voice continued firmly. Tom heard a snort of laughter, as he came to, and opened his eyes, ready to berate whoever was laughing at him, but was silenced by what he saw.

Before him was the boy who had disappeared those few hours before, holding the hand of a young man who stood with him. He was looking up at the young man who, in turn, was looking down at Tom, who instinctively grasped for his rifle but stopped when the young man spoke. 'You are English soldiers, yes? Giorgos', he said, looking down at the boy, 'Giorgos told me you were here, that you needed some help and perhaps you can help us. Giorgos said there were more of you, more than three'.

Tom peered up at him. 'First of all, mate', he replied, 'who are you? Where are you from, and what do you want? Yes, we are British soldiers, you can see that but who are you?' And how do you speak such good English, he thought. He nodded across at George, who held his rifle across his body, ready for quick action if it was required.

'I am Yannis Stephanidis, a soldier of my country'. He lifted up his left arm, which ended in a stump below the elbow, and with his right hand, pulled out what looked like dog tags, which were hanging around his neck on a thin chain. 'I was discharged from the Army and sent home, but I want to fight. Now these Germans come to my village, over there', he added, gesturing in the direction of Panadiki. 'They are looting, they have shot people who tried to stop them. I need your help, I cannot stop them'. His voice had risen in volume as he spoke and Tom could see the passion that animated him.

He continued, 'They have two of your soldiers as prisoners, one is hurt but not so bad. I heard the Feldwebel say that they will be taken down to a prison compound near Chania tomorrow, so you have little time'.

'And how many Germans are left there, I saw a dozen leaving, and the armoured car, but they must have left a few, I could see them'. 'There are seven', replied Yannis, 'perhaps too many. Giorgos said there were more of you '. 'There were more of us', replied Tom, 'but our orders were to get to Sphakia for evacuation, so the five who have gone were just obeying orders. The three of us here decided we should do what we could for the squaddies they have captured, which means attacking them in Panadiki and don't you worry about numbers, they don't know we're coming'.

He questioned Yannis, finding out where the German soldiers had found billets, where they were holding the two squaddies and how they were guarded. Yannis had explained that he had kept out of sight of the soldiers, knowing that he could make no difference alone, so he could tell them little. 'What about the other young chaps', asked George, 'Wouldn't they help you and will they help us?' he queried. Yannis looked back at him, a downcast expression on his face. 'There are no others', he answered. 'We all joined the Army, they were killed or captured. Only I have returned. Now, the village is old men, women and children'.

There was a brief silence, they could expect little help, that was clear. Tom looked down at the boy, and smiled. 'Giorgos, I think you can help us'. The lad looked up, uncomprehending. Yannis was concerned, 'What do you want him to do? He is just a boy'.

'Nothing dangerous, don't worry. Just to go back to the village and remember what he sees. Where the prisoners are, how many are guarding them, where the Jerries are billeted. Will he do that?' Yannis spoke Tom's words to the boy in Cretan Greek, the boy responding with a proud smile. He would.

'Please tell him', added Tom, 'he must behave normally, he isn't a spy, he just has to remember what he sees'. Yannis nodded, and Tom continued. 'Send him back now and fix a place for him to meet us later, an hour after sunset. Then it's down to us'.

Giorgos received his instructions from Yannis. Before he left to go back to the village, he turned solemnly to George and held out his hand. The corporal, touched at the boy's gesture, grasped it with his own and shook it firmly, smiling back at the lad. 'We're both George, eh! Go get 'em soldier' he murmured, as the lad disappeared among the trees.

'How long till sunset, Yannis?' Tom asked. 'Maybe two hours', was the reply. 'Then there's two hours to wait here, then an hour to get to the village and find Giorgos. We'll pool ammunition, rest up'. Then, looking directly at Yannis, he asked, 'Do you have a rifle for yourself somewhere, mate? And can you use it, I mean, with one arm, because we need you if you can'. Yannis held out his hand, gesturing for Tom to hand him his rifle, and then balancing it on his shortened arm, proceeded to use the other to remove and replace the magazine, then to work the bolt backwards and forwards then finally, to sight and take a dry shot. 'My rifle is hidden in the village, I can pick it up on the way in', he concluded, and handed the rifle back to Tom, who was nodding his approval.

'Ok, you'll do. Now, tell me, when we free them two lads, which way should we go after that? Come back here and follow the others or carry on through and find another way? We'll need to get a move on if we want to get to Sphakia before the Jerries'.

Yannis doubted that they had any chance of getting to the evacuation point in time, even now, but did not think that this was a good time to air that opinion. If he did, maybe they would change their minds about the attack and he did not want that to happen. He decided to simply answer the question.

'We must carry on through the village, towards Galatas, but head off south before we get there. There will be Germans there so we must leave the road, walk into the mountains. It will be a very hard two days to the coast at best, maybe longer'.

'What about food', queried Tom, 'Is there any food in the village that we can buy? I have a little money'. 'There is bread, some olives, cheese if you are lucky', replied Yannis, 'Water we will find on the journey'. Tom's eyes narrowed.

'We? Are you coming with us?'

'You will never find your way to the coast without me, and if you help my village then I must help you in return. I grew up here, I know the paths, caves where we can sleep or hide, I know people along the way who will help us. I will not leave the island with you though, my place is here'.

Tom and George exchanged glances, they needed help, that was sure.

'More rest', said Tom. 'If all goes well, we'll have a long walk in front of us. Davey, you're our lookout for the first hour. George, you take the second hour but wake me half way through. As long as all's clear at the end of George's watch, Yannis will lead us, nice and quiet, to the village. Understood?' All nodded in agreement, Davey moving off to watch over the approach from Panadiki, leaving Yannis, George and Tom to wait quietly among the trees.

Old soldier that he was, George was sleeping within a few short minutes, with Tom not far behind. Yannis could not sleep, Panadiki was his home, and it was his flesh and blood down there.

It only seemed like a moment before Tom felt a hand upon his shoulder, dragging him from his nap. He was faster to wake this time and quickly set about checking his rifle and ammunition. He thought he had about forty rounds, surely more than enough for this small action, if all went well. Ideally, depending upon what information young Giorgos was able to give them, they would be able to steal the two soldiers away without firing a shot, but how likely was that? More probable was a firefight, casualties and everything that went with it. Beside him, Yannis watched silently.

Inevitably, Tom began to ponder if he was doing the right thing, making the correct decision. Did he have any right to expect George and Davey to follow him into the village, putting their own escape from Crete at risk? What if either of them were wounded or killed? How would his decision-making look then? Bravado or worse.

He became aware that Davey, sitting across from him, under another olive tree, was looking at him with a resigned smile. 'Sergeant', said Davey quietly, 'If it was me being held by Jerries in that village, I should want to know that someone was looking out for me, and besides, there's Yannis's family to think about too. We had a couple of good nights in Panadiki didn't we, maybe with his kin, we should try to see them right. Me and George want to give it a go, so don't go taxing yourself none. We're volunteers, same as you'.

Davey paused, looking sharply over Tom's shoulder. In one lithe movement, he lifted his rifle to his shoulder and pushed a round into the chamber at the same time, ready to fire. As Tom threw himself down to one side, Davey took first pressure on the trigger then lowered the rifle into his lap as Yannis leapt in front of him and bore a small figure to the ground, a rifle clattering down beside him.

'Fuck me, Giorgos, I nearly shot you', he exhaled, 'Where did you spring from, you little bugger, and that rifle's bigger than you are!' The boy had returned.

The lad was terrified and it was a few moments before Yannis could calm him down enough for him to tell why he had returned against his instructions. Gradually, his story emerged, coaxed out between his tears.

He had returned to Panadiki. The German soldiers, of whom there were seven, took little notice of him, he was just another skinny ragamuffin to them, so he was able to walk around the houses and find out what had happened so far. His Mama told him that the two captured soldiers had tried to escape but the wounded man was too slow and they had not even managed to get out of the village. They had been recaptured and interrogated by an officer and an NCO in one of the houses, and the screaming that they had heard earlier was from them. He thought that they had been killed because all was now silent but the house was locked and he could not see them. The Germans had shot an old couple who would not let them search their house. It was stupid, said Giorgos, because the old couple had nothing to hide. They were beginning to search the other houses and he was scared that his mama and ya-ya would be hurt. He saw one of the soldiers looking at him and knew that he could not wait for Yannis to return, anything could happen, so he had run off behind the byres, collecting the hidden rifle from under the eaves of Papa's old shed and found them as quickly as he could.

There was a momentary silence, broken by George who, once more, engulfed the boy's small hand within his own. 'Yannis', he asked, 'Please tell the young man that he is a fine soldier and a credit to his mama. Tell him that we will do our best to keep his mama and ya-ya safe from the Germans'. 'And kill the fucking lot of them', he added under his breath.

Tom knew that they could not waste another moment, and rapidly issued his orders. 'Yannis, you stay with me, we'll approach the houses from the north. George, Davey? Giorgos will guide you to the south end, on the Galatas side. Wait for my firing if you can, and we should be able to drive any survivors into your range. If they hole up in one of the houses, well, we'll just have to clear it. You got any grenades?' Both George and Davey nodded in the affirmative. 'Not much of a plan is it, I know, but there's no time for reconnaissance. 'Any questions? No, then we'll move. How long before we can be in position, Yannis, ten minutes?' Yannis nodded, 'I think'. 'Then let's move, and George?' 'Sergeant?' he answered. 'Keep that boy out of harm's way, he wants to see his mam'.

Fifteen minutes later, Sergeant Tom lay in the lee of a large boulder, Yannis next to him, looking down at the village of Panadiki.

In the tiny hamlet about one hundred yards below, illuminated by the lights of a grey kubelwagen and an oil lamp, eleven people were lined up facing a wall, hands against the old stone, as they were roughly searched by two grey-clad German infantrymen, while another stood back, sub-machine gun in hand, watching for any sudden movements. With no more communication than the slightest nod to his friend, Yannis took the first pressure on the trigger of his rifle, checked his target then squeezed harder, enough to send the first shot crashing down into the group.

Chapter 13

The party of villagers and soldiers, now comprising fifteen souls, had abandoned the road immediately upon leaving Panadiki, crossing what might have been described as a meadow, except that it was littered with enormous boulders, some of which were the size of motor cars and larger. A narrow path zig-zagged between the rocks, heading inexorably upwards towards the head of a valley, softly illuminated in the light of the rising Moon. On another day, Tom might have appreciated the scenic beauty laid out in front of him but tonight, there were other things on his mind. Posting Davey as rear-guard, and with George escorting the centre of the slowly moving column, he moved up to the front of the group, where Yannis and his father were leading the way.

'Yannis', he called quietly, 'a word please'. The young man acknowledged him, said a few words in explanation to his father and waited for Tom to climb the last few yards to join him.

'Yannis', he began, 'I am sorry to say this but how long will you need us to escort these people? I have a duty to give my lads a chance to evacuate, those were my orders, and we need to get to the coast quickly or the last boats will be gone. With your people in tow, we can only move as fast as the slowest, and I get the feeling we'll be moving slower yet. What's in your mind?'

The young man looked across at Tom as he considered his reply. 'Sergeant Tom, six hours will see us to Peripetro, where my people can stop. They have relations there who will take them in, give them rooms to stay. When the Germans come to search, they will be the same as anyone else there, they will not know that they came from Panadiki. We should be there by four in the morning and the Germans will have many villages to search once they have discovered their soldiers. I would not expect them in Peripetro for a further twenty four hours or even longer'.

He paused, then began again. 'Please stay with us until we reach the village, Sergeant Tom, then I promise that I will lead you through the mountains to Sphakia. You have my word'.

Tom quickly considered the offer, then nodded his acceptance. 'Alright then, Yannis, that's agreed. George and Davey wouldn't want to leave the old folks in the hills anyway. But no hanging about in Peri-whatsit, we deliver the old 'uns and kids then we leave. No sleeping, no coffee drinking, we get on our way'. 'You have my word, Sergeant Tom, perhaps they will give us a little food and water to help us on our way but we will not, as you say, be hanging about'. Tom smiled his acknowledgment of their agreement and moved back down the column, pausing with George and Davey in turn to explain the plan.

It was a tough slog through the night as the party made its painful way towards Peripetro, along tracks ever more rough and tortuous. Within the first hour, the three soldiers and Yannis had relieved their older companions of the few belongings they were carrying in order just to keep moving. They had to reach Peripetro before daylight, the Germans might send out spotter planes and they would be so visible on the bare mountainsides.

The older women, though valiant and spirited, were finding the pace difficult and before long, were arm in arm with the younger men, supported as they stumbled along. One of them glanced across at Davey, her escort, and made a remark in her own language, provoking some quiet laughter from her companions. One of the younger women, smiling, leaned across to Davey and said, 'Agathe say she think her day with young man is over but no. If you are tired and lie down, she will warm you up!' At this, George hooted with laughter, leaving Davey to blush in his embarrassment. Fortunately for him, it was still dark and no one could see his discomfiture. It was good to know though that one of the younger lasses knew some English. He would have to be careful what he said!

Tom turned to Yannis saying, 'No offence, mate, but how can they make a joke after what they've seen today? Three of their old folks murdered by those bastards, and our two chaps?' Yannis smiled sadly. 'There are reasons, Sergeant Tom. They are grateful to you and your men for saving them, and they see that the one you call Davey is so young. All their own young men went away to war and only I have returned. When they look at Davey, they see their sons, their brothers, so they want him to know that he is important to them, as if their own. Also, you must know that we are a people who know suffering very well, we are proud but life is always hard. We have to live through pain often, and what better medicine than a smile? We feel the same as you but we show a different face, that is all'.

'Then you have my respect, Yannis, all of you', answered Tom, realising that he had misjudged them. 'I apologise if I have offended you or your family', he continued. 'Offended us? Never!' smiled Yannis. 'You saved my people from those devils, I could not have done that alone. No, your names will be spoken among us long after this war is over'. He added, with a grin, 'Perhaps, Sergeant Tom, the next baby in Panadiki will be named for you!' Now it was Tom's turn to laugh, and the people around him smiled too, happy that their rescuer could laugh with them, and share their peril.

The night passed, and first light was rising behind the mountains as Peripetro came into view. It was a true mountain village, with a single row of low, stone-roofed houses tucked below a sheer crag with further steep slopes looming behind it. A narrow stream, emerging from one side of the crag, ran along the length of the line of dwellings before disappearing out of sight as the ground dropped away. There was a smell of wood-smoke and the crow of a cockerel welcoming the new day but no people in view. After a discussion among the Panadikiots, it was agreed that Spiros, Yannis's father, would walk into the village alone and if all was well, he would call everyone down.

As Spiros made his careful way down the short slope to the houses, the rest of the party sank to the ground. All were drained of energy, and the old people in particular looked grey and exhausted. Hopefully, their journey's end had arrived.

When Spiros came back into view, beckoning them down, it was as much that the three British soldiers could do to get everyone on their feet and moving again. Giorgos was tottering with fatigue, almost asleep as he walked, and with a smile, George swept him up, carrying him draped upon his back, down to the houses and safety.

Peripetro woke quickly at the arrival of their guests, and there was weeping and angry words as they told their story to the inhabitants. The soldiers, not understanding the language, could not follow the account but respectful glances came their way from time to time. A smiling young woman brought them bread and cups of goats milk, and Tom could see that his two companions were beginning to relax and feel their tiredness, and he knew that if he allowed that to happen, and allowed his own weariness to take over, it would be hours before they moved on. Any further delay would make it more likely that they would miss evacuation from the island and what if German soldiers came to Peripetro? The villagers would be shot for harbouring them. That could not happen.

'Brace up, boys', he murmured to George and Davey, 'we're leaving now, can't stay here'. 'I thought you would say that, you young bugger', answered George with a smile. 'He's right though, Davey, time to go. See if we can catch that bloody boat home. Davey, you listening to me?' He nudged Tom. Davey's eyes were fixed on the pretty young girl who had brought them the bread and milk, and it seemed that his attentions were not unwelcome to her, judging by the shy smile upon her face.

'Private Williams', rasped Tom, in a quieter version of his parade-ground voice, 'Eyes front!' He and George chuckled as Davey jumped in surprise then moved reflexively towards attention before he first realised where he was, and then that his two seniors were grinning fit to burst! 'Davey, time to leave, lad', said Tom, quietly.

He sought out Yannis, who nodded his understanding before Tom even spoke. 'There is a small change of plan, Sergeant'. Seeing Tom's expression, he hurried on. 'We will leave now and I will guide you as I promised'. 'Then what's changed?' enquired Tom. Yannis looked embarrassed.

'Sergeant Tom', he started to say but was interrupted by a light female voice, light but determined. 'I am coming with you, I am your best guide'. The speaker was the young woman who had translated on the hillside for Davey, one of the two that they had rescued from probable execution in Panadiki.

Yannis looked apologetic. 'She is my sister, Sergeant Tom, my older sister. She will not listen to me'. Before he could continue, the young lady in question burst out in a rapid flow, a torrent even, of impassioned Cretan Greek. Tom hid a smile as Yannis, the recipient of this flood of words, seemed to shrink before his eyes, then found himself standing a little straighter as she turned to him.

'Sergeant Tom, I am Elena, the sister of this boy', she said, gesturing towards Yannis. 'I grew up in these mountains, I know the paths as well he does, better. We will guide you to Sphakia together'. 'But what about your sons, your husband?' spluttered Tom, 'what about them?' He almost wished the words back, as Elena's countenance darkened at his words. 'Husband, I have no husband, and what if I did? No husband would tell me what I could do!' Tom, never a faint heart, pressed on. 'And your sons?' Elena, perhaps understanding that she should not risk offending Tom, who undoubtedly had the authority to exclude her if he saw fit, moderated her tone. 'Sergeant Tom, those two boys, Giorgos and Petros, are the sons of my sister in law, not my sons. How could I have sons', she explained, 'I am not married', she added with a smile, 'nor even betrothed'.

'Be that as it may', continued Tom, 'I must ask your father if he thinks that we need you, and if you have his approval to guide us'. As he spoke, he could see the indignation building in Elena's face and before she could respond, he added quietly, 'There has been enough death among your people, Miss. I will not be responsible for more'. Elena visibly paused a little at his words and nodded her assent.

To Tom's surprise, Spiros readily gave his permission for Elena to accompany them. Through Yannis, he explained, 'Elena is the picture of her mother, God bless her soul. Our firstborn, she inherited her mama's courage, strength and beauty, she is her image. I could not stop her doing this for you, as I could not stop the year turning or the sun rising. All I ask is that she returns to us, if God wills it'. Tom was moved at the old man's passion. 'Sir, I will return her safely to your care if I have the strength', he said with feeling, not knowing how he would achieve it but sure that he must.

Elena had overheard the conversation and was looking somewhat triumphant, so Tom decided that he should make her position extremely clear. 'Miss Elena', he began, 'You have your father's permission to help us but you must understand, you will be subject to military discipline'. She looked blank at Tom's rather pompous and formal tone, so he took another tack. 'I am in command and you will follow my orders. If you do not wish to do that, you must stay here. If you come with us and do not obey my orders, I will send you home. Do you understand me, Miss?' She smiled back at him, disarmingly. 'Oh yes, Sergeant. I understand. You will tell me what to do and I must do it. Don't worry, I will be a good soldier'.

I'm not bloody worried, he thought, you're the least of my worries, but did not say it, he had to at least try to treat her as he would treat anyone else under his command and not rise to any minor provocation.

'Fine' he answered. 'I'm sure you can shoot so find a rifle and as much ammunition as you can carry. We leave in five minutes'. She saluted him, with a grin, and raced away to arm herself.

Five minutes stretched to ten, as the rescued took turns to hug and kiss their rescuers, making them promise to return once the war was won. It was clear to Tom that the farewells would last all morning if he didn't step in but in the event, he did not need to. Both George and Davey sensed that they could stay no longer and gently disengaged themselves from their new friends, young and old. Yannis and Elena, after kissing their father, joined them, leading them up from the houses along a rough path which followed the little stream around the side of the crag.

They had only walked twenty yards or so when George felt a hand pulling at his sleeve. It was his young friend, Giorgos, with tears trickling down his face. As George crouched down to comfort him, Giorgos put out his hand and placed its contents in George's rough palm. It was a tiny wooden crucifix, threaded onto a piece of cord. Roughly made, it was carved out of a single piece of olive wood.

George was a tough old soldier, seen everything, been everywhere, but it was as much as he could do to keep any composure at all. Blinking back his own tears, he asked Elena to translate his words to Giorgos. 'Young soldier', he said gently, 'You are a good boy and I thank you for this present. I will wear it all the time and it will remind me of you. Your duty now is to look after your brother and your mama. I promise that if I can, I will come to see you again. God bless'. After kissing the boy on the top of his head, George straightened up and without looking back, carried on up the path, placing the crucifix carefully around his neck.

He was followed closely by his comrades old and new, all deep in thought, contemplating the changes that the past few days had wrought inside them all. Within minutes, they had followed the track to the top of the crag and disappeared from the view of the villagers below them, standing in grateful but regretful silence.

Chapter 14

By the time that they had climbed the long slope behind the crag of Peripetro, full daylight was upon them. The cool of the night remained but it would be only minutes before the heat of the new day arrived. Elena, putting herself at the head of the party, set a strong pace despite the incline, and the slow progress of the previous night seemed to be well behind them. She had confirmed to Tom that they needed to leave Peripetro far behind them quickly, so that if they were spotted and pursued, then their chasers might not connect them to that village.

Tom had agreed without demur, he had no wish to increase the danger that the villagers were already in and it suited his purpose to try to make up for lost time and reach Sphakia for evacuation before it was too late. Perhaps it was too late already? They were almost a day behind the rest of the platoon survivors who had left them at Panadiki, and two days behind the main body. The Navy would be taking a pounding from the Jerries, that was for sure, and they couldn't wait for ever.

George caught his eye. 'Tom, I know what's in your mind, and don't fret. Either we'll find a boat waiting for us, or we won't. If there's none, well, they'll send another. Besides, it seems to me there's still a job to do here'. 'How do you mean, George?' answered Tom, knowing full well what he was meaning.

George paused, choosing his words with care. 'You know me, Tom, regular soldier, always do my duty as best I can, and our orders are to evacuate and fight another day and that's right. But if we can't get out now because the Jerries won't let us, then there's other ways we can soldier till we can find the regiment again'. Tom nodded. 'Go on'.

'Seems to me the folks here hate the Jerries more than we do, not surprising, invading their country without so much as a by your leave. The shootings, the cruelties we've seen, that'll be going on all over. These people will fight back, won't they, they won't let Jerry walk all over them but they're not soldiers, so we can help them'.

'They're not helpless though, George', commented Tom. 'Yannis was telling me about these Andartes, that's what they call their guerrilla fighters. He reckons there are numbers of them, fighting already. I heard they took down a good number of them parachutists between Maleme and Chania. Some of them will be old soldiers, like Yannis'.

'Then if it comes to it, Sergeant, if we can't evacuate now, maybe we should tag along with them, at least until we get another chance to leave. Apart from anything else, I don't see how else the three of us would survive otherwise, got to get food from somewhere, got to hide out somewhere'.

'Alright, George, I get the message', answered Tom. 'Tell you what, if we can't get off now, we'll speak to Yannis about finding a group of these fighters to tag along with. First things first though, we must get to Sphakia as fast as we can, and hope we're not too late'.

Yannis, walking behind them, and overhearing the conversation, smiled to himself. He still doubted that they would reach the coast in time to escape and if they didn't, he agreed with George, three trained soldiers, four including himself, would be a valuable addition to any Andartes group. He had given his word though, and would do his best, with Elena's help, to get them to Sphakia as quickly as they could.

Tom, following behind Elena, decided he ought to get to know her a little and find out what her plans were for getting them over the mountains. He was in charge, after all. The path zig-zagged through a boulder field, the stones ranging in size from football to wagon, and Elena would dip out of sight momentarily as she passed behind one of the larger rocks, then reappear for a minute before disappearing again. Tom stretched out his pace for a minute or so and was quickly on her heels.

Hearing him, she turned and smiled but before she could speak, Tom saw her look quickly to the north. At the same second, he began to hear a familiar drone in the sky. 'Everyone down!' he bellowed, 'and don't look up!' Pulling Elena by the sleeve of her shirt, they tumbled down into the shade of one of the larger boulders, and were able to wriggle down under its edge, until only the tops of their heads were visible from above. He knew that George would make sure that Davey and Yannis were well concealed too.

Ignoring Elena's close proximity, squeezed against him in the confines of the hollow under the great rock, Tom risked a quick glance down the slope. In the sky, appearing over the end of a ridge and flying slowly towards them, was an odd-looking plane, with a high wing and a long, fixed undercarriage. Tom was up on his aircraft recognition, identifying it as a Storch, Germany's slow-speed, short take-off and landing reconnaissance plane. He knew that it could quarter the mountainside at low altitude and would radio back any sightings to troops on the ground. They were being hunted!

'Stay down, don't move until I order' he roared finally to his comrades and ducked back into full cover, pulling Elena's head into his chest to keep her concealed. She started to wriggle but realising his intention, quickly relaxed and became still. They lay silently, as the rattle of the aircraft engine became louder and louder. Neither looked up as the noise reached its peak, both missing the shadow of the plane as it swept over their position and followed the upward slope of the rock-strewn cove. The rattle of the engine faded but no one moved and sure enough, within a minute, its volume increased as the pilot reversed his flight and followed the valley downhill, this time to the east of their hiding place. Again, the engine noise quietened and this time, faded completely away.

After more minutes of silence, Tom called out. 'George, can you see down the valley from where you are, anything there?' After a pause, the corporal replied, 'All clear, Tom. I can only see about half a mile, mind'.

Tom looked down at Elena, who had pulled her head away from his chest and was looking back up at him. 'What's the path like from here on, Elena? Is there any cover, anywhere to hide if they come after us?' he asked, unable to hide a grin at her flushed, overheated face. 'Same as this for about four hundred metres, to the top of this valley', she answered, 'then about five kilometres of open mountain until we start Samaria Gorge. Nowhere to hide until the gorge'. 'Then we can't move until it's dark, not with planes after us', he replied. She nodded.

George, Yannis and Davey, crushed together in the lee of an enormous slab of limestone, looked up in unison as Tom dropped down beside them. 'George, me and Elena are going to move up to the top of the slope, only about four hundred yards. I'll give you a whistle when we get there, as long as it's clear, then bring the boys up to twenty yards below us, I'll keep an eye out for you'. Turning to Yannis, 'She says there's no real cover until the gorge, that right?' At Yannis's nod of assent, he continued. 'So we have to wait until sunset then get down that gorge to the coast before morning. I was hoping we'd be there tonight but there's no chance now, so we'll just have to see how things stand this time tomorrow. I'm sorry, boys, our Good Samaritan act might have cost us our ticket home'.

Davey, who had been his usual quiet self until then, shook his head. 'No, Sergeant. You gave us the chance to leave, along with Rodri Jones, and we couldn't, same as you, isn't that right, George? And we couldn't leave those old dears either, not after what those Jerries were going to do to them. No, if we miss the boat then we'll keep ourselves busy until there's another one'.

Tom and George both looked stunned, as Yannis looked on. 'That was quite a speech, Davey', laughed George, eventually. 'We struggles to get more than half a dozen words out of you usually. Nothing to do with a certain lass in Peripetro, is it?' Davey didn't answer, he was too busy looking at his boots.

Tom winked at George and continued, 'That's the spirit, Davey, never say die. We have to look forward, not back. Right boys, I'll be getting back, wait for my whistle'. With that, he was gone.

Twenty minutes later, it was done. They were settled in fresh concealment, with eleven or twelve hours to wait before they could move again. They all knew that smoking and cooking fires were out of the question in case they were spotted, so water, bread and cheese would have to suffice. George took first watch, looking down the valley, while Tom, sitting in cover with Elena at the head of the valley, kept an eye on their evening's planned route.

Tom could see no movement, other than a large bird of prey, leisurely circling as it gained height above the mountains, carried by powerful thermals as the strong sunshine warmed up the air. He was thinking to himself how simple and uncomplicated a bird's life must be, when a gentle voice interrupted his thoughts.

It was Elena. 'Sergeant Tom, talk to me, please. We have many hours to wait before we can move again, and just looking at each other will become very boring'.

Tom smiled tiredly, replying, 'We need some sleep first, Elena. I've not slept for the past two nights, nor the lads. We're done in'. As she made to interrupt him, he held up his hand, palm facing her. 'That's my order, Elena. We must rest now, understand?' She nodded back to him, a little sulkily, he thought, but pressed him no further.

'OK then, my girl, you sleep first and I'll wake you in two hours. We'll watch two hours on two off until it's time to move'. More kindly, he continued, 'Here, roll up my jacket for a pillow, that'll help you get off, and we can chat later, alright?' She grinned, saying, 'I will make you keep that promise, Sergeant Tom. An Englishman's word is his castle, right?' 'Yes, it is, Elena, or something like that', he answered, grinning back at her. Satisfied, she lay back under the shade of the rocks that concealed them, and within a few minutes, Tom heard her breathing begin to settle as sleep came to her.

She really is a pretty thing, thought Tom, looking down at her. Her oval face, deeply tanned, was flawless, with a fine nose and, he knew, hazel brown eyes, able to blaze with anger or twinkle with humour at a moment's notice. Her lush, dark brown hair, tied back with a thin blue ribbon, was dusty after their trek and Tom found himself wondering how she would look with her hair down. Before he could take his observations any further, and consider how she fitted into the men's shirt and trousers that she was wearing, a little voice, fast becoming familiar, butted into his thoughts.

'Sergeant, you are very kind looking after me but you cannot watch the path and me at the same time', whispered Elena, with eyes still closed and a faint smile twitching at the corner of her lips. Tom felt himself beginning to blush, murmured 'Yes, ma'am', and turned his attention quickly to the track ahead, feeling foolish and that he had given himself away a little. Bloody old chump, he thought. Elena smiled privately to herself, with just a little satisfaction, and settled back for her much needed siesta.

It was mid-morning now, and as the heat of the day began to build, a haze rippled across the open mountain spread out in front of him. To Tom's right, the rubble strewn slope carried on upwards for, Tom estimated, another couple of thousand feet, appearing to top out at a long ridge which climbed further towards a distant summit. Directly ahead, a thin path wove its way between the rocks, large and small, that littered the mountainside, disappearing eventually into a fold of a crag about half a mile in front of him. Where it went from there, Tom could not tell, even using the Colonel's binoculars.

To Tom's left, the slope dropped away, at an angle of perhaps forty five degrees, for a good half mile, before easing down into a narrow valley, through which a stream had cut its way. Tom could see a few stunted trees along the near bank, which looked like oak through the binoculars, although very small, and above the far bank of the stream was what seemed to be a rough track, much larger than their own path. Big enough for vehicles, Tom wondered. Probably, and he was not going to investigate. The only vehicles along it would be German.

He could see no people, no sheep, not even a goat. Tom felt himself beginning to relax, his eyes beginning to feel heavy in the heat, which seemed oppressive for a man born and bred in Shropshire. Experience told him that he must be active in order to stay awake and do his job, so for the remainder of the next two hours, he visually scoured the landscape in front of him, systematically, with binoculars and without, and fortunately saw nothing to worry him. All was quiet.

George had appeared for a quick word, mid-watch, wanting a better estimate of their departure time from their hiding places. They agreed on nineteen hundred hours, it would not be dark by then but the light would beginning to dim, so their chances of being spotted were small.

As George stealthily returned down the slope, he looked down at the slumbering Elena. 'Sleeping Beauty', he stage-whispered, turning to Tom with a wink, before vanishing from sight.

Tom was glad when he was able to wake Elena, and yawning, she took his place. She was delighted with the binoculars, promising to rouse him if she saw anything unusual. How glad he was to take his place in the shade, still hot but at least out of the powerful sunshine. Head down, he was deeply asleep in seconds.

Elena took covert glances at Tom as he slept. He looked a fine man, she thought, but more importantly, she knew him to be a man of action and firm decision. He had not hesitated to kill the whole platoon of German soldiers, they were all dead before they could even begin to fight back. It was a pity that he had to leave the island to re-join the British Army, they could use a man with his skills and experience when the fightback against the invaders really started.

The one they called George, the older one, he was a killer too, she was sure. He was kind, how good he had been with little Giorgos, but his stare, when he thought no one was looking, seemed both hard and cruel. He would not be a man to cross.

The younger one, Davey, was not much more than a boy, despite his enormous size. She had noticed that he hung upon the words of his older colleagues, listening carefully and soaking everything in. There was a bond between him and George, she thought, like father and son, no, that was not right. Like older brother and younger, that was a closer description. He was cared for and guided by his elders but she could see that he had qualities of his own that were beginning to show. If he lived, and mentored by his friend George, he would become a formidable soldier.

And what about Yannis. He had seemed so young when he had joined the Division and left for the mainland to fight the Italians, her little brother. He was different on his return.

It was more than losing his arm. He was cold, bitterly angry. She could understand that, she felt it herself after the innocent lives lost at Panadiki, the old couple, her aunt, the two New Zealand soldiers. Somehow though, it was deeper in him, she guessed it was because he had seen so much more in his time at the Front. He had not talked in any detail, just told them about the death of Petros, in the same attack that had cost him his arm. If she was honest, and although she still tried to play the role of big sister with him, he frightened her.

And what of herself? Was she changing too? Almost certainly she was, although it would be more obvious to someone who knew her, looking in, rather than to herself, looking out. She too felt blinding anger and insult but also, perhaps, a little excitement? Was it a sin to feel that way when people she knew were being maimed and slaughtered around her, and she had the opportunity to fight back, to spend time helping these professional killers? No, how could it be? The Germans had invaded, murdered her neighbours, her fellow Cretans, it was no sin to fight back. It was her duty, and she would fulfil it, if she could.

All was quiet on the mountain and with a jolt, Elena realised that she had let Tom sleep on, half an hour more than his allotted two hours. She had not followed his instructions but, she reasoned, he needed sleep more than she did, after all, he had fought a battle at Chania before starting up into the mountains. If he shouted at her, she would shout back, she wasn't one of his soldiers after all! Nevertheless, the prospect of angry words from him, of failing in her duty, appalled her a little.

'Sergeant Tom, Sergeant Tom', she murmured, leaning over him, 'You must wake now, Sergeant Tom'. Tom's eyes flicked open, his pupils dilating, she noticed, as he quickly identified her. He sat up, rubbing his eyes. 'Sergeant Tom', she confessed, 'I let you sleep a little longer'. 'Just thirty minutes', she added rapidly, as she saw his face harden in disapproval. 'You should have woken me up, Miss', he grunted. 'Is all quiet still?' She nodded. 'Then no harm done', he concluded, 'but wake me next time, do you understand? We're all tired, God knows, but I must be able to trust you to follow my instructions'. Seeing her downcast, tired face, he added, 'Like I said, no harm done. Now, its three hours before we can move' he said, consulting his watch, 'time to eat and drink and', he added with a smile, 'have that talk'.

After he had pulled out the remains of the bread and cheese from his pack, passing Elena a share, along with the remaining water bottle, Tom settled on a warm boulder from where he could see both the valley in front, and most of the path that they had already trod. All was quiet.

There was a short hiatus, both feeling somewhat awkward, before Elena decided that it was up to her to break the silence before it became embarrassing. 'Sergeant Tom, tell me about your life, where you come from. I have never left Crete and I know almost nothing of England. I know you have a king, as we do, and that it rains every day. I know that your soldiers use a lot of bad words and some of you wear skirts but fight like devils! I do not understand you at all but I would like to'.

'Well, Miss', Tom replied, putting aside his usual reticence, 'I come from near a little place called Pontesbury, in Shropshire, Shropshire's a county, a bit like your provinces'. She nodded in understanding.

Gathering his confidence, Tom continued. 'It's a wonderful place, Miss. No big mountains like here, but plenty of rolling green hills, forests and rivers large and small. Yes, it rains a lot but not every day! Dad is a small farmer, sheep mostly, same as here. We had a few cows for milk and calves'. She interrupted to ask what calves were, then gestured that he should continue.

'Mam and Dad wanted me to work the farm, take it over when they got older, being as I had no brother or sister, but I couldn't'. He explained, 'England, the whole of Britain, was poor. Thousands, millions even, with no work and no money. Dad couldn't make a living for all of us, the prices were so bad, so I had to go. I didn't mind, Miss, I had worked with them for five years after leaving school and I was thinking there must be more to the world than feeding beasts'. Elena smiled, and Tom continued, encouraged.

'I got the bus up to Wrexham, about as far as we are now from Chania, and joined up with the Royal Welch Fusiliers. I was a Fusilier for nine years, Miss, along with George. He took me under his wing, taught me what proper soldiering was, he's like a brother to me. We was in France, the Fusiliers, through the winter of '39 until a year ago, just over, when Adolf and his tanks threw us out! Me and George was lucky to get on a boat at Dunkirk but that's another story. Couple of months after that, some of us was transferred to the Welch, and I've been with the Regiment ever since, Miss. A few months in Egypt then over the sea to here. The Army's been my home and my family for ten years, Miss, I've grown up in it'. He paused, aware of the feeling evident in his voice.

'So there you are, Miss. We don't wear skirts in the Welch, that's the Jocks from Scotland and yes, they fight like devils! You wouldn't want to be on the wrong side of any of the Scots regiments, hard men. The Army takes in people from all over Britain and the Empire, that's why it's so strong!'

Elena was impressed at Tom's passion but could not stop herself quietly asking, 'Then how did the Germans win here, Sergeant?' Tom sighed. 'Well, Miss, like all soldiers, we do what our officers tell us, and our officers do what the government tells them to do. The truth is, there were never enough of us, nor enough planes either. The Germans threw more at it than we did, and that's the truth. But, Miss, you have to understand that this is a battle lost, not the whole war. We'll come out on top in the end, like we did in the last one. We are not done yet!'

'As for the King', he continued, 'He's simply the idea of the country in one man, same as yours, I expect. We're fighting for our families, for our Mams and Dads worrying about us back home and of course, for each other. George has been watching my back for ten years, and now we're both watching Davey's. And Yannis and yours, of course, Miss'.

There was a pause as they both considered what he had said. Elena began, 'Sergeant Tom, will I tell you my story? You have been very honest and I should be too'. 'As you wish, Miss', answered Tom, taking a further check of their surroundings and seeing nothing amiss.

'Tom, my story is not so different to yours. My father is a farmer also, sheep and goats. It has always been a hard life in the mountains, little money, just enough food but no more. I was raised to help my parents, help the village but I knew I wanted to escape, to have a different life. It is difficult to be a woman in Crete, you are expected to marry, make your children and follow your husband. I told you that I am not married or betrothed, and that is true'. She hesitated, grappling with an emotion that Tom could not immediately identify.

'I was betrothed. My lover was Andres, a sailor from Rethymno, he had family in my village, an aunt. He was my way to change my life, but he died, not from the war but from a disease, on his ship, far from home, and I learned of his death only months later. I would have been married by now if he had lived, living in the city but it was not to be and I am left to decide what to do next with my life. I know that I cannot stay, I want to be more than a sad spinster or married to some old farmer. Then these bastard Germans invade my country, kill my neighbours. They would have raped all of the women if you had not saved us, Sergeant Tom, then they would have killed us, children too. But you and your men and Yannis were there and now we are alive and they are dead. What will life bring next to me, Sergeant Tom?'

She hesitated, looking drained and weary as she opened her heart to this foreign stranger. Tom, in turn, felt stunned, and more than a little overwhelmed. Was she expecting him to say something back to her, what could he say? What if he said the wrong thing, and upset her more? This was so far outside his experience!

He cleared his throat to speak, having little idea of the words that might emerge, but Elena must have sensed his predicament, adding gently, 'Forgive me. You have no more of an answer than I, for how can you know my fate, or I yours? I am grateful that you are here, even if you must leave us to re-join your comrades and if we never see you again, your names will be long remembered in Panadiki'.

Tom, hardened soldier that he was, felt her sincerity and chose his next words carefully. 'Elena, may I call you Elena, Miss?' 'Of course', she smiled. Tom continued, 'Elena, I'm not much for learning but I do know that life throws all sorts at us, from nowhere, and the measure of us is how we manage it. We make our little plans, of course we do, and try to make some sense of our lives but it rarely works out, does it? I didn't know I was going to be a soldier and to be honest with you, I did not ask or expect to come to Crete. The fight was hotting up in the desert and I was trained and ready to fight the Jerries and the Eyeties wherever I found them. But now, here I am'.

Tom paused, then continued. 'And here you are, Elena. Whoever would have thought it? Farmers' children from either end of Europe, meeting up and we're fighting the same enemy. There's no understanding it, I reckon all we can do, you and me and anyone else for that matter, is what we think is the right thing'. Elena was still and quiet, eyes fixed on Tom's face. He expected to be feeling self-conscious, talking like this to a young woman, but he didn't. Was it her, or the situation or a combination of the two? It did not seem to matter.

'The right thing for me, Elena, has to be to find the regiment. Our orders are to leave Crete and we must, one way or the other, but while we're here, we'll fight with you as hard as we can, I promise you that. George and Davey feel the same as me, I know'.

Elena's response was a sad but resigned smile. 'You are right, Tom. Fate has brought all of us together, and in such circumstances! How cruel the world can be! You have helped us, thanks be to God, but you must leave and I must stay, Yannis too. You cannot choose and neither can I'.

A single tear ran down her face, cutting a path through the dust that coated her cheek, but if Tom had been expecting her to be overtaken by her emotions, he would have been guilty of a gross underestimation of her character. She was passionate, yes, but also strong and resolute.

'We take the world as we find it, Sergeant Tom, you and I, yes?' Tom nodded his agreement. 'So we will fight together today, and tomorrow. After that, who knows? The world will turn, that is all we can say'.

'Yes, lass,' answered Tom, 'that's right'. They exchanged a further glance, a little prolonged on both their parts, then settled back to wait for evening. Tom watched the route and valley ahead but quickly found himself thinking that if only he had met Elena in different circumstances! Not only did he find her attractive, she was so vivacious and vital, but their conversation had revealed a strength and depth of character within her that, for Tom, raised her above any other woman he had known. If only…. Tom cursed himself for a hypocrite, he had keep his mind on the job and not lose himself in dreams. So much for taking the world as he found it! It was more complicated than he had thought! He turned away from Elena and concentrated upon his duty.

Chapter 15

Twenty yards further down the hillside, wedged between and under massive boulders eroded long before from the cliffs above them, Yannis, George and Davey perched, sometimes in companionable silence, sometimes in quiet conversation. They had taken turns to sleep, and to keep watch, and they all felt better for the rest.

George and Davey had gently extracted Yannis's personal military story from him, and looked at him with a deeper respect. They already knew that he was a fighter but his battle experience was real enough. His epic journey from mainland Greece impressed them mightily, as did his fierce determination, despite just one complete arm, to help rid his island of the Nazi invaders. It did not occur to either of them that, had Hitler managed to land an army on the island of Britain, they would have shown exactly the same devotion and the same bristling aggression.

Home was far away, families too, and like most soldiers, George and Davey had learned to live in the present. They tried not to dream of the future, knowing that they must follow Tom and the Regiment but had already committed to helping the Cretans in their fight along the way, as it were. Inside themselves, under their skin, the longer they were on the island and the more they knew and understood the inhabitants, the stronger their feelings were that they should do whatever they could, when the opportunity appeared, whatever the cost. Neither of them put it into words and would have struggled if asked to do so, but it was certain and clear within them.

Yannis had learned about the two of them, and what a contrast they were. George with his two decades of service around the world, in India, Palestine, Iraq and of course, France. His experiences in life were manifold - deadly violence, poverty and suffering but also generosity, nobility in adversity and the power of love and family. Combined with his military skills, George was a formidable man and Yannis understood directly that the longer he spent in George's company, the more he would learn and understand about how the world really worked. He may not look like a formidable fighting man, thought Yannis to himself, with his thin body and thinner hair, but his eyes and ears missed nothing and his rifle and bayonet, always close to hand, were as well maintained as if he was in barracks.

Davey was a different picture but no less impressive in his own way. At least half a metre taller than his older comrade, he was built, in Yanis's view, like a circus strongman, all muscle and bulk. His mother must have fed him well! He was so young, with his pale, sunburned skin and round, friendly features but immensely strong, judging by the loads he had ferried up the mountain. His fighting experience was limited to the past few weeks around Chania, Yannis had learned, but his watchful eyes and all round vigilance indicated that many lessons had been learned. He listened to George with great respect, deference even, but had his own views and wasn't slow to express them. They were a notable pair. He had a strong feeling, a certainty even, that there was more violence to come and that George and Davey would soon show their mettle.

And his sister Elena, alone with the sergeant for the day? A grin flashed across his face, wondering if Sergeant Tom had managed to contribute more than a word or two to their conversation! She could out-talk anyone! It never occurred to him, of course, that their little brother big sister relationship was limited to the two of them, by definition, and that Elena would behave differently in the company of a different man. He was correct though in concluding that she could look after herself and that Sergeant Tom would behave with discipline and politeness, befitting an NCO in the British Army.

Time passed, and the light began to fail. George set the other two to preparations to move, making sure that they had left no trace of their presence. It was entirely possible that they might be pursued, so it was good fieldcraft to leave as few signs of having been there as possible.

An ammunition count totted up to almost two hundred rounds of .303 for their rifles, as well as thirty rounds of 9mm for a Luger pistol that George had taken from the dead German officer at Panadiki. Davey and George, with six Mills bombs between them, donated two to Yannis who had used similar grenades against the Italians.

Between them, thought George, they could manage a mobile action or two, fire and withdraw, but they would never be able to sustain a static defence and any automatic weaponry would quickly overwhelm them. Tom would know that, and would plan accordingly, he would be looking to get to the coast with no more delay, and without any enemy contact.

George looked up, hearing a sharp brief whistle from the direction of Tom's lair, further up the slope, followed by a longer note, then the two notes, short and long, repeated twice more. Yannis looked puzzled. 'It's Morse, lad,' explained George, 'AAA, Tom is telling me all's clear. I'll acknowledge with the same, and we will move up and join them. And keep quiet'. His muted whistle achieved, the three moved silently up the twenty yards of path, to where Tom and Elena, armed and ready, were waiting for them.

Tom quickly briefed the others. 'Yannis and Elena to lead, I will be behind them, then Davey. George, take the rear. No more than thirty yards front to back, we can't afford to lose anyone. We need to move fast, get to the sea before daylight so five minutes break every hour, no more, less if we can manage it. If you do get separated, you are on your own, just make for the coast'.

'Stay quiet, don't talk unless you have to. We are going to evade Jerries if we can, not fight them. Listen for my orders, George will take over if I can't continue. Any questions?' There were none, and Yannis took the first steps into the gathering darkness.

Elena and Yannis led the group at a fair pace for the first two hours, following a faint path along the contour of the mountain. Everyone tripped and stumbled in the fading light but no one cursed or stopped walking. Gradually the line of the path moved down the slope towards the bottom of the valley, the river and beyond it, the rough road.

Their path met the river, and in the cover of some scrubby trees, they took a welcome rest. Davey, the youngest and fittest of the little group, scouted out to a radius of two hundred yards around them but all was quiet. There was time to finish the small amount of food that remained, washed down with cool, fresh water, then Tom quietly ordered everyone back to their feet. They had managed about half of the five kilometres to the gorge, and with a further sixteen kilometres to walk through the gorge itself, to the coast at Agia Roumeli, there was little time to spare.

The riverside path was easier to follow, with a more even surface than higher up the mountain, which allowed for faster progress. Another hour saw the river beside them disappear into the void, passing over a shelf of rock, into the gorge below. Yannis motioned to speak to everyone.

'My friends, you must stay on the path, and there is only one path. There are cliffs you could walk over, and fall many metres, so you must stay close to the man in front of you. I cannot find you if you are lost'. Elena said nothing but nodded her agreement. The three soldiers listened respectfully, recognising their local knowledge, and knowing that they were in their hands.

'I hope that we rest only once, it will be very hard, maybe seven hours walking. We will be near Agia Roumeli by five hours in the morning, still dark. Germans will not see us and they will not walk in the gorge at night with no guide. At the village, we have some family, uncle, aunt, kids. Elena will talk to them, learn about your Navy boats and your comrades'. Tom made to interrupt, looking with concern at Elena, who would be putting herself in peril on their behalf, but his objection had been anticipated.

She addressed him directly. 'Sergeant Tom, I will be in no danger. These are my people, they will help us. There is no other way'. She was right, Tom thought, but he still was not happy. He would have to find some way of giving her some protection, without endangering the whole group.

The journey through the gorge was a long nightmare, at least for the British element of the party. The descent was relentless, needing hands to negotiate the many drops and with an awareness, especially in the early stages, of the chasm so close to their path. Much of the track, though, followed the stream at the very bottom of the ravine, with the near vertical rock walls looming over them. It was obvious to everyone that in daylight, they would be open to attack, with little chance to defend themselves. They could be assaulted from above, surrounded from upstream and downstream, and annihilated with ease. No one dawdled and by 0400, the steep walls of the canyon had opened out into a wider, shallower valley, with the smell of the Libyan Sea beyond it. It remained dark, with a quarter moon providing scant illumination.

In this pale, dim light, Yannis motioned for the others to join him to brief for the next steps but on this occasion, Tom took charge, fixing each in turn with a calm gaze. Elena guessed that he would attempt to frustrate her plan, and took an indignant breath, preparatory to restating her case, and the lack of any other options, but Tom forestalled her.

'Miss Elena, you are correct, we need information before we can move on. Go and speak to your uncle, please ask him where any British soldiers might be now, are there any Royal Navy ships here or coming here, and ask him, where are the German army, are they here and how many? As much information as you can'.

Both Elena and Yannis looked surprised at Tom's agreement, having anticipated that he would object and would not trust their judgement. George and Davey waited, smiling, knowing that there was more to come from Tom. They knew his style!

He continued, 'Corporal, you are a quieter stalker than Davey, am I right?' 'Yes, Sergeant', answered George. 'Old poacher', he added with a grin 'Thought so. I want you to follow Miss Elena down to the village but keep out of sight. She knows you are there but make sure no one else spots you, understand? See her to her uncle's house, watch outside while she speaks to him then get her back here. Miss Elena, you have half an hour to get there, no more than twenty minutes in the village, less if you can, then half an hour back. It will be almost light by then, we'll have no trouble seeing you coming. You won't see us, we'll be out of sight, and George', he added, 'lend Miss Elena that pistol of yours, I don't want her carrying a rifle into the village, we don't know who is watching. Understood?' 'Yes, Sergeant, return by 0530', answered George. Turning to Elena, he grinned. 'Come on then lass, no dawdling, best foot forward', and they receded into the gloom, George ten yards behind and to one side. Tom knew that George would disappear, more or less, when they came closer to the village.

Tom, Davey and Yannis walked quietly back to the mouth of the gorge, and to the eastern shoulder that guarded the entrance. Scrambling up through shattered rock, they found a ledge about fifty feet above the stream, no more than the size of a large dining table but likely to give a better view down towards the coast and to Agia Roumeli. It seemed to Tom that the slope continued above them at a not too steep angle, so that a line of retreat back up the mountain was a possibility. He could just about distinguish some scrubby, stunted trees among the rocks, little oaks perhaps, which would also provide some cover if it was needed. Tom gave the first watch to Davey, telling him to wake him in three quarters of an hour, no later, for he would need to be wide awake and alert when George and Elena returned. Gesturing to Yannis to do the same, he rested his head on his haversack and was asleep.

It was only a nap, but Tom felt the benefit when, on schedule, Davey shook him awake. He was still weary but at least he felt alert again. How tired George must feel, he thought, ten years and more older than him. Yannis slept on, as Davey lay down beside him, while Tom looked south, in the direction of the village, from where Elena and George should be emerging within the next twenty minutes or so. Sunrise was not far away and already, Tom guessed that figures would be visible at about three hundred yards, and the light was slowly increasing as the minutes passed. It was overcast and humid and if Tom had been at home in Shropshire, he would have expected rain in an hour or so.

He sighted his rifle, resting it on the top of his haversack, and waited. For ten minutes, all was quiet, peaceful even, just the trills of waking birds and the occasional faint clang of a goat's bell in the far distance.

Then, from the direction of the village, Tom heard the rapid crack-crack-crack of a pistol, immediately followed by the deeper boom of a rifle, five shots in quick succession, mixed with the lighter rapid percussion of what were probably semi-automatic carbines. Joined by Davey and Yannis, snapped out of their sleep by the sudden clamour of firing, Tom peered into the muted light of the early morning. He could see nothing. They were startled as two loud explosive roars crashed out next, followed by more shooting, which was now sounding more deliberate, and less frantic. 'Grenades'.

'Sergeant', stuttered Davey, clearly agitated, 'shouldn't we go down and see if we can find them, help them, like?' Tom noticed Yannis shaking his head, he understood their position. 'No, Davey lad. George knows where to find us, and he won't leave Elena, and we won't leave them. We don't know what's happened, who's after them, how many. We have to wait for them, and prepare to be attacked by whoever is after them'.

He knew that Davey would feel better if he had something to do, ordering him to move fifty yards to their right, to give a better spread of defensive fire, then, remembering the Colonel's binoculars, he swept them up to his eyes. They were a precision instrument that worked well in poor light and the developing disaster became clear as he looked down the valley.

He could see George and Elena, dodging from cover to cover, with George snapping off rounds, sometimes single shots, sometimes five rounds rapid fire. Elena's pistol was useless at anything other than short range, so she was not shooting. George seemed to be supporting her anyway as they gradually retreated back towards the gorge and their comrades.

Less than two hundred yards behind the two of them, Tom could see at least six soldiers in pursuit, in field grey uniforms, topped with the distinctive coal scuttle helmets. Quickly he estimated the distance to the chasing Germans and shouted to Yannis and Davey. 'Five hundred yards, ten rounds rapid!' Their three rifles crashed out, and helmeted heads disappeared as the German infantrymen sought cover. George was seen to wrap an arm around Elena and dash for the shelter of the rocks below Tom. My God, they're slow, thought Tom, as George and the young woman zig-zagged towards them, rounds cracking past their heads. 'Pick your targets', roared Tom, and fired at a grey clad figure, half revealed behind a low bush. He grunted in satisfaction as his target was flung backwards by the force of his shot, lying still in the short grass, arms out-flung.

He could hear Yannis and Davey shooting for all they were worth, and the returning fire from their attackers seemed to be slackening. There could not be more than his rough count of six, thank God, concluded Tom, nor did they appear to have automatic weapons, which was a mercy.

He looked down. George and Elena had reached the bottom of the rocks but Tom could see that George would not be able to haul the young woman up the slope without help. He roared, 'Keep firing, lads, pour it on!', and vaulted down through the rocks, just managing to keep his balance and reach flat ground without falling flat on his face. Without a word, he picked up Elena in both arms and raced back up the incline into cover, George hot on his heels. He laid Elena down gently on the rough ground, she was conscious but appeared to be dazed. 'Just bad luck', shouted George above the tumult of gun shots. 'She got clipped by some stone fragments, one of their grenades was a bit close. She'll have a lump on her head, no more'.

Yannis looked anxiously across between shots. 'She'll be good', shouted George again. 'Big headache'. Yannis smiled in relief, then moved nearer to Tom as he was beckoned over, George taking his place in the firing line.

'Where now, Yannis? We can't stay here, can't go to the village, stupid to go back into the gorge. What's at the top of this slope?'

'A lot of wild land, Sergeant' he answered. 'And clouds', he added, pointing upwards. Sure enough, the overcast of the valley was showing as cloud on the mountainside behind them, obscuring everything more than one hundred feet overhead. Of course, thought Tom, we're still a couple of thousand feet up.

'Once we are on the plateau, Sergeant, they will not find us. There are caves, shepherd's huts. We can rest, I will find enough food for us, maybe ammunition also'.

'Then let's move, mate'. Elena still looked dazed, as Tom told George the plan, then ran across to Davey to give the same message.

Within minutes, they were ready to move. Rounds still cracked past them but their pursuers were no closer, perhaps they had taken enough casualties. Tom had organised a slow fighting withdrawal, with Davey, as the strongest among them, slinging the complaining Elena over his shoulder, the remaining three keeping up a steady fire as they moved backwards up the hill. Within two minutes, wisps of cloud were blowing around them and in a further minute, the valley below had disappeared utterly. The odd shot was still heard but mostly wide and in the distance.

An indignant voice, Elena's, made itself heard. 'Put me down, you English oaf! Do you think I am a goat to take to market?' Tom almost laughed out loud as Davey dropped her onto her feet, where she swayed but did not fall. 'Sorry Miss, Sergeant Tom told me to carry you. And I'm Welsh, Miss, not English'. At this, both Tom and George chuckled, despite their desperate situation, only to quieten down when Elena turned her glare upon them. She did not berate them but said, 'I learned nothing. The patrol saw me before I was near my uncle's house, I shot one but there were too many. The next thing I know, Corporal George is pulling me back up the mountain'. She turned to him, 'Corporal, thank you for saving me, and Davey? I am sorry, you are not an oaf and I thank you also'.

Before she could continue, Yannis spoke up. 'Elena, listen! Can you find your way to the Priest's Cave from here?' She instantly calmed and responded, 'Yes, of course'. 'Then guide them there. I will find Manolis, they must have food and drink and he will know what is happening with the evacuation, expect me back tonight, before dark'. He turned to Tom. 'Sergeant, we need help. Elena will take you to a cave where you will not be found. We have friends, good Cretans who will help us with food for a few days, warmer clothes for the night. They will also know about the evacuation. They are two hours away on foot. May I have your permission to proceed, Sergeant?'

Tom paused before replying. 'Is there any reason why we can't keep together, all go with you?' Yannis frowned, 'Manolis, his house is in a village further down the coast. There may be Germans there, and better his neighbours do not see you, too risky. Safer if you hide for one, two nights'. He was becoming agitated, as speculative shots from their chasers continued to crack and ricochet around the mountainside. He needed a quick decision.

Tom glanced across to George, who nodded almost imperceptibly. 'OK, go! We'll keep Elena safe', and with that, Yannis took off to the east, as far as Tom could tell, disappearing rapidly as the mist claimed him.

He turned to the woman. 'Elena, thank you for helping us. You're still groggy, we'll help you for as long as you need it, alright? No debate, let's go!' Grasping Elena by the elbow, and gesturing to Davey to be back marker, he turned uphill and the tramp to the Priest's Cave began.

It was intensely hard going, climbing in and out of ravines, skirting around cliffs and scrambling through rock fields. Scrub trees provided some handholds and leverage but eventually they ran out as the altitude increased. All of them were more or less exhausted after the efforts of the past few days, and were certainly not dressed for walking through wet clouds on the sides of mountains. Elena was shivering, despite Tom's battledress jacket draped around her shoulders, and he was also worried about George, who had had no sleep at all, as well as no food. Collapse could not be far away.

On the positive side, they were following no obvious path and Tom could not see how they could be successfully followed. There had been no more rifle fire, no hint of any pursuit. Aerial reconnaissance would be useless with all the concealing cloud, so maybe they were in with a chance after all! Elena seemed to know where she was going, although she hardly spoke, more often gesturing which direction to take. She was tired out and almost certainly concussed. On occasion she tripped or stumbled and would have fallen had Tom not held her up.

After perhaps three gruelling hours, at a steadily decreasing pace, Elena wearily muttered, 'Stop. We are there'. The three soldiers looked around them, seeing more rocks and clouds but nothing which distinguished this piece of mountain from any other they had passed. For the first time in hours, Elena smiled. 'Behind you, Corporal George, is a big stone, as big as you. See, it looks like a priest saying his prayers'. They all turned to look, George commenting that if he half closed his eyes and used a little imagination, maybe it was shaped a bit like a person on his knees. 'Behind the priest', she continued, 'is the cave entrance. It is small, we must crawl in and wait for Yannis and Manolis'.

Sure enough, behind the priest, there was a narrow, oval cavity in the rock, perhaps a shoulder's width across at its longest dimension, with darkness inside it. Elena lay on her belly and wriggled through the opening, vanishing into the darkness inside. Her voice issued from the hole, 'Come'. George and Davey followed her through, Davey with a squeeze, Tom passing their weapons through after them. After a final check of the surroundings, and finding all still silent, Tom followed them, leaving the priest alone to finish his prayers.

By the time Tom had squeezed himself through the entrance, Elena had begged a precious match from George to light the stub of a candle. From its faint light, they could see a narrow passage in front of them which turned a corner to the right after about ten feet. Surprisingly to Tom, and despite the tiny entrance, there was standing room inside the cave, enough even for Davey to stand upright without hitting his head on the ceiling. 'Come', said Elena once more, and she led them around the corner of the passageway, which led to a larger chamber that looked about twenty feet across. There seemed to be quantities of dried straw spread thickly over the floor, and all except Tom threw themselves down into it, Elena seeming to find sleep even before her body sank into the vegetation.

Tom issued some quick orders before he lost Davey and George to their much needed slumber. 'George, no watch for you, next six hours are your own. Davey, I'll wake you in three'. Putting out the candle, he made his way back through the cave entrance where he sat, back against the Priest, rifle across his lap, pondering their next steps.

Chapter 16

Yannis was alone in the cloud within a few seconds, his sister and the three soldiers immediately out of his view, their voices muffled and lost in the murk. The odd round snapped past him, as the Germans continued their hopeful gunfire but even that was left well behind as he kept up a steady pace. Despite a shortening of his previously fractured leg and one lung that had lost some efficiency, Yannis reckoned that he was likely to still be the better mountaineer of anyone that might pursue him, at least over these mountains. Not only had he walked them as a child but he had guided John Pendlebury, the English archaeologist, through them during the few years before the war.

Yannis knew that he had to keep at roughly the same height for an hour, to bring him around the shoulder of the mountain, before the descent to the village of Lavoutro, where his father's friend, Manolis, lived. He would have to avoid the road, with the risk of German troops hunting for them, and that would slow him down further. He had thought about leaving his rifle and ammunition with the others, for speed and deception, but in the end, how could he leave his precious .303 behind? It was difficult to conceal but there was no ready substitute for an accurate rifle if the need arose.

Scrambling in and out of ravines was tough and Yannis was relieved when he reached the stream that signalled the time to head downhill. He was really tired now, but was below the cloud within minutes and drove himself onwards.

The following two hours were tough, his pace relenting as the day warmed. There was always water to hand, following the stream as he was, but lack of food was having its effect. He would need to eat and rest before returning Tom's party in the cave. He hoped to God that they had made it that far.

Directly ahead of him, the ground sloped down, over a couple of kilometres, to the sea. He could see several kilometres of coast but not a single craft disturbed the water. No Royal Navy, not even a fishing boat. He had not expected to see any warships at this hour, they would be too vulnerable to air attack, but not even a fishing boat had ventured out. The sea was empty.

By then, Yannis was five minutes above the road that ran along parallel to the coast, connecting Agia Roumeli and Sphakia, and the villages in between, including his destination, Lavoutro. It was too dangerous to take to the road, even if no Germans were travelling along it. If he met locals, there would be questions to answer and who could he trust? Better to follow the road as it straggled along below him, cutting down to Lavoutro at the last minute.

He reckoned he was within a kilometre of the village, skirting through a grove of old, gnarled olives when the sound of engine and voices abruptly came to his notice. From the direction of Agia Roumeli to the west, around a corner in the road, came a small German scout car, another Kubelwagen, travelling at walking pace. It was open-topped, and instead of a back seat, there was a machine gun on a mounting directly behind the driver. The machine gunner was facing to the rear of the vehicle and as the vehicle came further around the corner, the reason became clear.

Shambling along behind the scout car were a large group of unkempt, unarmed soldiers, Yannis estimated fifty to sixty, with three guards on either side of the men, and two more following behind. He shrank closer to the ground but continued to watch the crowd of men as they began to pass him on the road below his position. He was too far away to identify regiment insignia but it seemed obvious that he was looking at Allied soldiers who had missed out on evacuation. Looking closer, the uniforms that some of the men were wearing looked similar to Tom's but as they were all plastered in dust, it was impossible to be sure.

Yannis saw that he could do nothing for them, making the obvious decision to remain hidden until they were far down the road. As the last of the column passed directly below, Yannis heard a loud cry and then a thump, as something heavy hit the road. There were more shouts, in German he thought, and he risked lifting his head a little higher.

On the road, some of the prisoners were piling into the two guards at the back of the column, they had knocked them to the ground and were trying to wrench their weapons away from them. It was a furious melee and in the confusion, as three of the other guards waded into the brawl, swinging rifle butts at heads and bodies, two prisoners unexpectedly broke away from the group and made to dash up the hill towards the shelter of the olive grove. There were shouts of 'Halt, halt!' from the guards, and roars of 'Go lads, go!' from the remaining prisoners as the two pounded up the hill, arms and legs pumping furiously.

They had managed about thirty yards when the inevitable happened. A heavy and accurate burst of machine gun fire from the scout car engulfed both men, blood and fragmented tissue misting around them as they shuddered and collapsed under the impact of the heavy bullets, finally lying destroyed and unmoving on the ground. As Yannis watched, horrified, he heard howls of pain and anguish from below, immediately followed by mayhem as more prisoners turned on their guards. This time though, the guards were prepared and the rapid rattle of machine pistols filled the morning air. In seconds, three more men lay on the ground, two still and dead while the third writhed in his agony, blood pumping out fast around him. This was ended abruptly when a guard stood over him and fired another burst into his chest. There was a short, stunned silence, then shouts of pain and anger as the guards pushed the men viciously back into line. The three bodies were thrown from the road into a shallow ditch that bordered it, and the prisoners, now cowed and shocked, were moved on.

Yannis lay in the silence of the grove. All he could hear in his mind for minutes afterwards was the repeated and unmistakeable thud as bullets slammed into flesh, all he could smell was burnt powder and fresh, spilt blood. He could not move. He had seen death in the Pindus Mountains with the Division but never like this. He and Sergeant Tom had annihilated the patrol at Panadiki but they had been armed and were attacking helpless civilians. This had been butchery, the massacre of disarmed men and he knew now, without the slightest doubt, that this would be a war of no quarter and no mercy from either side, until Crete was once again free.

The road was quiet in both directions as Yannis emerged from his hiding place and walked reluctantly down towards the road, stopping first at the bodies of the two servicemen who had made the break for freedom. Trying not to look into the faces of the dead men, he found their identity tags, two each hanging around their necks from what looked like bootlaces, and removed one tag from either man. He would give them to Sergeant Tom, perhaps he would be able to identify which regiment they belonged to. Burial would be undertaken by the villagers as soon as they knew what had happened, and they would do it today, before heat and wild animals took their toll of the remains.

After covering the faces of the dead men with what was left of their battledress tunics, he moved down to the road. All was still and deserted, and Yannis was able to do the same for the three corpses thrown like trash into the ditch.

Feeling shaken but with even more reason, he thought, to do his best for his British comrades, Yannis once again left the road and, taking advantage of the stunted trees and bushes that bordered it, made the final kilometre to Lavoutro. Setting himself down behind a heap of shattered boulders, he looked down at the view spread in front of him.

Lavoutro was a fishing village, a small one of perhaps thirty souls, with a single row of small houses built around the tiny, crescent-shaped bay which lay empty. The few boats owned by the villagers would normally be out at sea at this time, thought Yannis, perhaps that is where they were, fishing, but given the chaos of the past few days, who could say?

Most noticeable was the quiet. It was not silence, birds still sang and Yannis could hear lambs calling for their mothers, but it was far quieter than it should be. On earlier visits to see Manolis with his father, neighbours would be chatting with each other, children playing, dogs barking. Even when the boats were out, there would be a morning bustle. Not today.

The column of prisoners must have passed straight through the village, for no one was resting in the shade of a tree, and no one was drawing water from the village well. Yannis sat in silence, watching, for a quarter of an hour and in that time, it was as if the village had been deserted. Unable to use up any more time waiting, and thinking again of his friends, tired and hungry on the mountainside, he moved carefully down the last of the incline to the village, keeping as low and as quiet as he could but with his rifle cocked and ready to fire. He felt exhausted, so fatigued that he knew he could hardly have defended himself if he had been attacked or challenged.

His line of descent took him directly to the back of Manolis' small house. There were no chickens scratching in the dust, no washing out to dry, all very strange, but before he could tap on the old, peeling door that led, he remembered, into the kitchen, it opened a crack and a gruff voice hissed, 'Jesus, it's young Stephanidis! In God's name, why are you here? You've picked a fine time to visit! Come in before someone sees you!' A large, rough hand snaked out of the doorway, latched on to his shoulder and dragged him inside the house.

Yannis could see nothing at first, in the gloom of the kitchen as Manolis, for it must be he, shut the door behind him. 'Why have you come today of all days, boy? Don't you know, there are German troops everywhere? They are looking for the British, and found some, I think. There are none here but how will I explain you to them if they come again?'

While he spoke, Yannis was beginning to pick out details in the room. Manolis, an older man, dressed in a ragged shirt and dirty, torn trousers, stood in front of the door. He looked agitated, moving from foot to foot and running a hand, repeatedly, through his untidy mop of white hair as he talked. Opposite him, standing in the open doorway to the front of the house, was his wife, Agathe. As thin and gaunt as her husband, she scowled at Yannis but said nothing.

'Manolis, I know about the Germans, they are why I am here. Elena and I have brought three British soldiers over from Chania, to find their Royal Navy to evacuate them. We ran into Germans near Agia Roumeli, too many to fight so Elena has taken them further back into the mountains. They need food, supplies to keep them going until they can find a boat to leave, can you help us? I know this is a bad time for you also but these British are our allies, they saved us at Panadiki'.

Manolis looked unconvinced and said nothing, as did his wife, so Yannis tried again. 'Manolis, you are my father's friend. These soldiers rescued him and nine others, the Germans were going to kill them all! They might have lost their chance of rejoining their army because they helped us. How can we not help them in return? All I ask is some food to take to them, enough for a few days, a little wine, coffee if you have it, and some old clothes. Please, Manolis, it is a matter of honour!'

'Don't speak to me of your honour,' Manolis spluttered. 'You should not have come here at all, putting us in harm's way. I should send you packing but I will not, knowing your father and your mother, God bless her soul, for so many years'. Yannis sighed in relief and staggered, feeling fatigue sweep over him.

'Sit down, young man,' muttered Manolis, 'before you fall down. Wife, he needs to rest, give him something to eat, then he can lie on the couch for a few hours and get some sleep. I will have to speak to my neighbours, Yannis, and see what we can spare between us. Give me three hours'. 'Thank you, thank you' answered Yannis, gratefully, as Agathe led him further into the little house. 'There is no Royal Navy here to collect your English friends', Manolis added. 'They have been driven off by the Stukas and there are hundreds of English soldiers waiting to surrender. I advise your friends to do the same'.

As he left through the rear door, Manolis turned and asked Yannis, as if an afterthought, 'Where did you say the British soldiers were?'

Despite his near exhaustion, something in his heart told him to be cautious in his reply. 'Due north of here, I don't know exactly where, they will look out for my return' he said. Manolis grunted, and closed the door behind him.

After quickly swallowing the piece of goat's cheese and cup of watered wine that Agathe silently handed to him, Yannis lay back on the couch and was instantly asleep.

A few hours later, in the middle of the afternoon, Yannis felt a hand shaking him by the shoulder. He looked up, to see Manolis standing over him.

His brusque, impatient manner had returned. 'Get up, get up, Stephanidis! I have your food, not so much but all we can spare, and a pack to carry it in. Take it and leave, there are Germans close and you must not be seen leaving here. Go and do not return!'

It took Yannis a few moments to fully rouse himself but without delay or protest, he was soon on his feet, heavy pack in hand and ready to leave.

'Manolis, thank you for helping us. I will not forget and Father will know that you have honoured his friendship. I will not return, have no fear'. Manolis said nothing in reply, just moved to the door and opened it enough for Yannis to squeeze through. As he moved through into the daylight, he turned back to the older man.

'Where is Dimitri, your boy? Is he fishing?' Manolis said nothing, just shut the door firmly, leaving Yannis staring.

He turned, and seeing that the immediate neighbourhood still appeared to be deserted, took his first steps back towards the mountains. The pack was heavy but not beyond him to carry, and he was sure he should make it back to the cave before nightfall.

As he moved into the shade of the first olive grove, a figure moved in the shade and turned towards him. He stopped suddenly, realising that Agathe had been waiting for him. Tears ran down her face as she faced Yannis, and began to speak. Her voice was strained and quiet.

'Yannis, I loved your mother, God bless her, and your father as if they were my own and so I cannot let you go unprepared. Not everyone has your heart and courage in these terrible days. I cannot be sure but I think that the Germans know of you. Be careful, return to your father alive!'

Yannis was dumbfounded. 'What do you mean, what has happened, how do they know of me?' 'Our son, Dimitri, has been taken by the German soldiers, all of the young men have. They helped the British escape, used the fishing boats to ferry them to the big ships and they are being punished'.

She paused, re-gathering her resolve, then continued. 'My husband took four hours to collect that food and drink when you were asleep, it should not have taken half as long and he would not tell me why it did. I know him well after all these years, he will be trying to persuade the German soldiers to release Dimitri and what can he offer them? You and the British soldiers, he has nothing else. I saw a patrol of Germans head north about an hour ago'.

'You don't save your own son by betraying your friend's child!' Yannis was astounded and could barely speak. Agathe wept bitterly, covering her face in her shame, and he suddenly felt a rush of compassion for her, after all, Dimitri was her only child and he realised what it must have cost her to warn him, against the possible risk to Dimitri.

Yannis gently took her hands from her face and looked directly into her tormented eyes. 'Agathe, thank you for what you have done. If anything bad happens to me or to my friends, well, you did your best to help us, and I promise you, if I come through this alive, I will try to help return Dimitri to you'. He paused. 'But if I discover that Manolis is helping the Germans, then he is risking his life, you know this'. He could not say to Agathe that he would kill Manolis himself, given the opportunity.

She nodded in her misery, and scuttled off down the hill to the house, leaving Yannis to gather himself up for the hours to come. He would have to move fast! He had told Manolis that the party was located due north, whereas in fact the cave was north-west of Lavoutro and with luck, if any pursuers were looking to intercept him while on the journey, they might miss him altogether.

Within a few minutes, he was across the road and starting on the climb up the steeper slope of the mountain. It was tough work, carrying the combined weight of the pack and his own rifle, but the food and a few hours of sleep had restored him enough to make a strong pace. Every few minutes he stopped, ostensibly for a breather but really to check if he was being followed and each time, he saw nothing.

Within half an hour, he had rounded the shoulder of the mountain, reckoning that if any German soldiers were waiting to intercept him, they would now be well to the east, with the bulk of the mountain between them. With luck, he could still get to the Priest's Cave before dark, perhaps within ninety minutes or so.

After another hour, and aided by the absence of low clouds which had burned away through the afternoon, Yannis had reached a high valley strewn with boulders, a real rock field, and he knew that he was within about three kilometres of the cave. The weight of the pack was becoming a burden and he was beginning to relish the thought of when he might be able to take it off when a faint, mechanical buzz insinuated itself into his consciousness. As the buzz gradually became a roar, his soldier's instincts took over and he looked down the valley in time to see a single-engine fighter plane, in grey-green camouflage, come clattering over a ridge then straight up the valley towards him, no more than fifty feet above the ground. He had been seen!

They must have realised that he had taken a different route and had called for aerial reconnaissance! How stupid he had been, not anticipating this next step, at least as a possibility!

As Yannis dived behind a waist-high heap of rubble, the fighter opened fire and machinegun bullets smashed into the ground near him, sending rock shrapnel flying in all directions. Within seconds, the plane was past him and he was back on his feet, haring up the steep rocky slope towards an area of huge boulders, all jumbled together, as if they had just been tipped out onto the ground. As he dived into their shelter, dropping the pack as he wriggled into the tight, low space, deafening engine noise and the deeper, thunderous crash of cannon shells exploding around and above him overpowered everything, save the hot fragments of steel seeking him out.

Chapter 17

Staying awake on guard outside the cave, while the others slept inside, was nearly more than Tom could manage. The last few days and nights, ever since they had left the trenches outside Chania, had been relentless and, if he was honest, terrifying. Feeling exhausted and hungry while being pursued under fire was a soldier's lot but by God, it took everything out of you. He was tired through to his bones and was beginning to notice how sluggish his thinking was becoming. He wondered if he had agreed too easily with Yannis's suggestion to make for the cave but really, what else could he have done? He had to trust the Cretan's judgement.

Tom soon realised that sleep would be inevitable if he remained sitting, with his back resting against the Priest. He would walk a short patrol line instead, and maybe familiarise himself with the surroundings, in case they had to leave in a hurry. The cloud was beginning to clear and already visibility, at least down the slope, was up to half a mile. There was a risk that he might be seen by a sharp-eyed pursuer but experience told him that, against the backdrop of the cliff behind him, he would be difficult to spot, especially as there was no skyline to be silhouetted upon, and also his British Army khaki would help him blend into his surroundings.

Tom's patrol line was no more fifty paces to the left, and fifty to the right. It was bounded by a rock wall to the right, smooth, close to vertical then leaning out of sight after roughly one hundred feet. To Tom's eye, it looked unclimbable, if they were needing a line of retreat.

The left–hand boundary was a ravine, and that looked more promising. It was angled without being precipitous, it was dry, seemed to have a profusion of hand and footholds and ledges, and would not be difficult to climb, even weighed down with weaponry. It curved around out of sight after approximately sixty feet meaning that a short ascent would see them out of sight of any pursuers within a minute or two.

For two hours, Tom walked his line, not wanting to waste energy, and the time passed uneventfully. There was no movement around them. As he passed the mouth of the cave, he heard a quiet voice from inside. 'Sergeant Tom, may I join you?' It was Elena.

'Yes, you may but shouldn't you be asleep, is your head still hurting?' he answered. 'Bah, you are not my father! I will sleep again but I woke and wanted some air and also, you know, to pass water'.

'Oh', stuttered Tom, 'of course'. She smiled up at him as she passed by, taking herself into the shelter of the ravine, then emerging a few moments later.

Tom continued to pace his line and Elena fell in beside him. 'Sergeant Tom, may we talk some more? Or will I disturb you from your watch?' Tom, secretly delighted that they could share a little time together, replied solemnly, 'Yes, Elena but we must keep a good eye out as we speak, then in an hour, I must rouse Davey and get my rest'.

She laughed quietly. 'Now I am learning the real English! I must put my best foot forward while keeping my good eye out!' Tom grinned. 'It can be a funny language, Elena. I might have told you to keep your eyes peeled or your lip buttoned!'

'Ah, I understand 'good eye out'. In Greek language, if we want someone to look carefully, we say 'your eyes fourteen', I don't know why. I do not understand the buttoned lip though'.

Tom hesitated. 'Well, Elena, if George was talking too much or interrupting me, I might say to him, button your lip. It means stop talking'.

'But you would not say that to me, Sergeant Tom, you just said I could talk to you', she replied, with a twinkle of mischief in her eye. Tom was beginning to feel a little out of his depth but caught the glint of humour in her voice.

'Of course not, Elena. You can talk till the cows come home'. They both laughed again, continuing to pace slowly, Tom looking out, down and across the mountain without pause.

Elena cleared her throat delicately then asked, 'Tom, did you leave a wife or a sweetheart in England? I told you yesterday that I was not betrothed or married but you did not tell me about yourself. I did not ask you, I know, but today I am feeling brave so I ask you now'.

Tom glanced down at her in surprise, then quickly back to the horizon. 'No, Elena, I'm not married, and no sweetheart either. A girlfriend or two in my time of course but remember, I joined the army when I was nineteen, too young to be married'.

'And would you like to be married one day, Tom?' 'I would, Elena, but this war is getting in the way of ordinary life, isn't it? When we get this won, then perhaps things will change. Besides, same as every soldier, I could be killed any day, then I'd be a dead husband, no use to anyone'.

Elena was taken aback by his blunt words but continued. 'You do not think that people should take happiness when and where they find it during this terrible war, just because tomorrow might bring disaster?'

'No, Elena, I don't. If I could guarantee that I would survive all this, then yes, of course, but I've seen too many of my comrades die already and my turn will come, more than likely. It's better that I don't drag anyone else down with me'

Elena turned to return to the cave but half-turned. 'Tom, I think that you are wrong. You should know that nothing is guaranteed in this life. All the bullets might miss you then you break your head on the way home. Also know that love, if it finds you, cannot be denied'. Without a further glance, she crawled back into the cave, leaving Tom to ponder her words.

Perhaps she was right, he thought, but he was here as a soldier, not to find a wife. He must concentrate upon his orders, to rejoin the regiment, and everything else should take care of itself. He was still pondering when Davey joined him.

He gave instructions, and Davey knew to call him if anything at all happened. He crawled back into the cave, and by the light of the candle that Davey had left burning, he could see that George was still spark out, and that Elena seemed to be sleeping too, although her back was turned to him so he could not be sure. He took his boots off, what a relief that was, and flopped down in the warmth that Davey had left, and was flat-out asleep before another thought had passed through his mind.

Three hours passed, it seemed to Tom, in an instant, signalled by a rough hand grasping his shoulder. 'Time to rouse yourself, Sergeant'. It was George's voice, pulling him back from the depths of his exhausted slumber. 'Nothing to report, but the day has gone on. No sign of Yannis yet but maybe we should be looking out for him anyway. That's what Elena reckons, she knows how far he had to travel, and by the way, you're in her bad books, you didn't blow the candle out!'

Tom was coming to, realising how tired he still was. 'Alright, I'll be with you. What candle?' George chuckled and made his way back towards the cave entrance, leaving Tom to put his boots back on in the dark. 'Oh, that candle', he thought to himself.

He fumbled his way to the entrance and struggled out, only to be blinded by the late afternoon sunshine that streamed down onto their sheltered ledge. His vision slowly cleared, only to see the three companions all smirking at his discomfiture. 'All present and correct, Sergeant', grinned George. 'Oh, bugger off' he retorted, and retreated to the ravine to relieve himself.

'Is he angry, George?' whispered Elena. 'No, miss', was the reply. 'He's just a miserable sod when he wakes up, he'll be fine. I expect he could do with a brew, you know, a mug of tea. Come to think of it, so could I'. 'I think Yannis will have something for us, not English tea but something else', answered Elena. 'We've got some tea, miss, but I don't reckon we should light a fire, not until Yannis is back and we know it's safe. He might have someone chasing him'.

Tom joined them as they looked down the mountainside, in the direction that Elena thought that her brother might appear. They were all hungry but no one mentioned it, they would either eat when Yannis returned and if he did not return, then they would be forced off the mountain to find food elsewhere.

'Plane!' said Davey, alerting the others. They could hear the roar of an aero engine, out of sight and perhaps further down the mountain. As they looked unsuccessfully for any view of the plane, they all heard the unmistakeable ragged chatter of machine guns, then the engine noise suddenly multiplied as a fighter plane climbed into view, appearing over the cliffs at the bottom of the valley below, then turned again to retrace its flight, this time accompanied by the harsher clash of canon fire. It did not return, and the engine noise gradually faded away to silence. They all looked at each other.

Tom took charge. 'I reckon he was after Yannis'. The three nodded. 'Right. Elena, you come with me and we'll find him, you know the route that he'll be on. George, I want you and Davey to come partway but find some cover either side of the valley so if we're followed back up, you can enfilade their line. Got it?' They nodded, he knew that they needed no further instruction, not with George's experience and Davey's accurate fire.

'Come on, girl', he muttered to Elena, and carrying only their rifles, they started their way down the valley, not running because of the rocky terrain but hurrying, and breaking into a trot when it was possible. Even so, it was fifteen minutes before they reached the end of the valley and could peer down into the second valley below.

At first there was nothing then Elena exclaimed 'There!' and pointed towards a collection of huge rocks below. From around the edge of a jagged boulder a hundred metres away came the figure of Yannis, moving slowly uphill, rifle in his hand and an old canvas pack, a large one, slung across his back. 'He's bleeding!' shrieked Elena, and she ran down to meet him, stumbling on the rough ground but, Tom noted with military approval, keeping a firm grip upon her rifle.

He followed her to where Yannis had sat down, having seen them. Tom could see a gash to the side of his head which bled a steady stream of blood down his face and had coloured his shirt down one side. He looked pale and dazed.

Without a word, Tom pulled out his field dressing and pressed the gauze pad to the wound, then grabbing Elena's free hand, placed it over the pad, telling her to press hard while he tied off the bandage that would hold the dressing to Yannis's head. It would have to do for now.

'Take his rifle and the pack, Elena, and we'll follow you up'. As she hesitated, tears starting from her eyes as she looked at her injured brother, he hissed 'Go, we'll be right behind you'. She looked at him blankly, then nodded, stripping the pack from her brother's back and the rifle from his hand. Now fully loaded, with the pack on her back and a rifle in each hand, she straightened up and began to trudge back up the hillside. Tom, meanwhile, pulled Yannis's good arm over his shoulder, placing his own arm around his ribs. 'Now, young 'un, let's get you back'. With a heave, he started back up the slope, hoping to God that there was no one in pursuit, for they would be sitting ducks.

Yannis was half-fainting but of no great weight, so Tom was able to make steady progress. By the time he mounted the brow that led into the top valley, he could see Elena ahead, and George and Davey coming out of concealment to intercept her. He saw Davey carefully take the pack from her back, along with one of the rifles, before guiding her back up the valley towards the cave. George, then came down the slope and without a word, put Yannis's other arm over his shoulder and shared his weight. It was still a good half an hour before they reached the cave and carefully pulled and pushed Yannis in through the entrance. Tom went back outside, to give an early warning if pursuers came in sight.

By that time, Davey had quite rightly thrown caution to the wind and had lit a small fire. Surprisingly, the fire was inside the cave! Davey explained to George that Elena had told him that there was a natural chimney that led upwards and exited the cliff about sixty feet above them. Sure enough, there was a natural draught that drew in air through the entrance, and kept the atmosphere within the cave breathable.

Davey had heated a dixie of water in the meantime, and the first task was to clean Yannis's wound. George had some experience of 'field medicine', as he called it, and blotted away much of the blood and dust that had dried onto and around the wound. 'Ah', he said as he worked, 'just a nasty cut, lad, your skull is in one piece underneath, must be good and thick, you sure you're not from Yorkshire?' Yannis was gasping in pain as George worked away, his chatter distracting the young man enough that he managed to sit, still and unmoving.

'Now, lad', he continued, 'My mother was a seamstress and a very good one at that, taught me everything she knew. Give me a couple of minutes and I shall have you as good as new. Elena, please to hold your brother's head while I sew him up'.

She watched impressed as, in the candlelight, George opened his army issue housewife, threaded a needle with linen thread and began to sew up the wound, using the forefinger and thumb of one hand to pull the edges of the gash together, while placing neat, small stitches to hold it closed. 'There you are, my lovely', he said as he finished, 'the girls will find you much more interesting with a nice neat scar to show off!' Next, he tied his own field dressing over the wound, and sent Davey to relieve Tom, so that he could hear Yannis's story first-hand. While George was working on Yannis, Davey had boiled more water for tea, so by the time Tom joined them, there was a steaming dixie of tea to drink from, and pass around. Elena and Yannis had never drunk powdered tea with powdered milk before but it was strong and hot, reviving them little by little.

Yannis was still a little dazed and painstakingly told his story. As he described the shooting of the five allied soldiers, he carefully pulled the identity tags he had collected out of his pocket and placed them into Tom's open hand. Tom moved closer to the candle to examine them more closely, then sat up stiff and straight, a look of disgust and anger in his face. He looked directly at George, 'Two Aussies, one Kiwi but the other two we know'. He named Rodri Davis and John Williams, two of the platoon who had left them at Panadiki, to try to make the evacuation. George cursed and quickly standing up, blundered his way through the cave to the entrance, to join Davey outside.

Tom looked at neither Elena nor Yannis as he explained, 'Rodri was a regular, George and him had been mates for nearly twenty years. He never said but I knew he was glad when Rodri took off for the boats, he was good with a mortar but no shot with a rifle. He was Davey's mate too, he'll be mad. Williams, I didn't know him well, hadn't been with us long but he was one of us. He deserved better than that'.

He fell silent, Elena placing her hand on his forearm. He hardly noticed but eventually responded with a duck of his head and an acknowledging pat on her hand. Yannis gave the remainder of his account, and it was obvious to them all that the plane had been sent to reconnoitre, after Yannis had evaded his pursuers. Would there be radio contact between the plane and the patrol? Perhaps not. There was time to move on, further into the mountains, but Yannis needed some rest time and some nourishment, they all did.

Bringing himself back to the present, he said, 'Now, let's see what's in that pack'.

Chapter 18

Manolis, for whatever motive, had done them proud. There were two pairs of old trousers and two ragged shirts, a few candles, two loaves of bread, together with the inevitable goat's cheese, a few dried fish, some cooked potatoes, three large tomatoes, two bottles of wine and finally, a small earthenware bottle, carefully corked. Pulling out the cork, he took a sniff. 'Strewth, that's strong, like smelling salts!'

Elena laughed as Tom reeled backwards, eyes streaming. 'It is tsikoudia, I think. Our brandy, made in the village, very strong. You can drink it for pleasure or for medicine, very good for both'.

Tom divided the food and drink between them all, keeping back a loaf of bread and one of the bottles of wine in reserve for breakfast. Who could say when they could be resupplied? He took George and Davey's share, with his own, outside and ate with the two men.

They were both still visibly upset about the shooting of Davis and Williams. George, in particular, looked pale under his tan, and said little. They knew they must eat though, and made short work of the food that Tom had brought for them. Eventually, George looked up and said, 'Tom, any orders for us?' He was ready to work.

'Lads, we'll have to move on, get further into the hills', answered Tom. 'Yannis says there's no boats around Sphakia, just Jerries, so there's not much sense in going there for now. Maybe if we get down to the coast twenty or thirty miles further on, we can find a boat that'll take us. Trouble is, that patrol that Yannis was told about, I think they'll be sniffing about here before too long, that pilot will have reported back and it's possible that Manolis chap is helping them, he'll know about the cave. It'll be dark soon, so I think we'll be ok for now but I don't want them chasing us, we're too few and too short of ammo. I'd like to thin 'em out if we can. George, what do you reckon?'

George looked up, eyes glittering. 'I'm with you, Tom'. Alongside him, Davey nodded his agreement. 'What's the plan?' George added.

'I shall need your help, George, and you, Davey, to sort one out', Tom answered. 'There's only the three of us and we can't sit in the cave and expect to defend it, they would just hold us here until we surrendered, there'd be no other choice'.

Before he could carry on, a furious, female voice called out from the entrance to the cave. 'Three? Can you not count, Englishman? I can shoot Germans as well as any man, and my brother will be able to shoot again by morning. That makes five, or are English numbers different?'

Tom was taken aback at Elena's fury but was well used to dealing with insubordination. 'Miss Elena, your first responsibility must be to your brother. He can hardly stand unaided, never mind shoot. Before first light, you and Yannis will start up the mountain. I would send you now but he needs more rest'. She started to interrupt but Tom held his hand up. 'You agreed to follow my orders, Elena, so listen! The three of us will stay for an hour after you leave. We will engage any Germans, if any arrive, then we will follow you. You must not wait around to join in the fight. Do you understand?'

Elena remained angry but she could see from Tom's expression, reflected in the faces of his two comrades, that he would not be moved. 'I understand, Sergeant Tom. I will do as you say and keep my word but remember, this is our island and we will defend it!' She turned on her heel and, glaring once again in Tom's direction, re-entered the cave.

There was a short silence. 'You know something, Tom?' said George. 'What?' 'Imagine how sharp her tongue would be if she didn't like you!' It was Tom's turn to glare now but he couldn't keep it up and soon was grinning along with the others.

'George, do you reckon we'll be ok till morning?' he asked. 'I reckon so, we'll be hard to find in the dark and they'll be worried about an ambush. As long as Elena and Yannis are on their way at least an hour before dawn, we should be able to surprise them, if they come'. 'Oh, they'll come', answered Tom, 'I can feel it'.

Evening light was fading as Tom took the first three hour watch outside the cave. Davey would relieve him at midnight and George would cover the final part of the night. A groggy Yannis and a still displeased Elena were briefed to be ready to leave at 0500, Tom would be awake by then and would make sure that they were on their way in good time. They told him that they would follow the ravine that lay to the east of the cave, it was an easy scramble, even in the dark, for a few minutes, followed by a rocky plateau that would take perhaps forty minutes to cross. The cliff beyond the plateau was pierced by two further ravines and it was agreed that they would wait in the right-hand of the two, in cover, for a maximum of one hour. 'After an hour', said Tom, 'you will know that we are not coming, so you must try to get back to your family in Peripetro and live to fight another day'.

At this, Elena's tense features softened. 'Ah, my Sergeant, then you must be sure to prevail, for what could we say to our father and to Christina and to little Giorgos? That we lived while you died? No, we will never do that. You will live to fight another day, I know it'. At that, she quickly kissed Tom's cheek and turned away, busying herself with her small pack. Tom was both pleased and embarrassed at her reaction and stood still, not knowing what to say or do next. Yannis caught his eye and winked, Tom grinning back and moving out of the cave entrance, to begin his watch.

Tom's watch was quiet, with no alarms. It was a cool night at mountain altitude, with no wind, so sound would carry but Tom heard nothing. He was relieved to hand over a negative report at midnight to Davey, who asked, 'Will they come, Sergeant?' 'Davey', he answered, 'Yannis was sure that he'd been betrayed and I'm sure that fighter plane wasn't a coincidence so yes, they'll come but likely not until morning. Even so, keep your eyes and ears wide open just in case. Call us if you hear anything'. At that, Tom crawled back into the cave and was quickly asleep.

Davey's watch was uneventful and at 0300, he handed on to George. By 0430, Tom was up and about, checking that Yannis was fit to travel. He felt a little awkward around Elena but she seemed oblivious, quietly getting ready to move. Just as they were about to leave the cave, they were startled by the smash and ricochet of a bullet hitting rock, immediately followed by the crack of the shot.

Tom and Davey were out of the cave in a moment, rifles at the ready, joining George who was peering out into the darkness. More shots impacted into the cliff behind them, spraying them with rock chippings but well over their heads.

'Where's it coming from, George? Can you see?' hissed Tom. 'Can't see, mate, but judging by the ricochets, we're flanked, both sides. They must know where the cave is, we can't see them so they can't see us, stands to reason, they're just taking pot luck, must be close though. All downhill in front, so no problem from there, not yet. Hard to get the lass and her brother out though, they'd be walking into fire, not away from it'.

Tom felt crushed, and cursed his poor judgement. He had been complacent, he realised, thinking that the opposition wouldn't start an attack in darkness. Well, they had, and what was he going to do about it?

He became aware of a body wriggling down beside him, as more shots smashed into the cliff. It was Elena. 'Sergeant Tom, we cannot get to the ravine now but there is another way. We can all climb above them, out of their sight.' 'How, Elena?' Tom replied urgently, 'we need to move fast before they storm us'.

'Back in the cave. The chimney. I told you it leads to the top of the cliff, to the plateau, Yannis and I climbed up it when we were children, it is wide, easy'.

'Are you certain, lass? Big fella like Davey can get up it?' 'Yes, easy'.

Tom knew there could no delay, and issued his orders, hoping to God they would work.

'OK. Elena, get back in the cave and get Yannis up that chimney, we'll give you five minutes, we can hold them that long. George you next, then Davey. I'll follow you up as soon as I can but no firing until I get to you. Give me a couple of minutes after Davey, if I don't appear then get moving!'

Mouths opened in comment but Tom was having none of it. 'Go!' he exclaimed, and Elena scuttled back into the cave, calling for Yannis.

George and Davey lay down on either flank, and at a nod from Tom, began to take aimed shots whenever they saw a muzzle flash. It was impossible to gauge distance in such poor light, so the prospect of a hit was small but at least they might keep heads down and buy some time. The volume of fire coming did seem to lessen after a few minutes, and Tom gestured to George to follow the others, taking his place in the firing line. Ammunition had to be hoarded, so they couldn't blast away, just aimed shots. Five more minutes passed, and the light was starting to improve as full morning came closer.

'Davey, get moving'. The young soldier took a final shot then scrambled for the cave entrance, rock fragments dropping onto him as more shots thudded into the rocks above him.

Somehow, Tom had to give the impression to the attackers that there was more than one rifle defending the cave. All he could think of was to fire to either flank alternately, it meant moving almost continually and his shots could hardly be aimed but all he needed was a minute or two, then he would follow the others.

Tom's last shot was in the chamber, ready to fire, when he heard the scrape of boots on rock, behind him. Turning onto his side to curse Davey for not obeying orders, he was astonished to see the silhouette of a dark figure, rifle with fixed bayonet in hand, about to spring on him from around the corner of the priest's rock. While he had been concentrating on the flanks, this soldier had crept up unnoticed, from dead ahead.

Without conscious thought, and as the German trooper closed the last few yards upon him, Tom turned over onto his back, lifting his rifle as he turned and almost simultaneously squeezing the trigger. The trooper was already starting to lunge down with his bayonet as the bullet took him full in the chest. All his weight was moving forward and as he fell, his long blade was pointed unerringly at Tom's chest.

It was all Tom could do to swing the stock of his SMLE with as much power as he could muster, diverting the blade to smash onto the rocky surface beside him. The body of the trooper, now a dead weight, crashed down upon him, squeezing the breath from his lungs, and the edge of his coal scuttle helmet smashing across the bridge of Tom's nose. For a few seconds, shock left him motionless under the bulk of the shot soldier but somehow, animal strength kicked in and he rolled the body off himself and scrambled to his feet, rifle still in hand. Head ringing with pain and eyes watering, Tom stumbled into the cave.

The others had left a candle burning and he was able to find the chimney without any delay. As he started to climb, having extinguished the candle behind him, he could hear voices from above.

'Tom, is that you?' He kept climbing in the darkness, not the easiest of tasks, but before he could reply, a burst of machine pistol fire sprayed across the cave behind him. None of it reached him, he guessed he was twenty feet or so above the floor of the cave.

It could not last however. How long would it take them to discover the chimney passageway? Not long. Leaning into the wall of the chimney, keeping hold of his rifle with one hand and hoping to God that he wouldn't lose his foothold, he used his free hand to open a pouch on his battledress, pulling out a Mills bomb. Gingerly, Tom pulled the pin of the grenade and listened.

Below him in the cave, the firing had ceased. Tom could hear German voices, at first one then more. Thinking that he could not push his luck any longer, and that it would be only a matter of seconds before their escape route was discovered, he released the lever of the grenade, waited a couple of seconds then dropped it into the darkness below him, hoping that it would roll across the floor of the cave before exploding.

Tom was already on the move before the blast of the detonation roared into the space underneath him. He felt himself lifted off his feet and somehow deposited a few feet further up. Smoke billowed thickly around him, the passageway acting as a chimney once again.

Holding on to his last deep breath, Tom managed the second half of the climb in a rush, like a 'rat up a drainpipe', as George described it later. Willing hands yanked him the final few feet, Tom finding himself flat on his back in the fresh air, with a pillar of smoke seemingly bursting from the ground beside him.

George was talking to him urgently but Tom could hear nothing over the roaring in his ears, just see his friend's mouth moving. Elena was staring at him in horror, he didn't know why, surely she'd be happy to see him alive?

Tom staggered to his feet and fumbling in his pouch, pulled out another grenade, armed it and dropped it down the chimney, in case someone had survived the first blast. He could not hear the blast but felt the ground moving beneath his feet. The rising smoke abruptly stopped.

The chimney had emerged onto a flat, rock step, perhaps the ledge of a presently dry waterfall. The ledge ended abruptly, and Yannis and Davey were flat on their bellies at the edge, firing down rapidly.

Tom and George joined them, with Elena lying down alongside her brother. A scene of slaughter was spread out below them in the strengthening light.

Tom guessed that the patrol had broken cover when his defensive fire had ceased, only for some of them to walk straight into the maelstrom of his first grenade. A couple of survivors had staggered out of the cave, into the hands of their comrades but before they could move far, Yannis and Davey's accurate firing was killing them where they stood.

Tom's hearing was gradually recovering, as the sharp, rapid crack of the rifles proved. Elena shouted in his ear, 'Tom, are you wounded?' 'No, Miss. Bust my nose again, nothing else'.

'Are you sure, Tom?'

Tom looked down. His tunic was drenched in blood, not long spilled. He looked up at her and smiled, 'Not mine'.

Yannis had stopped firing, having run out of targets but George saw him stiffen, nudging his sister then pointing down into the valley. Stumbling away, down the hill, was a man with a mop of white hair, dressed in an old jacket and ragged trousers. It was Manolis, who had led the Germans to the cave!

Yannis looked enquiringly at his sister, who nodded quickly. Before Tom could comment or intervene, Yannis had sighted on the fleeing old man and fired. At about three hundred yards, it was an easy shot for a marksman and Manolis dropped on his face, a red wound blossoming in the centre of his back. It was not a killing shot however, and he was seen to raise himself up on his arms but before he could move further, another bullet took him in the back of his head, blood and bone and brain tissue spraying over the rocks around him.

Before Tom could speak, Elena silenced him with a fierce look. 'I told you, Tom, we defend our island. He betrayed us as much as he betrayed you'. Tom acknowledged her with a dip of his head, she was right. This was war, and he knew that he would do the same in his own country, without any hesitation.

Ammunition was virtually exhausted, and with little prospect of finding more .303 rounds on an island abandoned by the British Army, Tom decided that they would have to use captured German weapons from now on. Again, he cursed himself. Machine pistols and rifles had been available at Panadiki, when they had wiped out that first patrol, but they had left them, thinking that they would be leaving the island within twenty four hours. Still, there were plenty more, below them on the mountainside.

'George, can you and Davey collect rifles for us all, and as many 7.92 rounds as you can carry. Don't bother with any other calibres. Any food you can pick up too. If there's time, pull the bodies into the cave, it might give us a bit more time if they can't be spotted. We'll cover you from up here, quick as you can. If they send a plane, well, you'll have to hide yourself, same as us'.

George had been expecting the order, and knew that Tom was still too shaken by the explosion to be of much use himself, so he and Davey made their way to the top of the ravine then down to the carnage below. Within the hour, they were back, fully loaded, Davey having to make another trip down to the foot of the ravine to collect the remainder of their haul.

George reported to Tom, 'Five good rifles, Tom, they look new, and one spare. Three or four thousand rounds and half a dozen of them tater masher grenades'. He grinned, 'And Davey has something special'.

'Oh yes? Davey, what have you got there?' The young soldier was just emerging from the top of the ravine, and doubled across to Tom. 'Machine gun, Sergeant. Corporal says it's an MG34, takes the same rounds as the rifle. Spare barrel, tripod too but I reckon I can fire 'im from the hip, can't be that different from a Bren'.

'I think you'll find it's about twice as fast as a Bren, Davey, so if you ever fire it, short bursts only, could be useful. One thing, Davey'. 'Yes, Sergeant?' 'You carry it'.

George told him that his grenades had killed probably four troopers in the cave, it was difficult to be sure because the explosions had done so much damage to the bodies, the blast in such an enclosed space would have been enormous. The second grenade had finished the job by blocking the chimney, probably permanently given the size of the boulders that had been dislodged. All the bodies had been piled inside the cave and with Davey's enormous strength, they had toppled the priest rock against the entrance, effectively closing it off.

'How much food?' 'Three days if we take it easy, Tom, no more than that'.

'And we need a full day and a night's rest, George', added Tom, 'I don't know about you but I'm knackered. Perhaps Yannis knows of somewhere out of the way where we can rest and decide where to try next'.

He paused, then continued. 'Seems to me, the longer we stay, the more trouble we'll bring down on Elena and Yannis and God knows who else. I don't want that on my conscience, do you? The sooner we're off their hands, the better'.

'Oh aye', answered George. 'They're civilians, well, Yannis is a soldier of course but Elena isn't, even if she thinks she is! And there's the families, they're at risk too. No, we got to leave, early as we can'.

'But first, a rest. Hey, Yannis?' Yannis looked up from examining his new rifle. 'Yannis, where to next? We need a rest but somewhere quiet. Anywhere in mind?'

Yannis smiled, even smirked a little. 'Of course, Sergeant Tom. We cross this plateau, good hiding in the rocks if we hear a plane, then an easy climb up the ravine to the south. We will follow the mountain for half a kilometre, there is a shepherd's shelter, small and dirty but hidden away. They would not find us in a week'.

'Then let's move, it's still early but someone will be looking for that patrol soon. Split the food and ammo, George, everyone carries their own weapon. Move in five'.

The sun was clear in the sky as the five made careful progress across the flat ground to the foot of the ravine. It was going to be a hot day, and the sooner they could find the shelter, the sooner they could rest. Tom didn't notice that Elena followed closely on his heels, with eyes for no one else.

Chapter 19

They had reached the shepherd's shelter with no alarms. It was a low, stone structure, about the size of a small garden shed, roofed with heavy stone flags balanced upon outsized, rough wooden beams. There was no window, just a low doorway that could be sealed against the chill of the night with a rough, plank door. Concealed in a twisted fold of ground, it would not be discovered unless a searcher stumbled upon it by luck. Its drawback was that, hidden as well as it was, it overlooked nothing.

George had insisted upon taking the first sentry duty, and the sergeant was not in any state to gainsay him. Yannis had reckoned that Tom was concussed, both by the blow he had taken to the face in the struggle outside the cave, and by the grenade explosions. His nose was certainly broken and heavily swollen, and as he lay on the floor of the hut, with bruising blooming around both eyes and cheeks, George had commented, 'Tom, you look like one o'they panda bears, even your mother wouldn't know you!'

Before Tom could rouse himself to a comment, Elena intervened. 'Corporal George, they are honourable wounds received in battle, you should not mock your sergeant!' George, knowing even if Tom did not, that she held a torch for him, watched astonished as she cradled Tom's battered head in her arms. 'See', she said, 'how his fine nose is now as crooked as a cow's horn', and with that, she abruptly grasped the end of his nose in a strong hand and twisted it, audibly grating as it moved, back into a straight line! Tom squawked with pain, then passed out!

'Oh God forgive me, George, I had to do it! He could not breathe with it all twisted like that, and he would never have agreed if I had asked his permission! Will he forgive me?' The corporal, suppressing the urge to roar with laughter, assured her that Tom would forgive her, almost certainly, given a little time to think about it, only to be interrupted by a thick, congested voice rising from the floor, 'Don't bet on it!' Elena shrieked and threw her arms around Tom's neck, and the last George heard as he beat a retreat out of the hut was Tom's protesting voice, muffled in Elena's bosom, or so he presumed, muttering, 'Careful, lass. You'll bust the fucker again!'

Yannis had laughed with the others, having experienced her brand of medicine in the past, then put himself to thinking about what needed to happen next. Tom, covered in blood, now including some of his own, was fully conscious again and caught the eye of Yannis.

'Sergeant Tom, before you sleep, we need to decide what we should do next. Should I tell you what I think?' 'Fire away, Yannis', he answered. 'You've not let us down so far', smiling back at the dishevelled young man, who looked more like a vagrant than the efficient professional killer that he was turning out to be.

'We need to find a boat for you, and not meet any more Germans if we can, we have been fortunate that no one has been wounded or killed yet. It will not be easy, they will know that there will be British soldiers trying to escape the island, and how else but by boat? And when you get to sea, you will be on your own'. Tom nodded his agreement, encouraging Yannis to continue. 'We have enough food here for a couple of days but you will need more to take with you on the boat, at least for five days because you might need to get all the way to Egypt'. He hesitated, prompting Tom to encourage him to continue, 'Come on lad, spit it out!'

'Sergeant Tom, there is something else I must do and it might help us find a boat for you'. What next, thought Tom but held his tongue, and Yannis continued.

'That traitor, Manolis? His wife, his widow now, is a good woman, she warned me of his treachery. Their son, Dimitri, is a fisherman and has a boat but he is imprisoned by the Germans because he helped some of your soldiers to escape. I promised to Agathe that I would try to help him return to her if I could, and I will do that. I am thinking that if I can free him, he could get a boat for you'.

'You mean if we can free him, Yannis', interjected Tom. 'If that is the best way to find a boat, then that's what we'll have to do'.

Yannis was relieved that his idea had not been rejected out of hand. He had to find a boat and he had to find Dimitri, so perhaps there was an opportunity to do both.

'One question', said Tom. 'Will you tell Agathe that you killed her husband? That could turn her against us'.

'I have thought about that. I will have to tell her, my honour tells me that I must. I cannot kill her husband, then pretend that someone else pulled the trigger! My heart tells me that she will wish her son to be free again, more than to seek revenge for her husband. He was a hard man, cruel, he used to beat her but he was also the father of her only son so who knows, really?'

'Yannis, here's my answer', said Tom, after a pause. 'When you are ready, and not before tomorrow, because you need to rest as much as any of us, take yourself down to the coast and find a boat for us. If you can find one to hand, all well and good. If you can't then you might need to go through the widow and plan to rescue the lad. Take Davey with you, find as much food as you can and I think we could do with some more local clothes too, we can't mix with folk if we're still in British uniform. Take a day, do what you can and get back to us. We'll make a final decision then. Alright?'

It was alright, and the rest of the day and night passed quietly. It was as much as anyone could do, to take a turn on watch, then eat and sleep. They heard aero engines but always in the distance, none came close. Tom's face felt as if it had been kicked by a horse and was bruised and swollen but he had a shrewd feeling that it was superficial and would fully recover in good time. At least his nose was straight again! Yannis's stitches, applied so carefully by George, were holding, and although the wound was itching, there was no infection.

Yannis and Davey were ready to move an hour before sunrise. They dressed Davey in a shirt and trousers that Manolis had given to them, they were a tight fit but with his tanned and dirty skin, unshaven face and growing hair, he could pass for a Cretan farmworker, at least at a distance. He knew that all the talking would have to be done by Yannis, he would just have stand there and 'look gormless' as George put it! Yannis pulled a stained old trilby down over his stitched forehead, if he was forced to remove the hat, he would have to think of an explanation for the healing wound.

Just before they left, George handed Davey the Luger pistol, telling him to tuck into the waistband of his trousers, under his shirt. 'Eight rounds, mate, semi-automatic, just pull back this toggle, that cocks it, and keep pulling the trigger. I hope to God you don't need to use it'.

Handshakes all round, with a kiss for both from Elena, and they were on their way, an easy climb down the mountain, so Yannis said, followed by a two kilometre walk west to Lavoutro. That would be as good a place as any to start their search.

It felt strange for Tom and George and Elena, left on the mountain. They could do nothing to help Yannis and Davey, and all three of them were feeling that they should be down on the coast with them but also knowing that a party of two had a better chance of a successful reconnaissance than a group of five. They would just have to be patient, take the chance to rest and recuperate, eat what food was left and be ready to move when the call came.

As ever, they took turns at sentry duty, two hours on and four off, with Elena taking a full share. Once again, their luck was in. There was no sign of German soldiers seeking them out, although Tom knew that this could not last for much longer, and as yet, no sign of an aerial search. It seemed most likely that German troop numbers had not yet built up enough to set up an extensive hunt. Probably what soldiers there were, were fully engaged in rounding up the numerous British, Australian and New Zealander strays that had made it to the coast but missed their rescue. Their misfortune, thought Tom, might improve their own chances.

The penny had finally dropped with Tom, concerning Elena's feelings for him. He could no longer miss the frequent glances in his direction and indeed, her proximity inside the cramped shelter. It was complicated further because he had also come to realise that he returned much of those feelings. Other than the obvious physical attraction, and the knowledge that she was as unattached as he was, he admired her courage and her spirit, her refusal to be cowed by this dreadful invasion of her homeland and her determination to do whatever was necessary, not just to survive but to fight back! He wondered if it was simply the shared experience of their extraordinary situation that was throwing them together. He hoped that it was more than that, that although the conflict was responsible for their meeting, perhaps their mutual attraction would have shown in other, less remarkable times.

When Elena exchanged with George for her first sentry duty, Tom took the chance to speak to him about it. At times like this, and despite the difference in rank, he knew that George, with his advantage in years, was more worldly-wise and experienced, and would listen without mocking or taking advantage and might even be willing to provide a little common sense advice.

Sure enough, George listened carefully, with no jokey remarks or belittling of Tom's obvious sincerity and desire to do the right thing. What Tom did not fully appreciate was George's immense respect for him, both personal and professional. They had served together for ten years, George watching his younger comrade grow, through honest effort and intelligent learning, from green trooper to resourceful and inspiring, yet personally humble, NCO. George would never have taken the field promotion to corporal, had Tom not been next in his chain of command.

'What do you think I should do, George?' finished Tom. 'What would you do?' George had anticipated the question, had considered it even before Tom had initiated the conversation, and did not take long to consider his answer. 'Tom, it is simple but not easy. Simple because the choice is so clear but not easy because neither you nor Elena will be happy with it'. 'Go on', said Tom.

George took a deep breath, recognising that Tom probably knew what he was about to say, and that there would be no unsaying of it. 'Tom, you have to rejoin the regiment with me and Davey, and go wherever they tell us to go. Elena cannot go with you, may not even want to go with you because she will need to stay here and will want you to stay, but knowing that you can't'. He paused, then continued. 'So, you are both equally buggered. Best thing is to be honest with each other, so she and you know where you stand and agree that you have to part. Once you've both swallowed that, well, maybe you can come to some sort of understanding for the future, whatever that might be. All damned hard, when there's a war on, but what choice do you have? Worse for both of you if you say nothing and go your own way, you'll be regretting it for years'.

Tom was silent, then looked straight at George. 'Thank you, George. You've put it into words better than I could and of course, you're right, old friend. There's nothing else I can do, I just wish there was more time to know her better and so on but there isn't'. His face was pale, under his deep tan, but George could see that he had reached a conclusion.

'George, would you spell Elena for half an hour, ask her to come in here for a word?' 'Yes, Sergeant', George replied, and walked the several yards outside the shelter to where Elena lay, rifle by her side, watching in the direction that Yannis and Davey had taken, hours before. Elena began to bridle at the message, for she was proud to stand her watch but, seeing something unexpected in George's face, she simply nodded, walking slowly and deliberately into the shelter.

It seemed to George that a little discretion was called for, so took himself off a further ten yards. At quiet times like this, he could not but think of his wife Rachel, sitting patiently in Welshpool, waiting for the war to end. They had been married for fifteen years and for most of those years, they had been apart, separated by George's postings. Their infrequent time together, however, had resulted in three beautiful daughters, their pride and joy. George remitted virtually all of his wages for their upkeep and lived from letter to letter. His last leave had been a year previously, his last letter a month ago, and God knows when or where he would receive the next one! It didn't do to dwell on it, he knew, but sometimes it was unavoidable. Ah well, he thought to himself, better that they were there to worry about, than not being there at all. Rachel was still comfortably in his mind when he became aware of Elena's approach, moving quietly to lie down beside him.

'All's quiet, miss, not a peep anywhere'. He could see that Elena had been weeping, her red eyes showed that, but there were no more tears now. Perhaps it was his imagination but if anything, he could detect a deeper contentment mixed with the sadness. As he rose to return to his rest in the shelter, he hesitated, then looked down at her. 'He's a good man, Miss Elena, the best'. Elena smiled back, tears filling her eyes once more. 'Yes'.

When George lay back down in the shelter, Tom was already asleep and it was not long before George joined him.

They were on their third cycle of watches, after 2000 hours, when Tom heard the quiet strains of 'Abide with me' in a soft tenor, wafting up the hillside. 'Advance and be recognised', Tom called, to be answered with 'Private Williams D., Sergeant, and my mate Yannis, returning from patrol'. Only the starlight enabled Tom to pick out Davey and Yannis together, stumbling up the last few steps of the incline. They both looked all in, but also unwounded and quietly satisfied.

Yannis had not felt so exhausted since he had fought with the Cretan Division in the Pindus Mountains six months previously. The missing forearm wasn't the problem, it was his mended leg and his damaged lung. Constant climbing up and down mountains was putting intense pressure upon both, particularly as the rest of the party were depending upon him. He had had to find food for them, as well as investigate the prospect of locating a boat for their escape, while remaining undetected by the enemy and by any potential traitors. True enough, he had the seemingly inexhaustible strength of Davey to rely upon but the real responsibility was his.

Elena could see her brother's extreme fatigue and helped him remove his large pack and sit down on the still-warm ground, Davey beside him. Tom was impatient to hear what they had achieved but waited while George gave them both a reviving mouthful of tsikoudia. They had eaten before starting the climb back to the shelter, they said, so none was offered, and Yannis started his account of their long day.

He and Davey had made it down to the road before full daylight, but their final step to Lavoutro, the final thirty minutes, had to be concealed and discreet. Fortunately there was no traffic at that hour and they reached the edge of the visit without alarm.

As they had climbed down the mountainside, Yannis had decided that their first stop in the village must be to Agathe. His reasoning was that she had already shown her sympathies in warning him about her husband, and he had promised to liberate her son Dimitri, if he could. She would know that her son's best chance of life lay with Yannis. What he could not be sure of was her reaction to the news of the death of her husband, which he must surely give her. Would she betray them? He did not know for certain.

He explained his idea to Davey, who simply asked him, 'Is there a better way?' Yannis told him that he knew nobody else in the village, did not know who to trust and that if they promised to take Dimitri with them, Agathe would surely help them. They needed information, where the boats were and where Dimitri was confined, just to start with, knowledge that only someone local could provide. So no, there was no better way. Davey response was simple, 'Let's do it then'.

Yannis took the same route to the back of the cottage and was hopeful that they were unseen. Davey's bulk and height made him stand out, Yannis could not think of another Cretan that matched him for size but that was a risk they had to take.

All was quiet. Yannis knocked quietly but repeatedly on the door, murmuring, 'Agathe, Agathe, it is Yannis, please let me in'. There was no response, then he heard a thin voice from behind the door. 'Yannis? I thought you were lost and would not come back! Why have you come?' It was Agathe.

Yannis knew that what he said next would decide their future. 'Old mother, I said I would do what I could to bring Dimitri back to you, that is why I am here. I need your help to do that'. He heard a quiet sob from behind the door, then the door opened enough for him to slip inside, followed closely by Davey. Agathe embraced him, crying 'You said that you would return for him but I had given up hope. My husband….' She stopped speaking as she saw the bulk of Davey, filling the doorway.

'Who is this? Mother of God, you have brought a giant with you!' Yannis quickly explained Davey's presence, quietly amused when Davey solemnly took her hand in his huge paw, whispering 'Hello, missus'.

Agathe looked back to Yannis. 'I know that my husband betrayed you, for when you left with that food, he went straight to the Germans. I followed him, for I know his nature. They gave him money to help them, he showed it to me. He thought that those supplies he gave you would slow you down, and the soldiers would able to follow you and catch you all. He was wrong, wasn't he? For you are here and he is not. Is he dead?' 'Yes, he is dead', answered the young Cretan.

There was no sorrow in her eyes. 'Then that is right. He was a bad husband but I would not have wished him dead before his time. But betraying his own people for money, I would have killed him myself'.

Yannis started to speak, intending to tell her of her husband's death and his part in it, but she interrupted him before he could say more than a very few words. 'Do not tell me how he died, I do not wish to know. It is enough that he has paid for his dishonour'.

She looked up at him, clear-eyed. 'Tell me what you want, what you wish to know'.

She told them that Dimitri was held, with four other young men from the village, in an old net-store, down by the beach. They were under constant guard, usually by just one soldier but sometimes by two. Agathe and other wives and mothers were allowed to bring them food and water every evening but no one knew if the men would eventually be released or punished further.

The three village fishing boats had been impounded by the Germans and were presently moored a kilometre to the west of the village, in a small cove. They were ready for sea, Agathe thought, because the Germans had seized them before they were due to go out into the Libyan Sea to fish.

'Agathe, if we liberate Dimitri and the others', said Yannis, 'they will have to leave Lavoutro, they cannot stay'. 'I know this', she replied. 'They would all be killed. What will you do with them, take them with you?'

Yannis had not fully thought this through but the answer was evident. 'When the English soldiers have left us, I will return to the mountains with Elena, so Dimitri and the others can come with us. They will be hunted but no one knows the peaks like we do, the Germans will not find us'. Agathe could see that this was the only solution.

They moved on to supplies. Agathe suspected that, if the five young men were to be released, their parents would happily give up some of their carefully hoarded food, both for them and for the British soldiers. She would have to speak to all of the families but now that Manolis was dead, she anticipated that they would trust her. He had been well known as an angry and bitter man, and not to be trusted, whereas she was long known for her truthfulness and sense of honour. Their sons liberties were at stake and surely, that fact alone would make up their minds.

Could Yannis take the risk of more people knowing of their plan? It didn't seem that they had much choice in the matter. They could not release Dimitri without releasing the others, and if they did that, more supplies were needed. One thing was very clear, any delay would increase the risk of detection and failure. They would make the escape tonight.

His decision made, he hoped that his plan would stand up to the inevitable pressure of action, and of course, Tom and the others were relying upon him.

Agathe was sent on her travels to the other families, while he and Davey remained in the house, resting and eating what little food they could find. She returned briefly at about midday, to tell them that she had spoken to three of the four families, all of whom had agreed to support the rescue of their sons. Her final visit, in the afternoon, would be to the young wife of the last of the men, and she thought that this one might be problematic. She explained that they had been married for less than two years, and had a young baby. Calista, the young mother, would not be happy for her husband to disappear into the mountains, leaving her alone to care for their child. What should she say to her?

'You must tell her that she and her child will come also. We will find a home for them in one of the villages, far away from here. There are many kind people who will take them in'.

Seeing that the two men were still hungry, Agathe brought out some dried meat and hard bread that had been concealed in a cavity in the chimney. Initially they refused, feeling that they could not deprive her of what little food she had but she insisted, reminding them that they had a mountain to climb up and down yet, before they could put the escape in motion.

Agathe was away for longer than they had thought likely but within two hours, she had returned. Calista had been terrified for her baby whichever choice she made but eventually, she had seen that this was the only way to save her husband and to give them a chance of a life together.

Yannis instructed her to tell the others to bring as much food as they could spare to her house, when darkness came. They must then return to their houses and not stray, whatever they might hear happening outside. Calista and her baby must be ready to leave their house at any time after midnight, but must remain inside until they were collected. He had also decided that the captives were to be given no warning of the rescue attempt, he did not want yet another group of people to be in possession of such potentially dangerous information. The less people that knew the plan, the better, and certainly, too many people knew already.

'We will return by eleven tonight, kyria, or very soon after. Feed the captives as usual but say nothing about any rescue! Tell the families again that they must not say a word to their sons, it is for their own safety'. There was one final question to ask her.

'Agathe, do you wish to accompany your son into the mountains? He will not want to leave you here alone'.

She smiled ruefully and answered, 'I will stay here, young man, it is my home, and I am too old and too fat to walk over mountains! Besides, Dimitri does not know about his father's treachery, nor of his death. How could he? He has been locked up for four days. No, I will remain, with the other families, and we will help each other. Surely the Germans will leave us in peace?'

Yannis was not so sure but could see that her mind was made up. He and Davey took their leave, after Agathe had quickly checked that no one was about outside, neither villagers nor soldiers. Within minutes, they reached the road and crossing it, were quickly out of sight among the scrub and rubble of the mountain.

As they plodded upwards, Yannis reflected upon their day's work. They had a plan, a simple one which might just be good enough. Weaknesses? Yes, of course. The whole enterprise depended upon surprise. If the Germans got wind of their operation then they could be hugely outnumbered. They could deal with one or two sentries without any trouble but if there were more, then their chances of a quiet extraction would be gone. They just had to hope that the families would say nothing.

Would the young men cooperate? Probably they would, after four days detention and an uncertain future but there was no way of knowing in advance. There would be no time to argue or persuade, that would be for sure. They would have to come, or take their chance.

Yannis was concerned for their families too. He had seen in his own village what the Germans would do to get information, they would torture and shoot without hesitation. What would their reaction be if any guards were shot in the rescue? Agathe and the other villagers would not be left in peace.

He was not unduly concerned about the escape into the mountains, they were all young, and even with Calista and her baby, given a couple of hours and darkness, they could disappear. There were more caves and gullies and ravines; with a few day's food in hand, they would not be found.

Davey's deep voice broke into his thoughts. 'Yannis, this boat. I'm no sailor, I don't know about George or the sergeant. How are we going to find our way back to the regiment?'

'Good question, Davey, good question. I'm no sailor either. We haven't thought about that, have we? The boat will have an engine and a compass, I suppose but is that enough? I don't know. It's down to Sergeant Tom, I think. We will see what he says'.

They carried on, Yannis walking more and more slowly as he was overtaken by his fatigue, but eventually he knew that they must be close to where Tom and the others were waiting. Once again, Davey spoke, this time quietly. 'Mate, we need to let 'em know it's us coming in, otherwise they might shoot us'. He was sure that they would not but they would be challenged and it would be as well to give them some advanced warning, for it was now fully dark.

His pals had no idea that Davey had a fine singing voice, he had always felt too embarrassed to mention his singing in school and chapel but it had been his passion since he was a child. Without further discussion, he began to sing.

'Abide with me, fast falls the eventide; the darkness deepens, Lord with me abide. When other helpers fail and comforts flee, Help of the helpless, O abide with me'.

An amused voice came out of the darkness. 'Davey, you could have chosen something a bit more bloody cheerful!' It was George. Tom gave the standard challenge and they were back, welcomed with relief and pleasure

Once their story had been told, everyone looked to Tom for his reaction. His response was immediate. 'Yannis, Davey, you have done us proud! Now we have a plan. It isn't perfect but it never is, is it, and I don't think that you could have done any more. Unless anyone can come up with a good reason not to, we'll go with it. George?'

'Good for me, Tom. What about the boat though, I'm no seaman and nor is Davey and you used to be a farmer! I can fettle an engine alright but drive a boat? Never done it'.

'Me neither, George, but I think we have to give it a try, it's our best chance. Give it a few more days and this island will be crawling with German troops, and we'll never get out. Maybe one of the fisherman will point us in the right direction, I don't know, but we must try'. There was no disagreement.

Then Tom added, 'I'm concerned about the families though, I don't trust the Jerries not to take it out on them if there's casualties. We shall have to try to take out the sentry without killing him if we can, but maybe that won't be possible. Yannis?'

'I think the same, Sergeant, but Cretans are very stubborn people, they will not want to leave their homes'. He repeated what Agathe had said. 'I agree, if we can hurt the sentry and not kill him, ok, the Germans might not harm the families'. His voice filled with passion, 'But this is war, and innocents, as well as the guilty, will die!' There was a brief silence, as the others digested the truth behind his words. He was correct, war respected no one.

'We leave in ten', ordered Tom. 'Weapons, as many rounds as you can carry, grenades. Yannis, you're knackered'. Yannis started to complain but Tom fixed him with his best sergeant's stare. 'You stay chummed up with Davey, he'll manage your rounds and you carry your rifle only. Don't argue! We need you in good shape for the jail break'.

He turned to his corporal. 'George, I want you to stick close to Elena'. This time, both of them started to speak but Tom was taking no opposition. 'Sorry, both, but I need to keep an eye out for everyone, for all of you'. George immediately understood, Tom needed to be a little separate for the operation, to enable him to see the whole picture and to give the best orders. Elena did not understand but George knew just what to say. 'Come on, my girl, we don't need no whippersnapper Sergeant looking after us, we'll show him how it's done! Did I ever tell you, you look just like my eldest daughter'? Elena grinned and then laughed, the awkward moment passing. 'What is whippersnapper, George?' she asked. 'Well, Miss', he replied, winking in Tom's direction, 'A whippersnapper is a boy who thinks he's a man, he might shave and wear long trousers but really he just wants his mam'. Tom grinned, and turned to sort his ammunition, trust George to save the day!

They were ready in five minutes and set off, with Davey and Yannis leading the way. George and Elena followed, with Tom in the rear. There was no conversation, only the careful, irregular tramp of their boots on the rough ground, and the occasional faint clash of weaponry. It was a clear night, faintly illuminated with pale starlight, enough to pick out their path downhill.

An hour had passed by the time that they reached the road. Yannis was feeling another level of exhaustion by then but knew that he simply had to keep moving, the rescue and escape plan was his and he had to see it through. Recovery and rest could come later. Looking around him, it was clear that everyone was suffering, either more or less, but all looked purposeful and determined and Yannis took strength from that.

Then, from somewhere deep inside himself, he felt a slow flood of pride, rising and rising, the realisation that he was a vital element within a group of fine people, all fighting together for the right reasons, not just for country but for each other. It wouldn't help him if bullets came his way but somehow, it all made more sense. He didn't fully understand it, just assuredly knew that he would not let anyone down. The fatigue could be put to one side, at least for now.

They had to walk parallel to the road for the final half hour, to avoid any traffic, both German and Cretan. Headlights and a clattering, noisy engine were the first signs of an open lorry, carrying a small patrol of German infantry, but they had plenty of warning and were able to shrink back into the darkness, away from the road, and it carried on its way. It was a further relief that the lorry was heading away from Lavoutro, not towards it, so perhaps the likely opposition had been reduced, rather than increased.

Agathe was waiting at the door of her cottage and hustled them inside, hugging Elena when she recognised her in the soft light of the oil lamp. The five arrivals filled the room, until Tom told Davey to watch from the front of the house, while George took the rear.

Yannis questioned Agathe, with Elena providing an English translation for Tom. Provisions for the boat, and for the group who would escape across the mountains, had been collected. Agathe had asked that the food was provided in small packs, one for each man and woman, and there they were piled near the door, a selection of bags and packs, some of an old military pattern, others homemade from whatever materials were to hand. Calista, she said, would carry what her baby needed.

The prisoners had been fed at the usual time by their families, and Agathe had loitered to ensure that no one had given any hint of the forthcoming rescue attempt. She said that the 'boys' were frightened, knowing that the Germans would not keep them confined in the net store for much longer, but would they released or punished or even executed?

There were two sentries on duty tonight, taking turn and turnabout, either patrolling the area or guarding the door to the store. She thought they would be relieved at six in the morning but sometimes the routine varied, so she could not be sure. She said that the sentries were not good men, they inspected the food that the families brought and stole anything that took their fancy. They were both armed with rifles and grenades, nothing more.

'Is there a path, a track from the net-store to where the boats have been taken?' asked Tom. Agathe said that there was, a good track all the way. Tom gave his first order.

'Agathe, Elena? Can you get to the path from here without disturbing the sentries?' The translation took a few seconds but yes, they could. He continued, 'Please to take these packs to the path, a few minutes' walk past the store, then wait there so that we can pick you up on the way to the boats'.

Elena was vexed. 'Why I cannot join the rescue, Sergeant Tom? You have a reason?' Tom had guessed that she would not be happy at his decision and was ready to explain. 'Elena, that food is vital for all of us, to make the escape successful, that's why I need you to safeguard it. Besides, that leaves four of us to tackle two sentries, should more than enough'. She could see his reasoning and reluctantly agreed, translating the plan for Agathe's benefit. They agreed that Agathe would help her carry the eleven packs to the path, collecting Calista and her baby en route but would then return home, she was too old, she said, to run about in the darkness. She would have liked to see, with her own eyes, her Dimitri free but would be satisfied to know that he was out of German hands and besides, he would contact her when he could, he was a good son.

Tom's next step was a quiet instruction to his corporal. 'George, can you do a reccie down to that store, Agathe will point you in the right direction. No more than half an hour, quicker if you can, check that there's no more than two on sentry, and which one we should take first. Right?' George pulled in Yannis as his translator, learned his directions and within a minute, had disappeared into the darkness outside.

As Elena prepared to leave with the packs of food, she turned to Tom and Yannis, fixing them with a bright, fierce stare. 'Be sure, my dears, that you are not hurt any more. What a sight you are, you look like pirates, not soldiers, all battered and cut and bruised!' She paused, both men aware of her gathering emotion but, quickly kissing them both, she turned and followed Agathe through the door.

Yannis turned to Tom. 'Sergeant Tom, you know that my sister likes you very much, and you her, I think?' Tom was taken aback but knowing the honesty was called for, particularly when they would all soon be in action, paused then replied, 'Yes, I do know she likes me, Yannis, and the liking is returned, she knows this'. He anticipated Yannis's next question, and continued, 'We have spoken, no more than that'. He sighed. 'She understands that I must do my duty and leave the island, and I understand that she must do hers, and stay. All I could promise to her was that I will return, at the end of the war or before, and we will see if we feel the same way'.

'You will keep your promise, Sergeant Tom?' questioned Yannis, 'you will return?' Tom, reminding himself that Yannis was her much-loved brother so of course he would be concerned for her, simply replied, 'Yes, I will'.

'Then we will look forward to that day', smiled Yannis. 'Since her betrothed died, she has not looked at another, and the years pass in sadness. She finds you, but we are surrounded by war, so she must wait longer'.

Tom nodded. 'I did not want this to happen, Yannis, not in war-time, I even told your sister, but I find that some things in life just come along, whether the time is right or not, so there we are'.

They both paused, there would be other opportunities to speak. 'What are your orders for me, Sergeant?'

Chapter 20

George returned from his reconnaissance, confirming that there were two sentries at the net-store. As Agathe had told them, one guarded the door while the other patrolled the area but that turned out to be theory rather than practice.

'They've got lazy, Tom, they don't think anything is going to happen. Half the time, they are both sitting by the door, smoking! Sitting under an oil lamp too, so their night vision's ruined. Best way to take 'em down would be to wait until they're both at the door, then approach from the other side, the back, of the store'.

'How many of us?' asked Tom. 'One from either side should do it, with a third up front in case anything goes wrong', answered George. 'Bayonets if we can't disarm 'em, no shooting unless we have to', he added, 'keep it nice and quiet'.

'OK then, you and Davey do the sentries, me and Yannis will be fifty yards out as your reserve. Once they're down, we'll break in and Yannis will talk to his mates, tell 'em what's happening. Hopefully, we'll be on our way to the boats in a few minutes. How will you know the sentries are both at the door, you'll be out of line of sight?'

You'll see them, won't you, from front on?' George answered, 'Give us an owl screech, worked in the desert, didn't it? They won't know any better'.

Tom pulled Davey in from the back of the house. He explained the plan, adding, 'Give me that machine gun, lad, and the ammo. You won't need it to get your sentry and don't worry, I'll look after it!'

They were as ready as they would ever be. George, with the advantage of his earlier look-see, led their silent advance from the house and in a couple of minutes, gestured for Tom and Yannis to cut left, while he and Davey continued onwards.

He reckoned that they were at least a hundred yards to the north of the net store, in deep darkness and as long as they were quiet, there was small chance of discovery. They continued walking for two more minutes, to ensure that they were beyond the store, before gesturing to Davey to cut directly south alongside him. Within another minute, George could just make out the shape of the building, with a faint light illuminating the front of the building to their left. Both he and Davey slowed down further and split up, reaching the back of the building and taking a corner each. If one of the sentries decided to patrol around the circumference of the store, then they would have to dispose of him as quietly as possible, before going for the guard at the front door.

Tom and Yannis should be in position by now, he reckoned, and the signal could come at any time. Sure enough, the tell-tale owl screech cut through the quiet night, to be answered by the screech of another owl directly behind them! Tom's screech was so lifelike, it had fooled one of the local inhabitants!

Gesturing to Davey that they should deliver their attack after a count of ten, George moved silently along his side of the building, bayonet in hand, confident that Davey would be doing exactly the same on the opposite side, counting down to the second when the attack would begin. As he neared the end of the wall, he could hear the quiet conversation of the two guards and could smell that familiar cigarette smoke.

As the tumbling numbers in George's head reached zero, he launched himself around the corner, into the warm light of the hanging oil lamp. Then everything happened so fast!

George was a split second ahead of Davey and for the smallest fraction, he had the undivided attention of both sentries. The first soldier, who had been sitting relaxed and easy, jumped up, his hand reaching for the carbine that leaned against his chair. He was going to fight! George had little choice, if he wanted to survive, and his bayonet, held sword fashion and with all his momentum behind it, plunged into the neck of the leaping soldier. The blade fully impaled his neck, slicing through both carotid arteries and everything in between. His body crashed to the ground, with George on top of him, desperately trying to haul his blade out of the ghastly wound.

Almost simultaneously, the remaining sentry who had been leaning against the door, carbine in hand, lifted it as George started his ferocious attack upon his comrade. As his finger began to tighten on the trigger, to fire into the corporal's unprotected body, his face tightened in an excruciating expression then blanked, as Davey's bayonet punched into his back, emerging through his chest with immense force. His finger spasmed in reflex as he died, and as he fell backwards, with Davey's arm tight around his neck, three shots crashed out from the carbine, flying harmlessly over George's head.

'Damn and blast', grated George, 'that's fucking torn it!' as Tom and Yannis ran up, the young Cretan immediately starting to search the nearest corpse for the keys to the store, from where shocked and frightened voices were beginning to be heard.

Tom quickly took command. 'Well done, now let's get a move on. Yannis, tell your lads they can either go with you into the mountains or out to sea with us but they've got a minute to decide. No arguing, they are dead if they stay. George, Davey, get out fifty yards in the direction of the village, I want an early warning if those shots were heard'.

By then, Yannis had the store door open and was surrounded by the five young fishermen, full of questions, and all speaking at once. What was going on? Who had fired the shots? Could they go home?

Calmly, Yannis held up his hands for silence, then explained, in a few words, the choices in front of them. They could make up their minds on the way to the boats but no one could stay, the Germans would kill anyone who was left.

To the astonishment of Yannis, and that of the other fishermen, one of the men, Andros, refused to move. 'No, I will stay, the Germans will not hurt me or my family. They already buy my fish, drink coffee at my father's kafeneion. They would have released me tomorrow, I took no British out to their ships and I will tell them that'.

Before he could say any more, Yannis had lifted the barrel of his carbine, jabbing it hard into the young man's stomach. He hissed, 'You would stay and take their money, you snake! Either you come with us or I will shoot you now!' The lad really had no choice and agreed to stay with the group but it was a forced agreement, and Yannis knew that he would have to be watched with care, lest he betrayed them all.

Yannis nodded to Tom that they were ready to move, and a quiet whistle brought George and Davey in from the perimeter. They had heard some engine noise, could be the Germans responding to the shots, so there was no time to waste. Young Dimitri, with a ready charm more like his mother than his father, took the lead and the group, now more than doubled in size, hurried along the sandy path, with George taking up his usual tail end Charlie position. Yannis was positioned in the middle of the group, directly behind Andros but concentrating upon keeping his own footing, as much as upon the unwilling escapee in front of him.

Their quick pace brought them to where Elena, Calista and the baby were waiting. There was the briefest, tender reconciliation between the young family before Yannis caught Tom's eye and hustled the group back into motion, after handing out the small packs of food from their families. As he counted the group past him, he noticed, with a dreadful lurch inside, that Andros was missing. As he looked around in panic, Tom noticed his agitation.

'What's wrong, lad?' 'That little shit has gone back, he'll betray us, he knows where we're going first. I'll catch him, look after Elena', and with that, he was gone, hurrying back down the path towards the net store.

Elena looked in bewilderment as Yannis disappeared into the darkness. 'Tom, where has he gone?' Tom's explanation did not satisfy her. 'I must go too, my brother!'

'Elena, you must not. These boys need you to guide them into the mountains if Yannis is …. delayed'. As she hesitated, he added, 'Yannis will make it, Elena, if anyone can. He is as fine a soldier as I've seen. Now, come, we must move!' She knew he was right, but leaving her brother to whatever fate befell him was the most difficult thing she had ever done.

Their race to the boats continued, men and women and baby all together, fumbling through the darkness. After a further quarter of an hour of progress, the crackle of rapid gunfire, back in the direction of the store, broke out. George could identify the roar of a machine gun and the slighter snapping of multiple carbines, interrupted by the flat percussion of a grenade, then the mayhem of the firefight resuming. Yannis had found his men.

Hard as it was, and wishing nothing more than to go back to fight alongside his Cretan friend, Tom and George chivvied the party back into movement. Elena was weeping quietly and Tom held her hand as some sort of comfort for them both, knowing that it was not enough but all that he could provide. Within another minute, all the firing behind them had ceased.

Before long, their surroundings changed. The scrub that surrounded the path gave way to open, short grassland which then dropped steeply down to the sea, and there, pulled up onto the beach were four small fishing boats, two open and two half-decked. They gathered at the boats, with Elena taking over the translation duties in her brother's absence.

Unsurprisingly, all of the young fishermen wished to stay on the island. They worried for their families and wanted to make them safe if they could, and to fight back against the invaders. They were helpful though, in organising the best boat for the soldiers' escape. The best half-decker was chosen, not for its looks, which were battered and flaking, but for the strength and reliability of its engine. The gas tank was full, having been fuelled up for fishing before the Germans had impounded it, and a dozen spare cans were moved across from the other boats, along with containers of fresh water. Dimitri, with his limited command of English, nevertheless managed to convey to George how to manage the engine controls and crucially the compass, even contriving to suggest a course of east-south-east, which would send them in the rough direction of Alexandria, the nearest British base in Egypt.

Tom could see that George and Davey had everything in hand and turned to Elena, who had not left his side. How ironic that such a terrible conflict had brought them together, two people who seemed made for each other, and was now separating them, perhaps for the remainder of their lives.

'How long will you wait for Yannis?' he asked. 'We can't wait', she answered. 'He knows the route that we will follow into the mountains, he will meet us when he can'. Neither could put into words the possibility that he might never meet them, that he might already be dead.

After a short moment, she spoke again. 'My Tom, you promised me that if you are alive at the end of this terrible war, you will come to find me. Will you keep your promise?' 'Of course, Elena, I will come to you if I am able, I won't break that promise. Perhaps they will send me back to Crete to fight again and I will find you then'.

He paused, then continued. 'Elena, we have known each other for a few days, only in this terrible war. I pray that we have the chance to meet again in peaceful times. Stay safe, my dear, if you can and that day will come'. They embraced quickly, aware that George and Davey were on board and waiting, and the four fisherman waiting to push the boat into the sea.

Elena smiled sadly, she knew her man and was sure that he would keep his word if he possibly could. Neither felt that this was the right way to say goodbye but what else could they do? Tom had his duty and she had hers, the war was in control of both of their destinies. A brief kiss signalled their separation, and Tom climbed slowly into the boat. In a minute they were afloat and in another, underway, slowly moving towards to the end of the cove and the open sea. As Tom watched, Elena's face faded quickly into the darkness. All she was left with was the put-put-put of the old engine and the quiet lap of the waves upon the beach.

Elena was still for a moment but knew that they could stay no longer. She looked at her companions. Calista's young husband carried the baby, who seemed quiet and contented, at least for now, Calista smiling behind him. The four fisherman, two carrying rifles taken from the guards at the net store, were quiet, dipping into their supplies, no doubt hungry after a long day in their little prison. They would need their energy, she thought, for the climb into the interior of the island.

'We must leave now', she announced. 'We must be many kilometres into the mountains before daylight, or the Germans will find us. Don't stop to rest until I say, and we have a good chance of success, also don't eat all of your food now, you will need it later. Any questions?'

One of the young men answered. 'Miss, we should disable our boats, stop the Germans from following your friends'. Why hadn't she thought of that? They rapidly removed rotor arms from the three engines and for good measure, removed the bungs in the bottom of the boats. Anyone who managed to push the boats into the sea would sink in short order!

Elena looked back along the track for a final time, hoping against hope that Yannis would appear, then resolutely turned west, gesturing for the others to follow her. Within seconds, they were gone and the beach was quiet once more.

Chapter 21

Yannis knew that he would have little chance of catching Andros before he reached the net store. His injuries had not reduced his endurance but his speed was gone, it certainly would not compare with that of the younger man. With the start that Andros had, and his quickness over the ground, Yannis would be a couple of minutes behind him, if the net store was where he was headed. What could he do?

As he raced along, something of an answer appeared in his mind. Simply chasing the young man along the path would leave him open to danger, Andros could hide and strike him down as he passed, or he could run straight into any German troops investigating the earlier firing. Instead of running east along the path leading right up to the store, it would make sense to turn off north a half kilometre beforehand, just for a hundred metres or so, before moving east again. That would bring him level with the store, yet out of sight of Andros and of anyone else. He knew that there would be no buildings or trees between him and the store, so if that was where the traitor was running to, he would see him, or at least hear him.

If Andros was heading for somewhere else, perhaps back to his home, then he would have to leave him for another day, it would be impossible to recapture him tonight. But Yannis would not forget.

Making his best guess of his position, Yannis turned north as planned, stumbled on in the darkness for a minute then headed east again, slowing down in the rougher going off the path. It wasn't long before Yannis sensed that the ground was opening up, between him and the sea, and that therefore the net store would soon be in front of him.

Yannis stopped, hoping that his heartbeat and his breathing would quickly return to a normal rate, allowing him to listen for and locate any movement. The atmosphere was clear, pale stars and a thin slice of moon providing a minimal, soft illumination and straining his eyes, he could just make out the shape of the net store, faint against the night sky, perhaps a hundred metres away.

He had hardly settled before a shadow flitted across the side of the store nearest to him, swiftly followed by a rising scream of 'nicht schiese, nicht schiese!' Before he could draw another breath, rapid fire burst out from the left of the building, carbines and a light machine gun by the sound of it, cutting off the scream abruptly. It sounded as if the Germans had found Andros before he had, and his best choice was to sit quietly for now, and to see what might happen next.

There was a babble of German voices from the direction of the store, quickly followed with a shout of 'Ruhe!', probably an NCO quietening down his patrol. Voices continued though, now raised in anger, Yannis guessing that they had found the bodies of the two slaughtered sentries. Someone must have had a flashlight, for he could see a light moving around, sometimes lost behind figures, sometimes lighting up the building. It did not give enough light, however, for him to estimate how many soldiers were in the patrol.

Yannis reckoned he should attack, to show them that their unwanted stay on the island was going to be painful and expensive. They could not see him in the dark which would give him an early advantage, but what if a dozen angry soldiers were waiting for him, and not the three or four that he estimated he could manage? He would be outflanked rapidly and that would be the end of it. He needed to get closer.

The terrain between him and the store was flat, comprising rough grass, thyme and other bushy herbs, interspersed here and there with a few rounded boulders. Crouching low, Yannis moved rapidly across the ground, with his carbine slung on his back for quietness. The final ten metres of his advance were as silent as he could make them, and he dropped quietly into the lee of one of the boulders, perhaps only twenty metres or so from the store.

No one had seen or heard him, there was still chat among the soldiers of the patrol, much louder at this shorter distance. It was still impossible for him, in this poor light, to see how many troopers he was up against but then, to his amazement, one of the two oil lamps hanging beside the door to the store burst into light! The other lamp was out of his view, further around the corner of the little building, as could be other men, but in the light from the first lamp, four soldiers were clearly illuminated. What were they thinking of? Here was his chance!

His carbine was at his shoulder in seconds, and silently cocked. Twenty metres was point blank, and his Walther spat out the ten rounds within a few seconds, all he had to do was to keep pulling the trigger. At that range, the soldiers were blown off their feet, the impact of the heavy bullets smashing them into each other, leaving them sprawled and devastated upon the ground, their blood joining that of their comrades. None had managed to fire a shot but before Yannis could move, he spied a shrouded barrel poking out around the corner of the store, immediately followed by short bursts of fire. Someone was fighting back but they couldn't see him and didn't know where he was. None of the bursts had come anywhere close to him.

An unknown hand extinguished the oil lamp and Yannis knew that he had to move. He did not know how many of the patrol had survived his attack but the risk of being rapidly flanked and surrounded was there again. It was time to go!

He had brought a couple of German stick grenades with him, recovered from the annihilated patrol that had attacked them in the mountains. Pulling the detonator cord on the first, he overarmed it in the direction of the hut, hoping that it would miss the corner of the building and threaten any soldiers hiding out of his sight. Yannis ducked to avoid the blast, which roared and buffeted over his head. There was no immediate resumption of firing, no screaming of men in pain, perhaps he had put them out of action, perhaps not. He quickly armed the remaining grenade and this time, lobbed it in the direction of the pitched roof of the store. It was guesswork in darkness but this time, the blast burst out on the other side of the building, his missile had rolled down the far side of the roof before exploding.

Yannis was up and running in a second, and this time, he could hear the tormented cries of wounded men behind him. He could not know if he had destroyed the patrol or not, but knew for certain that he had not when after only a brief few seconds, machine gun fire crashed out across the field. They could not see him but that volume of fire, hosed across his likely path, might easily put an end to his escape.

Ducking even lower, Yannis dropped behind a small boulder, only a couple feet in height but offering some temporary shelter. As occasional shots ricocheted off that rock, and off others close by, he concentrated on thumbing a further ten rounds into the carbine's magazine. He would need to be quick, for if there were survivors other than the machine gunner, they would already be moving to outflank and expose him. In the darkness, and with an unfamiliar rifle, the reloading took longer than otherwise.

The machine gunner was now firing in short bursts, trying to preserve his barrel from overheating and distortion, and in one of the pauses, Yannis was able to wriggle down between two rocks, eventually lying prone, directly facing the net store before the gunner recommenced firing. Every fifth round or so was tracer, enabling the gunner to gauge where his rounds were going, but also, along with the muzzle flash, informing Yannis of the location of the gunner. Some of the shots were close but now, well over his head.

Wasting no time, but sighting as carefully as he could, Yannis fired off five rounds, allowing the carbine to settle back onto his forearm after every shot. The only real sight picture to aim at was the bright, white flash as each tracer left the barrel and his concentration was total. He knew that his first shots must be close, for he was still less than one hundred metres from the store, but it was on his fifth shot that his skill paid off. The machine gun abruptly began to shoot directly into the air, only for a few rounds, then stopped. Surely, he had disabled the gunner!

He was on his feet and running in another second, hoping against hope that there would be no more automatic gunfire chasing him, and that there would no Germans waiting for him as he tore inland.

Behind him, Yannis could hear an engine starting, of course the patrol must have arrived in a truck. As deeply tired as he was, Yannis put on more speed, for if he was cut off before crossing the road, there would be no escape. Assuming the Germans had enough troops to hand, he would be penned in, trapped against the coast, and that would be the end of him.

A few minutes of lung-wracking effort found him stumbling onto the road that he had crossed hours earlier with his comrades, but before he was able to reach the other side, he was surprised by the roar of an engine, then dazzled as headlights swept around a corner not fifty metres away!

Head down, he kept running and burst through brush on the other side of the road, hearing shouting behind him and the screech of brakes as the lorry skidded to a halt. The ground directly in front of him angled immediately upwards, through an olive grove, leading eventually into the mountainous interior of the island, and Yannis felt immediately at home. They would have their work cut out tracking him here!

As he continued climbing, leaving the shelter of the trees, snap shots cracked past him, but he knew that he was invisible to his pursuers, lost against the dark loom of the hill. Tired as he was, Yannis somehow was able to tap into the energy of his youth and raced onwards in the darkness.

Elena was tired. She and her four charges had moved quickly through the remainder of the night of their escape and were a few kilometres into the mountains before daybreak. The young fishermen had accepted her authority and leadership without complaint and they had made good progress. They were young and fit of course, she thought, and perhaps they would soon leave her behind!

In the early morning light, in the shelter of a rock field, Elena had allowed a longer rest, fortunately so because no sooner had they stopped than the throaty roar of aero engines was heard in the brightening sky to the east of them. Elena just had enough time to ensure that all were tucked away out of sight under a spacious overhang, before a sleek, grey aeroplane, twin-engined, flew directly over them then carried on to the west. They stayed hidden for a further half an hour, for the plane might have reversed its course but it did not, and Elena then hustled everyone on, for they could still be pursued on foot.

The remainder of that pitilessly hot day was spent creeping from rock field to rock field, never far from shelter, refusing the temptation of easier travel lower down the mountain. Elena was headed for yet another refuge, the Cave of Hestia, the goddess of the home and family, and although this was a longer route, she was confident that they would reach it before nightfall, unless the Germans intervened.

There was another Luftwaffe overflight in the afternoon but they had spotted it early enough and were well hidden when it swept over them. Elena was as sure as she could be that they had not been detected and they moved on with a minimum of delay.

Light was just beginning to fade as Elena led her deeply fatigued band around the final corner of the path leading to Hestia's Cave and abruptly stopped, rigid in her tracks. The young man behind her stumbled into her, knocking her forward, and as she regained her balance, she started to laugh, and ahead of them, another voice joined in.

'Elena, my dear sister, where have you been?' Yannis had outpaced his pursuers with ease, for they were not mountain troops, and had made his way to the cave, guessing that Elena would make for it too, for they had visited it many times in years past. He was close to exhaustion, as they all were but they had a little food and would be safe here for the night. It would take months, if not years, before German infantry learned their way around Crete's rocky heights.

Brother and sister embraced, and brought each other up to date. It seemed miraculous that they were both unharmed, considering the stand-up fights that they had been involved in, and both of them knew that this could not last, could not continue. This was already a savage war and many would die in the fight to liberate their island.

Yannis hesitated, then spoke quietly to his sister, 'I pray God that Sergeant Tom, and my friends George and Davey have found refuge, and are safe'. 'So do I, so do I, brother', she answered, and they both stood, looking south to where the bright ribbon of the Libyan Sea was visible, squeezed between the mountains and the sky.

Later in the night, as his companions slept soundly around him, Yannis became aware of quiet footsteps moving towards the entrance to the cave. He sat up, only for his sister's soft voice to urge him to sleep, she was taking some air.

He watched silently as Elena sat down in the entrance of the cave, looking south once more and there she remained, until the sun started its next day's travel.

Chapter 22

Tom took care of the navigation, having plenty of experience of using a compass in the desert. Once they were clear of the cove, and illuminating the binnacle with a dim torch, he steered east-south-east, recommended as a rough course for Alexandria, the nearest British base. He didn't imagine that they would make it that far, it was far more likely that they would run out of fuel and sink or be machine gunned and bombed by a German plane. There was a small chance though that they would meet the Royal Navy along the way, and that was a gamble worth taking.

George had the cover off the tiny engine of just a few horsepower, checking the lubrication as it thumped away. He looked towards Tom, thumbs up and a grin plastered over his face. It looked like he was happy with the engine, and pleased they were on their way back to the regiment, thought Tom, even though there was still a long way to go.

Davey, content that he had managed to hold on to the MG34, his excellent German machine-gun, was sitting in the bows, busily stripping it down and cleaning every component. Tom knew that some maintenance would not only improve the reliability of the weapon but it would also familiarise Davey with its workings, which would help if there was a jam or if he needed to change the barrel under fire.

It wasn't possible to accurately estimate how long the fuel would last. They had started with a half-full tank and had seven cans donated from the other boats. If they could get through the night, and the whole of the next day and night, so perhaps the next thirty hours, Tom reckoned that they would be in sight of the Libyan coast, and would be able to follow it towards Alexandria. Surely there would be friendly vessels somewhere along the route?

The night was warm, balmy even, and as far as Tom could tell, they were making good progress. George had asked him not to flog the engine because although it was running well, it looked elderly and he didn't want to push their luck. Tom had dropped the revs about twenty minutes out, giving a quieter, smoother ride, and now, a few hours later, the early sun was just cracking the horizon in the east.

Looking back, Crete was gone, dropped now below the skyline. Ahead, there was no loom of approaching land, which came as no surprise. They were closing the African coast, but at an oblique angle, so it would be hours yet before any land became visible. Fortunately, the sea was still calm and although they were all confirmed landsmen, none had been troubled yet by seasickness.

Dawn, just as on land, was a dangerous time at sea, and Tom was pleased to see that, without need of an order, George and Davey were on lookout to either side of the boat, George to port and Davey to starboard. Tom still had the binoculars and used them to look back towards the island, for surely that would be the most likely direction for any pursuit to appear from, but for now, there was nothing. Was that a faint view of a mountain top there in the haze? Perhaps not, but his thoughts immediately turned to Elena, hopefully walking towards safety among those same mountains. He could still conjure up her smiling face, it would fade in his memory, he knew, as more time passed but for now, it was clear. He knew that lingering on the danger that she and her compatriots were facing would not help anyone, but it was so difficult to dismiss from his mind.

He looked up as George spoke. 'She'll be good, Tom, have no fear. Smart girl' he grinned, and Tom nodded, trust George to be able to read his feelings!

There was a breakfast to eat, of olives, old cheese, bread and water, which they took at their posts. The views to port and starboard were still clear but as Tom, binoculars to his eyes, quartered the horizon back to the north, he looked and looked again. What was that black dot, high up in the sky? Very small as yet, it could be a bird but as he continued to look, it grew larger and larger. Turning back to the boat, he throttled back to a quiet tick-over.

'Lads, there's a plane coming our way in the next minute or so. Get your arms out of sight and we'll see if we can con them'. The other two quickly obeyed, Davey pushing his machine-gun against the gunwale, close to hand. They were in shirtsleeves and Tom pulled on a greasy old cap that he had found under a net.

He looked back. The plane was closer, and above the burble of the idling motor, Tom could hear the increasing buzz of a low-powered aero engine. As he looked, no binoculars this time, he began to make out a single, high wing, with a long, fixed undercarriage hanging below. It was a Storch, that familiar, low-speed German reconnaissance plane. Someone must have guessed or discovered that they had escaped by boat, and had sent it out to find them.

'They'll come low and slow, lads, so give them a friendly wave and maybe they'll fuck off. If they don't, Davey, get that pop-gun of yours going. They're not armoured'. As he looked again, the plane was within half a mile and closing. It kept coming, then curved out to the west, beginning to circle slowly around them. They were so close that Tom could make out the pilot, with an observer sitting behind him in the well-glassed cockpit, taking a long, slow look as they passed in front of the boat then passing down the port side. 'Keep waving, George. Davey, start moving one of those nets around, look like you're doing something'.

The ungainly little plane, trundling through the sky, passed around the stern and for a moment, Tom thought that their ruse had fooled the German crew, but as he continued to wave, he could see the observer standing hunched in the cockpit, facing the tailplane, as he worked on a rearwards facing, fixed machine-gun.

Tom took in what was going to happen and shouted, 'Davey, get your canon ready, but out of sight until they're well in range then let 'em have it, I want 'em in the water. George, hold on tight, I'll see if we can make ourselves hard to hit'. With that, Tom opened the throttle and simultaneously swung the rudder to move the boat sharply to starboard. The gunwales on that side of the boat almost dipped under and George was tipped off his feet, only his firm grip on the engine cover stopping him from being thrown overboard.

He kept an eye on the plane, which was still circling. Their machine-gun, Tom could see, was mounted to fire through the rear window aperture. He guessed that it would probably be able to swing to fire perhaps thirty degrees either side of the tailplane, which would make it difficult, if not impossible, for the observer to hit the boat with any accuracy, and impossible to defend the plane if there was any return of fire. They must think we are unarmed, he realised! Their ruse had worked but the Germans still wanted to sink them!

Swinging the boat to port, he shouted to Davey, 'Fire on my order, Davey, not before. They're going to get really close!'

The Storch had an amazing ability to fly slowly without stalling and it tightened its circle, giving the observer a chance to hold the boat in his sights for more than a few seconds. Tom estimated it was still around three hundred yards away when it opened fire, and he swerved again to starboard. No rounds hit the boat and it seemed that the observer had asked the pilot to come in even closer, for the angle of the plane changed and it moved in another hundred yards. This was point blank range!

'Davey, no time for the tripod. Shoot when I say!' From the corner of one eye, he saw that Davey had one hand on the stock of the machine-gun and was cocking it, ready to shoot, with the other. His main attention though was on the observer, and as the angle opened, to bring the boat into the range of the fixed gun, he roared, 'Shoot, shoot!' , trying to keep the boat straight and steady to give Davey the best chance of a hit.

It seemed to Tom that Davey and the German observer opened fire within the same second, so it was impossible to watch one and then the other. He did see that Davey had cleverly led the plane with his burst, with the result that the plane flew straight into the volley of bullets. Davey must have followed the plane around because his shots tracked along the length of the cockpit, from the pilot, shredding the observer in passing, then chopped into the tail and stopped.

Black smoke gouted from the Storch's engine, and Tom could see that the pilot was in trouble. He turned to Davey, to tell him to give them another burst, but what he saw in front of him took all his words away. Davey had been firing from the waist and he stood, facing towards where the plane had been. Tom had not been aware of fire from the observer, nothing had come near him, but Davey had caught a burst through his chest. He was drenched in his own blood and Tom could sense, but not see, the huge exit wounds that the bullets must have created.

Before Tom could move, Davey's head turned towards him, looking at him with unseeing, dead eyes, then toppled backwards against the gunwale and pitched over the side into the water, still clutching his machine gun.

As Tom and George ran to the side of the boat, the Storch plunged into the sea, breaking up as it hit the water, but their attention was on Davey, and he had gone.

In the clear water, shaded now with a cloud of blood, all that was visible of Davey was his body, sinking quickly into the depths, more blood leaking from his body as he sank into the darkness. Tom went to dive after him, knowing him to be dead but wanting to at least save his body, to complete his final responsibility as the boy's sergeant. Before he could move however, he felt George gripping his arm. 'No, Tom. Let him go. He done his duty, let him go'.

Neither of them cared about the plane, which had sunk, leaving only a little floating wreckage. They had been through so much together, thought Tom, were on their way back to the regiment and now he had lost Davey. He knew that losing your men, losing your friends, was what happened in wartime but that did not make it any easier. Had he made Davey a target by giving him the job of shooting the plane down? Would George have been the target if he'd been the machine-gunner? It would have been as bad to lose him.

George spoke in his ear. 'Tom, he was doing his job, as we was doing ours, you know that. Now, we got to get on, we'll mourn him later'. Tom looked up quickly, ready to react in his grief but knew, as he opened his mouth, that George was right.

'OK, George, let's get on. I wanted to get him home though'.

'Not in your power, mate, not in your power'.

Chapter 23

Tom went back to the helm, opened the throttle and set the course while George checked the boat and engine for any damage. It was with a grim face, a few minutes later, that he stepped back to the stern, to report to Tom. 'Boat's been hit, Tom. There's a few holes letting in water, I plugged the ones I could see but I reckon there's more, water's still finding its way in. There's only three cans of petrol left, the others got shot up, don't know how they didn't explode. Engine is alright but I reckon we should slow down, that might ease the flooding and stretch out the fuel a bit longer'.

Tom cursed their luck but of course, it could have been much worse. One exploding fuel can would have been the end of them altogether. He throttled back, keeping enough way on the boat to keep her on course and little more. George opened up the engine compartment again and began bailing, hoping to expose more holes that he could plug. It was now full daylight, and both men understood that they would not be able to hold off another attack, if one came. They could no longer manoeuvre, and their weaponry was down to two carbines, a pistol and a couple of stick grenades. Anything larger than a rowing boat would out-gun them.

In another couple of hours, George had managed to plug more holes, using rags he had found lying around and the leaks had slowed further. Any increase in speed though would force the plugs out, and they would be back where they started, so they could only continue at walking pace. If the weather changed, and the sea roughened up, they would have no choice but to speed up and take their chance or they would founder anyway. Both men worked silently, the loss of Davey still raw in both of their minds.

As Tom steered, he kept watch all around their patch of sea and was not surprised when, again to the north, a small white wave with something of a shape behind it appeared. 'Boat coming up, George', he shouted. 'Yes, a fast patrol', he continued, as the wave and shape resolved into a sleek, grey patrol boat, rapidly overhauling them. 'Bloody pilot must have got a message off before we shot the bugger down', commented George.

'We can't fight these off, George', said Tom. 'If they fire on us, fire back but otherwise, well, they've got us'. George's face was set in frustration but he gave a nod and waited.

The patrol boat, about forty feet in length and swastika flag flying, began to circle them as the plane had done earlier, they could see larger calibre machine guns tracking them, as well as sailors with hand-held automatic weapons. There was no firing, no speaking, just acute tension as Tom and George waited together for whatever was going to happen. As far as Tom could see, it would be captivity or death, one or the other.

Tom spotted some movement on the patrol boat and immediately, a heavy machine-gun started to fire. He could feel big rounds slamming into the hull of their wooden fishing boat, smashing the engine and ricocheting into the air. Without time for thought, he grabbed George and they both flopped over the side of the boat, with the hull and engine between them and the bullets that continued to smash into the vessel. The firing continued, and their little boat started to settle, then abruptly capsized. It was as much as Tom could do to pull himself and George away from the heavy gunwale as it crashed down into the water. To his surprise, the remains of the boat continued to float, and both men instinctively clutched at it again, it wasn't much protection but it was all that they had. All that effort, thought Tom, and we're going to end it here, drowned or shot.

George was still next to him, grasping one of the ribs of the boat as it disintegrated around them, and he caught Tom's eye. 'Nowt like a swim on a hot day, Sergeant!' he quipped. Tom couldn't help but smile, if you had to die then why not do it with your best comrade next to you? He noticed that George was clutching his crucifix with one hand, the crucifix given to him by little Giorgos to help him on his journey.

Spitting sea water from his mouth, Tom was about to answer when a howling, deafening roar almost drowned out everything around them, only rivalled by the deep, percussive crack-crack-crack of what sounded like canon. The machine-gun fire that was destroying the boat around them abruptly stopped but multiple guns could still be heard firing. They seemed no longer to be a target, so Tom decided to take a look at what was happening and, gesturing to George, he grappled his way along the shattered hull to the stem, holding onto the boat with one arm as he looked across to the patrol boat.

A stunning sight met him, and as he looked the howling roar previously heard repeated itself, deafening him once again. Two fighter planes, Hurricanes he thought, were taking turns at strafing the patrol boat from stem to stern. Only one gun was firing back now, and as they watched, for George had joined him, even that fell silent. Still the planes shuttled in and out, smashing more rounds into the remains of the boat, and it sank lower and lower in the water, black smoke pouring from it as fire took hold of the wreckage.

An idea struck Tom. Gesturing for help from George, he pulled himself up on to the stem of their boat, still floating but at an angle, weighed down towards the stern by the remains of the engine. There must be a big air pocket keeping it afloat, he thought, as he scrambled out of the water and perched himself precariously on the prow. As the planes came for another pass, Tom waved vigorously with both arms, hoping against hope that either of the pilots would spot him. They roared past, much to his disappointment and disgust but as he watched, one of the Hurricanes peeled back and flew low and slow over him, perhaps for another look. He continued to wave and even shout and sure enough, the lethal little fighter waggled its wings as it continued back eastwards.

Hauling George up onto the prow to join him, they looked across to the remains of the patrol boat. It was utterly destroyed, the remnants burning rapidly down to the waterline. Ammunition was still cooking off in the heat of the conflagration, and bodies and parts of bodies floated around the wreckage, some drifting in burning patches of fuel. The smell of death and destruction was nauseous and overpowering and both men were amazed by the sheer devastation delivered so rapidly by just two planes.

'All we can hope for, mate, is that this bugger floats long enough for someone friendly to find us', said Tom. Already the heat of the day had built up and without water to drink, both men knew that their survival time would be limited, even if the sea remained calm and the wreck did not sink.

Tom had an idea. 'George, one of us needs to keep a lookout but what if the other goes down into the water, keeps a hold on the boat, you can't burn up if you're in the water, can you?' George looked thoughtful. 'There's no fucking great fish around here, is there?' he asked, 'because if there is, I'd rather stay up top!' Tom laughed. 'I don't think so, George, but I'll tell you what, I'll go first and if some monster has me for his breakfast, you'll know to stay up here!' With no more delay, Tom slid back into the water. The water was not cold, but it was not a hot bath either, and he guessed that ten to fifteen minutes would be enough before he needed a warm-up in the sun. If they could last out for a couple of hours, that would hopefully give any possible rescuer enough time to come looking for them.

He had not been in the water for more than a couple of minutes when George called down to him, with urgency in his voice.

'Tom, there's someone in the water, from that patrol boat, I reckon. I saw an arm moving, looks like he's in trouble, he's hanging on to a box or something'. Tom pulled himself slowly to the bow and looked in the direction that George was pointing, but he was too low and could see nothing.

He answered, 'George, I can't see a thing and besides, what do you want me to do? He was trying to kill us a few minutes ago! Let the fucker take his chance'.

There was a short silence. 'Then I'd better help him, Sergeant', answered George in a stiff, formal voice, and started to move down towards the water.

Tom picked up the disapproving tone in his friend's voice, he also knew that George was not a strong swimmer and might need rescuing himself. 'The bloody man knows me too well', he thought to himself.

'George, stay where you are. I shall paddle over and have a look. Just you keep me heading in the right direction and I'll see what I can do, alright?'

Tom struck out towards the remains of the patrol boat with an easy breast-stroke, George directing him around patches of oil and larger pieces of debris. He could not avoid all of the oil, as well as the pulverised wreckage of human bodies, and just concentrated upon keeping his mouth firmly closed, breathing through his nose and listening out for his corporal's instructions.

Within a slow five minutes, Tom had reached the floating box, with its hardly-conscious passenger slumped over it. The lad, for it looked to Tom that the survivor was a teenager, was beyond speech but he looked up at Tom as the sergeant swam up next to him. His blond hair was drenched in oil, mixed with blood from a deep-looking gash around the crown of his head. Tom could see no other wounds, even ducking under the water to check the boy's legs and torso.

'Now lad', said Tom, 'I don't speak German and maybe you don't know any English'. The boy continued to look up, seemingly uncomprehending and Tom realised that all the effort must come from him. He looked across to George.

'He's alive, mate, so I'm going to swim this thing over to you. You keep us in a straight line, and I shall need you to get the lad out of the water'. Making sure that the boy had a grip on the box, Tom lay on his front in the water, his hands hard against the box and began to kick.

He could no longer see George, who was now out of sight behind the bulk of the box and its helpless passenger. Neither could Tom steer a course around the oil and filth floating between them, all he could do was to try to propel the box in as straight a line as he could manage, and hope that his strength held out for long enough. He could not avoid oil splashing over his face, some of it entering his nose and mouth as he gasped for breath. He spat and spat but was left with a foul, burning dryness and a pain that would not shift.

It was draining work, and the cold seemed to be seeping into his muscles when he felt some movement from the youngster lying on the box above him. The boy's body slid down towards him, and as Tom, alarmed, put out an arm to stop him from slipping into the sea, he was amazed when the lad's thin legs started to kick against the water.

'There's my good lad!' exclaimed Tom, 'kick on and we'll soon have you out'. He slapped the boy gently on the shoulder, and was rewarded with the beginnings of a pale smile. To be honest, the lad's efforts made little difference to their progress but Tom felt encouraged and redoubled his own efforts. Nevertheless, by the time that the box bumped up against the remains of their boat, he knew that exhaustion was not far away.

It took the last of his energy to push the boy into George's strong arms and out of the water. Tom had nothing left and knew that he could not follow him and climb out himself. His hands lost their grip and he felt himself slipping further and further down into the water. There was nothing he could do, he thought, as the water closed over his head and he felt himself sinking, his breath bursting within him.

Without conscious thought, and in an instant, or so it seemed, Tom's head was back above the surface and he took a huge breath. George, hanging onto the remains of the boat with one hand, had grabbed Tom's hair with the other, and yanked him up to the surface.

'Now look here, Sergeant', he smiled, 'how would I tell Elena that you drowned rescuing a German, when it should have been me?'

Tom grinned back, spitting out water before he could reply. 'Better me than you, Corporal, you swim like a brick, don't you? You old bugger, you knew I wouldn't let you do it'.

George continued to smile but Tom could see a sad edge to it. 'We lost one good young 'un this morning', said the corporal, 'seems to me we should do our best to help another one, Jerry or no'.

Tom nodded. 'This fucking war'.

With more help from George, Tom pulled himself up to the keel of the boat and lay across it, the sun gradually warming him through. Their prisoner, for that was what he was, Tom surmised, lay in the same position, looking across at him. His eyes were open, looking in Tom's direction, and he attempted to speak.

'Danke, mein herr, danke', was all he could manage but Tom got the gist. He grinned back in response, and that was the last thing he knew for an hour, as sleep rapidly overtook him.

Chapter 24

He was woken by George, shaking him by the shoulder. His mouth and throat felt raw and painful, a combination, he thought, of thirst and the effects of swallowed oil. 'Tom, wake up, my lad. Ship coming close, don't know if it's theirs or ours, take a look'.

Tom sat up, noticing that the young German sailor still slept, and that George had draped a piece of canvas, rescued from the sea, over him, as shelter from the worst of the fierce sun. He looked across at his friend, 'What a piece of work you are, old mate'.

'Less of the old, Sergeant! Now, take a look at this ship'.

Tom looked past George. In the near distance, perhaps a mile away, he could see a bow-wave and behind it, a grey ship. It must be a warship, he reckoned, but he just could not scale it to size, there was nothing to compare it with and besides, he was a soldier, not a sailor. 'Whether it's theirs or ours, George, it doesn't matter. We can't last much longer', and with that, he started to wave both arms above his head. George joined him, borrowing the canvas from their young German friend to hold in the breeze.

Someone on the warship must have seen them, for the bow-wave quickly diminished and at about a quarter mile distance, the ship was stopped, just moving up and down with the gentle swell of the sea. Tom couldn't see a flag, for the vessel was still bow-on to them but any doubt about the nationality of their rescuers vanished quickly.

A small boat was rapidly and efficiently lowered into the sea, and within a few seconds as it seemed to Tom, oars were propelling it quickly in their direction. One man stood in the bows of the boat, Sten-gun in hand, watching them carefully.

At about twenty yards distance, the little cutter slowed down as the occupants took a good look at the three haggard survivors. The sailor with the Sten shouted back to his officer sitting in the stern, 'Sir, looks like three wogs to me, fishermen I expect, not armed'. George was beginning to frame an indignant reply but Tom, with a wink, nudged him into silence.

A decision must have been made, as a few strokes of the oars brought the rescuers alongside. Strong arms pulled them safely into the boat, one after the other, accompanied by some of the lower-deck banter and abuse that Tom and George had learned to expect.

The armed sailor stared down at them, 'Sir, two wogs for sure but I don't know about the little 'un, he's a bit pale for a goat-shagger'. The laughter among the small crew quickly changed to a stunned silence as Tom lifted his head, looked his abuser in the eye and said quietly, 'If you calls us wogs one more time, you ignorant fucking sailorman, I shall shove that Sten right where the sun don't shine!', adding, in his best Sergeant's voice, 'And get your bloody hair cut!'

Tom could hear George unsuccessfully attempting to stifle a laugh, and it burst out in a rush. Within a second or two, the whole crew, even the abuser, joined in. The young officer in the stern, evidently a sub-lieutenant, when he had controlled his own laughter, gave the necessary orders to return to the ship, and Tom gave him a swift briefing, including their rescue of the young German sailor.

The sub was first up the ladder, reporting to an older looking officer who rapped out immediate orders for their reception. Gentle, firm hands propelled the three of them rapidly onto the deck, then swiftly through a companionway and then down two further ladders, friendly hands placing their feet and hands on and off the steel rungs. As they were shepherded into a brightly lit, small room, which Tom guessed was the sick-bay, the whole ship around them vibrated and leaned over. Before they could react, a cultured voice cut in above the racket, 'Nothing to worry about, chaps, just the Captain turning for home, bit of a rush on. We're out on a bit of a limb, middle of the day and Crete just over the horizon, prime target for those nasty Stukas, you see? Now, let's have a look at you, the young one first, if you please'.

The voice came from a tall, thin officer who, as he spoke, was fastening himself into a green surgical gown. Bespectacled and bald, he chatted continuously as he examined the German sailor, then clipped away the hair around his head wound, preparatory to cleaning and sewing the gash.

'I'm Lieutenant Walker, known as Bones to my pals, ship's doctor to HMS Touareg, this very fine Tribal-class destroyer. We've been lurking about off Crete overnight, in case there were any chaps like you, in a spot of trouble. Captain had to turn back for Alexandria before light, those nasty Stukas, but then we received a message from the RAF, people in the water after an attack from a German patrol boat. So we turn back and there you are! Three of our foot-sloggers, just waiting to be pulled out of the drink, and here you are, marvellous!'

Tom thought that he should interrupt the flow while he could, introducing himself and George then adding, 'Sir, the blond lad you're sewing up is a German sailor we pulled out of the drink, as you might say. We don't know anything about him'.

'A German, marvellous!' answered the lieutenant, immediately breaking into what Tom and George guessed was fluent German. Hesitantly at first, the young man answered him but before long, an animated conversation ensued as the doctor continued to clip and sew.

Eventually, after a long ten minutes, the doctor turned back to Tom. 'Well, Sergeant this is very interesting. Yakob here is eighteen, on his first voyage. He's a radio operator, fresh out of training, an apprentice you might say, learning his trade. He's a conscript, nothing unusual about that but the interesting thing is he's Jewish, and we know how much Herr Hitler hates the Jews! Somehow he's kept his origins quiet but he reckons that his Petty Officer was suspicious of him. It doesn't matter now, of course, because he's dead, along with the rest of the crew! Tells me he's no Nazi, Adolf had already shipped off most of his relatives to concentration camps before the war started. He managed to pass himself off as a non-Jew, easy enough with that blond hair, I suppose, managed alright until he was conscripted. Called himself Albert Adler, good Aryan name'.

George had an obvious question but was too embarrassed to ask. He nodded at Tom, who guessed what the question might be. 'Lieutenant', he started, 'isn't there some surgery that Jewish boys have, how could he hide that?'

'Eh, what's that, Sergeant? Oh, you mean circumcision. Yes, I'll ask him'. Another conversation ensued, the boy blushing, then the doctor turned back to Tom. 'Says he was sickly when he was young, his mother wouldn't let the Rabbi near him, didn't think he'd stand the operation. After that, Mum went off the idea altogether. Just as well, he says'.

'Aye, just as well', replied Tom. 'But his war is over now anyway', he continued.

'It is', agreed the Lieutenant. He spoke again to the young man, whose response this time was a resigned nod. 'I've told him he'll have to be confined to a cell until we get back to Alexandria. He will be interrogated there, then shipped on to a POW camp. I told him he should stick to Albert Adler, there's plenty of Jew-haters are POWs'. Turning to his assistant, who had stood quietly in the background, passing sutures and instruments to Walker as he needed them, he said, 'Johnson, my compliments to the First Lieutenant. Our young German friend is fit enough to be accommodated in a cell until we get back to port. Could he arrange this please, at his earliest convenience?'

'Now, who's next?'

Both Tom and George were contaminated with fuel oil. They were given milk to drink, to absorb and neutralise any oil in their systems, although the surgeon thought that is was probably too late to be of much use. Their eyes and skin were flushed with fresh water and they were ordered to gargle with salty water every four hours. 'It's not very sophisticated treatment, Sergeant, but it's the best I can do, you see. We'll send you for an x-ray when we get to Alex'.

Their treatment finished for the present, Tom and George both noticed that Yakob had left the sick-bay, presumably transported to a cell. In deference to their Army rank, they were guided to the Petty Officers Mess, where they fed and watered, as well as questioned by their curious hosts.

One conversation in particular stayed with Tom. He was approached by the PO who had described them in the boat as 'two wogs and a goat-shagger'. He apologised, explaining that had he known that they were British, he would have treated them with more respect, no offence intended. This was not good enough for Tom, who was able to translate his deep fury into words, and managed to suppress the urge to beat him where he stood.

'PO, those wogs, as you call them, are some of the best people I have ever come across in all my service. If it wasn't for them, me and George would be dead on that island. They risked their own lives, and their families' lives, to get us across to the coast and into that boat. Would you do that for strangers who had just fucked up the defence of your island? Me neither'.

The PO stepped back, aghast at the anger and passion that he had provoked.

Tom continued, but wanting to bring his words to an end. 'If you ever get the privilege to fight alongside one of these wogs, PO, you'll find out exactly what I mean, and you'll be a better man for it'. He had no wish to further humiliate the petty officer who, after all, had been one of the party that had plucked them from the sea, so finished on a more conciliatory note.

'Have a drink with me, mate, and let's leave that in the past, shall we? Sergeant Tom Lane, Welch Regiment', he concluded, holding out his hand. The PO hesitated, then obliged with a firm handshake. 'Phil Watson, Petty Officer, Gunnery. You don't mince your words, Tom, do you?'

It was Tom's turn to be embarrassed. 'Sorry, Phil, but you touched a raw nerve. Truth is, I would've called them wogs until three months ago, like we did in Egypt. Now, about that drink'.

'Can't stop, mate. I should be at my station now but I told the subbie I needed a word, knew I'd made a prat of myself. Besides, I needed a haircut'. They both roared with laughter and agreed to get that drink later.

Tom caught George's eye. 'Let's have a look at Yakob, see how he's doing'. The mess steward collared a passing seaman, who led them down two more sets of ladders, to a space deep in the forecastle. An armed seaman, standing in front of a locked door, would let them go no further, nor would he unlock the door. 'No orders, sir'. They were at a loss. 'I'll ask the jimmy' said their guide and disappeared back up the ladders.

'The jimmy?' asked George. 'First lieutenant, mate, next to God' answered the sentry with a grin. They did not have long to wait as, a few minutes later, feet were seen and heard, climbing steadily down the ladder, followed by the rest of the officer in question, a tall, broad individual in working gear with an impatient look on his face.

'What the fuck is going on here, Brown? These chaps want to see their prisoner do they? Well, for fuck's sake, let them in. Their responsibility, not mine, and I can't see how one sick prisoner is going to get past two pongoes anyhow'. Turning to Tom and George he continued, 'Alright, gentlemen? You can have half an hour, door open, then I'm afraid he'll have to be locked up again. Fortunes of war and all that'.

'Sir, thank you, much appreciated', answered Tom, automatically coming to attention and saluting the superior officer. The jimmy laughed, 'Not sure you should salute an officer when you're dressed like a tramp but we'll pass on that! When you've finished with your prisoner, someone will show you to the bridge and you can meet the Captain, tell him your story'. He nodded, and was gone.

The sentry, Brown, unlocked the door. Inside the steel cell, Yakob was lying on his bed, a shelf, illuminated by a weak lightbulb. It was stiflingly hot, with no through ventilation, and sweat was pouring down his body. He had been provided with a bottle of water and an empty plate was on the floor, evidence of a recent meal. On seeing his visitors, he stood up, a pale smile upon his face, and moved towards them. With some hesitation, he stuck out his hand, saying quietly, 'Thank you, my friends, thank you, for saving me'. Yakob knew some English! He explained that he was in his first year at University, studying English, again having convinced the authorities that he was of pure Aryan stock, when he had been conscripted.

The fact that they could now converse with him left Tom and George even more delighted and pleased that they had saved his young life, rather than left him to drown. His bitterness at the Nazi government was evident, both of his parents had been arrested and imprisoned, as had two cousins. He had no knowledge if they were alive and without contact with them for two years, he feared that they were dead. 'The Nazis are not Germany', he explained, 'but stupidly, we Germans put them into power, and there will be no peace until they are defeated'.

Their exchange was cut short by the raucous and deafening blast of a klaxon right above their heads. The staccato racket made normal speech impossible between them. Brown leaned across to Tom, bawling in his ear, 'Action stations, there must be an attack. My station is on deck, I'll have to lock him in, no duties for you so you'll have to go back to the sick bay'.

Tom, never a sailor, was horrified to think of Yakob, locked up alone in a steel box while his compatriots tried to destroy the ship and everyone in it. He didn't know that, at Action Stations, all watertight doors were closed and that everyone, apart from a lucky few on deck, was locked in their own steel box. 'We'll stay here with the lad', he bawled back, 'Good a place as any'.

Brown, quickly reflecting on the First Lieutenant's words, and the need to hurry up on deck before the hatches were closed, nodded and ran to the ladder. A minute after he disappeared, the klaxon stopped, replaced by a massive vibration and roar as the ship's turbine ran up to full speed. There were also successive thuds as watertight doors were slammed and latched, leaving them isolated and alone, just the three of them.

Tom and George had experienced some terrifying moments together, in France and Egypt and Crete but they agreed afterwards that the following ten minutes were the most harrowing of all.

The ship was not on an even keel for more than a few seconds at a time, the Captain seemed to be throwing it about at random and it pitched and rolled without respite. Tom and George were thrown to the deck, where they stayed, quickly to be joined by Yakob, who was thrown from his bunk. They held on to each other, feeling almost paralysed by the uproar around them.

The noise outside, both on deck and in the sea was both deafening and terrifying. There was an almost continuous and rapid thud-thud-thud of different calibre guns firing, Tom guessed anti-aircraft, interrupted on two occasions by a deeper, more resonant boom as something exploded in the sea around them. They expected the sea to come roaring in as the hull gave way, to be drowned in an instant, but it did not happen. George swore afterwards that he heard powerful metallic crashes against the hull, he wondered afterwards how he could have heard anything among the deafening cacophony all around them.

The passing of time was immeasurable in these conditions but gradually they became aware of changes in the ship's motion. Although the engines seemed to be working as hard as ever, the sharp changes of direction seemed to decrease, then even out, and then stop, to be replaced by a more predictable motion.

From the speaker came a different klaxon tone and within a few moments, they heard hatches opening and could see feet on the ladder, it was Brown returning to his guard duties.

'We got ballocksed by two Stukas. Lucky for us, they didn't hit us. One near miss, caused some damage up top. Only three casualties, and they were when the Captain was chucking the ship about! Managed to shoot up one Stuka, damage the other. Anyway, the skipper's heading straight for Alex and with a bit of luck, we shouldn't see any more Jerries'. He added apologetically, 'Sorry but your prisoner will have to go back in the cell now, standing orders'.

Tom turned to Yakob. 'You sit tight, old mate, and we'll see you later'. Both men gave what passed for reassuring grins and turned back to the ladder.

Chapter 25

Tom sat back in the Sergeant's Mess, RAF Ramat David, just outside the city of Haifa, cold beer in hand, after a good dinner that had included fresh fruit, vegetables and even meat that didn't come out of a tin! George sat alongside him, looking replete and relaxed, no sentries to set or weapons to clean. How they had managed to find themselves here, less than a fortnight after their rescue from the waters of the Libyan Sea took some believing, even now.

HMS Touareg had slipped into the harbour at Alexandria at two bells of the afternoon watch the day following the confrontation with the Stukas. There had been no more attacks, ASDIC had detected a submarine but it had turned out to British.

It had been a busy twenty four hours on board for the two soldiers. Tom had briefly spoken to Lieutenant Commander Smith, the skipper, then spent an exhausting ninety minutes with the First Lieutenant, who had interviewed him in detail about their escape across and from the island. He was particularly interested in Tom's opinion of the fledgling Cretan Resistance. Were they determined to resist? Was it worth supporting them? What was their attitude to the British, to the Germans, to the Italians? He answered as fully and as honestly as he could but could not help wondering why a naval officer should be asking such questions of an army NCO. Surely that should be left to the Intelligence Officer of the Welch Regiment, whenever and wherever he found them?

The interview concluded with intriguing questions; if Tom was given an opportunity to return to Crete to fight again, what would be his response? Tom reply was definite. 'I would welcome the chance, sir. The regiment has unfinished business there'. That was absolutely true but to himself he thought, 'Elena!'

'And what about Corporal Parry? Do you know what his view might be?' Tom smiled grimly, 'You would have to ask him, sir, I can't speak for him, but he lost some good friends down there', and left it at that.

The two of them had spent a little time with Yakob, obtaining permission to 'air' him for a few minutes on deck and even teaching him a few useful English words, the kind that he wouldn't learn in university! He had solemnly shaken their hands as they finally left him in the cell, thanking them again for their kindness in saving him.

The Royal Navy was famous for its open-handed hospitality, and Tom and George were treated royally if briefly, as the ship was still in dangerous waters. Neither of the men had seen pink gin before, so a couple of large ones each were an education. They cemented their peace with PO Phil Watson over a glass, and once again, at his request, recounted the story of their action and escape. Phil listened intently, he had lost shipmates in action, and perfectly understood the pain and regret that they were feeling. They parted company good friends, promising to meet again if the chance arose, not knowing then how soon that would be.

At the dockside, they said their goodbyes, then moved off, expecting to find Army Liaison somewhere near, and then to return to the regiment. Instead, they had only taken a few paces when a tall, rather scruffy figure in desert fatigues stepped in front of them.

'Hello, chaps', he said in an educated, rather plummy voice. 'I'm Lieutenant Colonel Dawson, Intelligence Corps. Do I have the pleasure of speaking to Sergeant Lane and Corporal Parry?' Tom replied for them both, 'Yes, sir, I am Sergeant Lane and this is Corporal Parry'.

'Good, gentlemen, please follow me, there are some people you need to meet'.

Tom was not going to be hustled so easily. 'Excuse me, sir, but I don't know you. How do I know that you are who you say you are? I could swallow this easier if someone on Touareg had told us to expect a Lieutenant Colonel from the Intelligence Corps but no one did. So sir, with respect, you will have to do better than that!'

Dawson looked momentarily nonplussed, then roared with laughter. 'You will go far, Sergeant! OK, let's visit Army Liaison and see if they'll vouch for me!'

Army liaison, just a few yards away dockside, and populated by a captain, a major and two privates, confirmed the Lieutenant Colonel's identity without hesitation, leaving the two men with little or no choice.

Thoroughly bemused, they followed the colonel to a Humber staff car waiting, apparently for them, inside the dockyard gates. The journey through the dirty, crowded streets of Alexandria was silent and short, Tom and George exchanging puzzled glances, what was this all about?

The car eventually drove between high walls and gates slammed behind them. They were in the dusty courtyard of a bungalow, untidy-looking with doors and windows flung wide open. The heat was stifling, especially after days at sea, and they were bustled in through the door, along a corridor and into a large room, dimly lit by two lamps that were perched upon a large table. A ceiling fan above the table turned slowly, stirring the hot air but not producing any noticeable cooling.

Behind the table sat two men, clearly waiting for them. One, a middle aged but fit-looking individual, was in British Army uniform, an officer, and both George and Tom immediately came to attention in front of him. He looked at them with bright, sharp eyes, commenting, 'No time for that, gentlemen, stand at ease, in fact, take a seat and I'll introduce myself and my colleague, and tell you why you're here. Go on, sit down'.

'I'm Colonel Sands, same mob as Lieutenant Colonel Dawson'. Tom looked around but Dawson had not followed them into the room. Sands continued, indicating the civilian alongside him. 'I can't tell you this chap's name because I don't know it myself! What I can tell you is that he works in the secret end of the business and they're looking to get some bodies back into Crete, see if they can help the resistance cause a few more problems for the Jerries'.

At this point, the civilian, a chubby, bald man, sweating in the heat, interrupted. 'The First Lieutenant on the Touareg was impressed with your, ah, skills in evasion and signalled that we might want to take a look at you. We, ah, always have an eye open for talent'.

'Any questions so far, chaps?' asked Sands. 'What about our regiment, sir? Where are they, and do they know what's happened to us?' answered Tom.

'The 1st Welch, or the remainder of it, is resting and re-fitting. There will need to be quite a draft before it can go back into action'. Tom interrupted, 'Sir, how many made it?' knowing that the number would be small.

Sands paused, 'For your ears only', he muttered, glancing fiercely at both men in turn. 'Seven officers, one hundred and sixty one other ranks. Six hundred and fifty dead, wounded or missing'. Both men felt utterly stunned, eighty per cent casualties! The regiment had been their family and now? For all intents and purposes, it no longer existed.

Sands continued. 'I can guess that you will want to return to your unit and there's no question, they could do with your experience and they know that you are speaking to us. Hear us out first. I should make it very clear that we are looking for volunteers, so if you decide that what we are offering is not for you, you are free to return to your duties with your regiment'.

Tom looked across to George and received his assent, no words needed to be spoken. 'Sir, we'll hear you out'.

'First off then', said the civilian, 'tell us about your travels, from when you left the line at Chania'. They did that, Tom and George sharing the narrative, answering the many questions that both men threw at them.

This time, it took more than two hours to complete their account, and both men felt not only exhausted once more but emotionally raw at reliving Davey's death. Surely this was the last time they would have to go over it in such detail!

The anonymous civilian took over. 'I cannot tell you too much, ah, as yet but we are looking to drop a small party onto the island to assess and back up the resistance. We are looking for battle experience, leadership, people who can talk and persuade if necessary. There will be training to give, ah, in weapons and fieldcraft. You would be in command of the team, Sergeant. There are other skills we're looking for that you don't have but there's a little more recruiting we need to do yet. We're thinking a three-month stint, could be less, could be more. How does that sound?'

Again, Tom spoke for both of them, knowing the lines upon which George would be thinking. 'Sir, could we have a little time to discuss your offer? A couple of hours perhaps?'

Sands looked displeased but not surprised. 'You can have an hour, and not a minute over! There's a mess in the building, get yourselves something to eat, have a word with the steward and he'll find you some kit, get you out of that bloody awful fisherman's garb, then get back here! Dismissed'.

It was not a difficult decision. Both men knew that they had not finished with Crete and its people. They were both professional enough to understand that revenge for Davey could not be allowed to be part of their decision, but both of them relished the chance to even the score. Elena came into Tom's mind of course but realistically, he knew that he could be in Crete for three months and never see her, and neither would he want her to be exposed to further danger on his account. That is, if she had escaped with the other fugitives from Lavoutro.

They returned to the officer and the spook within the hour and told them, yes, they would volunteer. They were given a week's leave, cash and an address of a quiet hotel, and ordered, on pain of severe punishment, not to breathe a word to anyone of their proposed mission. They were given permission to write to immediate family, to assure them of their wellbeing, but to no one else. Tom requested that he write to Davey's parents, he thought they deserved more than a War Office telegram. Permission was granted, on condition that Tom gave no information regarding the circumstances and location of Davey's death. They were to report back in seven days, at 0900, when they would receive further orders.

The week passed quickly. They ate and slept, then ate and slept again! The fleshpots of Alexandria held no attraction for either of them, so the days were spent in beneficial indolence, regaining energy and strength. Both men wished that Davey, after all he had been through, had survived to be with them, but they did not dwell upon it for there would be more losses before the war was won.

Meeting Colonel Sands at the end of their brief leave, the two friends were given railway warrants that would see them to Haifa, in Palestine. They would be met at the station but were told no more.

The journey to Haifa, mostly along the coast of the Eastern Mediterranean, through scrub and desert with an occasional green plantation, was slow. The summer heat was intense but cold drinks did little to moderate the high temperatures. The journey was broken for the night at Tel Aviv, so at least a bed and dinner were available. For a while, the war seemed far away but they knew it was an illusion and that they would be back in the middle of it soon enough.

To their surprise, they were met at the railway station in Haifa by RAF transport and shuttled to the airfield and base at Ramat David. This northern area of Palestine, near to the border with Lebanon, was far less humid than the Nile Delta, and was altogether a more comfortable billet.

As junior NCOs in a long-established regiment, both men were used to looking after themselves and it came as a surprise when they were treated as visitors of some worth. They shared a room but they were used to crowded dormitories or congested tents, so it felt like luxury to them. They were able to shower, with clean uniforms laid out for them by the mess servants and then to partake in a freshly-cooked dinner, with a cold beer or two to tuck into afterwards.

George cocked an eye at Tom, 'Do you get the feeling they're fattening us up for Christmas?' he commented. Tom grinned back, 'You might be right, mate, but let's enjoy it, shall we?'

They were thinking about a second beer when a servant came across, message in hand. They were summoned to the Officers Mess and told to wait in an ante-room. They had only been waiting for minutes, a little impatiently, when to their surprise, Colonel Sands' civilian came into the room.

'Good evening, gentlemen. I trust you are being well looked after?' Without waiting for a reply, he continued, 'I am in the process of recruiting two more members for your team, had a bit of difficulty finding people with the requisite, ah, skills but I've got hold of one, and he will be joining you, ah, in a moment'.

'Your training for what we want you to do starts tomorrow, gentlemen, and you will be pleased to hear that the first new skill for you to learn will be, ah, how to parachute from a plane'.

'Oh no', groaned George, 'that's my fucking nightmare, throwing myself out into all that fresh air!' 'Ah', asked the civilian, 'does that mean you won't do it, it is, ah, an essential part of the mission'. George, with a wan smile, answered, 'Oh no sir, I'll jump. I have plenty of nightmares, parachuting is just one of them!'

At that moment, the door opened again, and to the astonishment of the two men, Petty Officer Phil Watson walked in.

'What the hell are you doing here, Phil?' exclaimed Tom, 'Are they going to throw you out of a plane too?' Phil laughed, 'Jimmy got hold of me, this lot needed someone with sea experience, bit of navigation, did I fancy a change? They didn't tell me you were in on it though, or I would have said no!' He roared with laughter at his joke then added, 'Throw me out of what plane? I'm a sailor!'

The civilian, who instructed them to call him Mr Smith, explained the need to parachute to Phil, who just shrugged his shoulders. 'Bring it on', he commented, 'what's one more stupid thing to add to my list?'

Tom had a question. 'What other skills do you need, Mr Smith, for the team? The three of us, we might know someone, depending on what you want'. Smith grimaced. 'I doubt you can help us, Sergeant. I'm looking for a wireless operator, for your communications, but someone who speaks German like a native'. He added, patronisingly Tom thought, 'I don't expect you will know anyone who, ah, fits the bill, eh Sergeant?'

Tom, with a wink and a grin to George and Phil, answered, 'Oh, I think I do, Mr Smith!'

End-piece

I hope that you have enjoyed reading 'Sergeant Tom and the Battle of Crete', the first in a series of novels that document his war, firstly in Crete but moving on eventually to other theatres.

I chose Crete because although it was a 'sideshow' in terms of the war in Europe, arguably making little difference to the general progress toward Allied victory, it generated so many stories of valour and patriotism, especially from the native Cretans and their allies, and in such a small and manageable geographic area, that nowhere else would do. If you want trouble, invade a Greek island and see what happens!

The people of Crete are still immensely proud of their efforts to resist the German invader, and rightly so. I was fortunate enough to be visiting the island in 2011, when the 70th anniversary of the Battle of Crete was celebrated. Veterans from all of the engaged forces attended, there were exhibitions and talks, and of course, homage was paid to the brave combatants who did not survive the fighting. I found it very moving and powerful.

For a feel of the atmosphere, visit the Commonwealth War Graves Commission cemetery at Souda Bay, next to Chania. It is serene, beautiful and very sad, particularly when the young ages of many of the dead are noted. John Pendlebury, the archaeologist who was tasked to begin the organisation of Cretan resistance well before the German invasion, is buried there.

The Battle of Crete did not end with the expulsion of the Allies and the German military victory. The Cretan population was immeasurably offended by the invasion and resistance started as soon as the parachutists drifted down to earth. Their opposition was implacable, despite the Nazi tactics of torture and mass executions. This novel begins to describe some of the Cretan reaction to invasion, and this theme will be further examined in 'Sergeant Tom: Return to Crete', the next book in the series.

Finally, although this is definitely a novel, relying largely upon my imagination and invention, I used documented events and people as the basis for much of first part of the story, centred on Chania. I changed the names of those involved because the detail of their actions had to be of my own invention, contemporary accounts tending to be rather 'broad-brush', and I had no wish to offend any surviving relatives. In reality;

- The First battalion, Welch Regiment was based around Chania and formed the rear-guard for the withdrawal of Allied forces.
- Captain Evans, with a Bren gun, destroyed two gliders that had landed in front of their position. Troops in his company destroyed two more.
- A monastery, taken by German parachutists, was counter-attacked and re-taken by three platoons of D Company.
- Corporal Myrddin McTiffin led his section to silence a heavy machine-gun, all of his men fell but he carried on alone and killed the entire crew of seven. For this act of gallantry, Corporal McTiffin received the Military Medal.
- The Commanding Officer, Lieutenant Colonel Duncan, was indeed last seen firing a Bren gun at the advancing Germans, as he helped to cover the withdrawal. He was captured and became a POW. I have been unable to discover if his exemplary leadership was officially recognised, I hope that it was.
- The Welch Regiment disembarked 21 officers and 830 other ranks on the island on the 18th February 1941. Only 7 officers and 161 other ranks reached Alexandria on 1st June. That represents a casualty rate of 80%, of which 250 were killed. Their sacrifice is still remembered in Crete today.
- Soldiers from Australia and New Zealand fought with great distinction against the German forces. Second Lieutenant Charles Upham and Sergeant Alfred Hulme, both New Zealanders, received the Victoria Cross for gallantry in the defence of Maleme and Galatas (In 1942, Upham, by then a Captain, was awarded a second Victoria Cross for his actions in Egypt).
- There are many documented instances of Cretan civilians taking their defence into their own hands during the initial invasion, attacking paratroopers and glider troops with improvised

weaponry and enormous courage. Often led by their local priests, they inflicted substantial casualties but were subject to terrible reprisals in the following weeks and months. Resistance continued throughout the German and Italian occupation, right up to the final liberation in May 1945.

Glossary

The Andrew: Nick-name for the Royal Navy, said to derive from an officer in the Impress Service, one Andrew Miller.

Boys rifle: British anti-tank rifle of .55 inch calibre. It was effective on armour up to 23 mm thick, such as might be found on an armoured car. With a five-round magazine, a maximum of ten shots per minute was possible.

Bren gun: A light machine gun of .303 inch calibre, used extensively by British armed forces. The name 'Bren' derives from Brno, Czechoslovakia, where it was designed, and Enfield, United Kingdom, where it was built.

Bully beef: A type of corned beef.

Chania: The second largest city in Crete, situated 90 miles or 145 km west of Heraklion, on the northern coast of Crete.

Gunfire: Black tea with a generous slug of rum, first noted in the British Army in the 1890s.

Heraklion: The largest city in Crete, situated at roughly the mid-point of the northern coast.

Hurricane: Hawker Hurricane single-seat fighter aircraft, in service with the RAF, in various forms, all through World War 2.

Junkers Ju 52: Three-engined transport plane, used by the German Luftwaffe for the movement of passengers, parachutists and supplies.

Junkers 87: See 'Stuka'.

Kubelwagen: A light military vehicle, built by Volkswagen and based upon the original 'Beetle'.

Lance–jack: Slang term for Lance-corporal.

Luger: A semi-automatic pistol, used by German armed forces for many years.

Messerschmitt: A German aircraft manufacturing corporation. Two of their aircraft feature in this story; the 109, an excellent single-seat fighter and the 110, a twin-engined heavy fighter/fighter bomber.

MG34: General purpose machine gun, in service with the Wehrmacht throughout World War 2.

Mills Bomb: Hand grenade, British issue.

NCO: Non-commissioned officers, for example, Lance-Corporals, Corporals and Sergeants.

Petty Officer or PO: A naval non-commissioned rank.

Raki: See 'Tsikoudia'.

Sangar: A temporary fortified position, with breastworks of stones or sandbags.

SMLE: Short Magazine Lee Enfield Rifle, of .303 inch calibre, in service with British armed forces in various forms from 1895 to 1957.

Sten gun: A submachine gun, used by British and Allied forces throughout World War 2.

Storch: Fieseler Storch (English: Stork) liaison and reconnaissance aircraft, used by the Luftwaffe, and known for its excellent short take-off and landing capabilities.

Stuka: Junkers Ju 87, a single-engined German dive bomber and ground attack aircraft.

Tsikoudia: Also known as Raki, a clear spirit, distilled from grape pulp and skins, after pressing for wine-making.

The Welch Regiment: Known as The Welch (an archaic spelling of 'Welsh'), an infantry regiment of British Army from 1881 to 1969.

Any mistakes or misrepresentations in this book are entirely my own. I hope that they do not detract from your enjoyment.

Joseph Taylor   August 2017

,

Printed in Great Britain
by Amazon